"This is a delicious chunk of crime-fiction candy. I devoured it. Atmospheric, dark, hard-hitting, relentless and thrilling with unexpected laughs. A story that'll stick with you days after its conclusion. Bravo."—Mark Pelletier, *BookTalk*

"Smith conjures up a cast of memorable characters, all flawed and many despicable, but all drawn with vivid detail and humanness to deftly expose the brutal, seedy nature and cost of organized crime and corruption. As in life, everyone's in the mix, hand-in-hand waiting for the payoffs: politicians, police, lawyers, journalists, and criminals. And the police personalities and dialogue are bang on, amongst the very best I've read from an author who hasn't actually served in law enforcement."
—A.B. Patterson, author of the PI Harry Kenmare novels and former detective sergeant and corruption investigator

"Vern Smith's dialogue is thoughtful and thought-provoking. This is a book you will recommend to friends, and it deserves a wide readership. You will look forward to reading more of this talented author's work."—Nick Chiarkas, author of *Nunzio's Way*

MORE PRAISE

"Reading Vern Smith is to be reminded that urban America is more than the sum of its con jobs; it is a texture built of rips and stitches, a circus tent under which some of its wackiest animators hold forth—from Phyllis Diller to Carl Stalling, from Erich Sokol to Ishmael Reed. *The Green Ghetto* is electric, eccentric, extracellular madness."—Michael Turner, author of *Hard Core Logo*

"*Under the Table* is a clever noir that will keep 'em guessing. Wickedly funny, you'll laugh even though you know you shouldn't. Much like the sketch show that it portrays, *Under the Table* entertains with dark humor, quirky characters, and celebrity appearances, while poking fun at the absurdity of societal constructs. Quippy and smart, Smith's prose is electric and crackles across the page."—Meagan Lucas, author of *Songbirds and Stray Dogs*

Editor: Krysta Winsheimer of Muse Retrospect

Book Design: Gary Anderson

Cover Photograph and Design: Garth Jackson

ISBN: 979-8-9869930-1-0
Run Amok Crime, 2023
First Edition

Printed in the USA

SCRATCHING
THE
FLINT

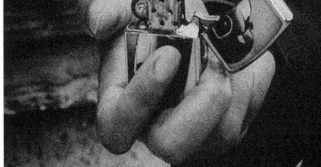

A NOVEL BY
VERN SMITH

For Big Al

ONE

Doyle Allenby closed his eyes, shook his head, no, and said, "I'm taking the deal."

Helen Tyndall sighed, thinking, poor Doyle. It was the way he sat across from her tugging at the billy-goat tuft on his chin. Same fancy shave as wild Billy Koch, the Blue Jays' closer, only Doyle was prettier, what with three shades of farm-boy blond jutting out all over. Nice fat bottom lip, too. Man, it was going to be a shame if she couldn't talk him down.

Saying, "Please Doyle, don't do this," Helen played with the dimmer on her desk lamp, dialing it below 60 watts. She was trying to be soothing, telling Doyle to relax, promising to get his cellphone records tossed on illegal search and seizure. Fido, the service provider in this case, was supposed to see a warrant first. And the poor kid from billing, he'd already signed an affidavit saying this Detective Cecil-Something-or-Other pushed him around, talked to him real bad. The Fido guy was forced—that's right, threatened with physical harm to his person—to cough up the paperwork.

"It's Cecil Bolan, you mean." Doyle looked down, twisting a gaudy ring on his right hand, Leamington Lions, SOSS 1987-88 Basketball Champions. "I know him from way back, high school, and he's trying to make things as right as possible for me. So I don't know how many times I have to say, I'm taking the stand, taking the plea deal."

Helen held an open hand to her face, pulling it away. "Go with my plan and we'll have you back in uniform writing up double-parked Hummers—they can't help it—before this is out. After that, in conjunction with your union, I'll recover your lost wages. Next, I'll get the union to pay your legal fees, slap 'em with failing to represent if they think twice."

"Wait." Doyle held up an index. "I thought Jean-Max Renaldo was paying."

"Point is, the longer we wait, the more options appear. See? My first loyalty is to you."

Me, Doyle thought, blowing her off with a puff of air.

Almost pleading, Helen said the crown would offer something better just before court. Next date was five months away and who was to say it wouldn't be another five? More, perhaps.

"Let it play out," she said.

Let it play out? Sure, Doyle was going to sit back while Pam Jenkins took his place and copped a plea of her own. If Doyle did that, it would be Pam Jenkins and Doris Sabo testifying against him. Goddammit, there were only three green hornets left, and someone, one of them, was for sure going to jail over all this, right along with Jean-Max.

"Look." Doyle rested an elbow on the edge of Helen's desk. "I'm going to testify. That's final. And maybe, oh mama, I'm here in Toronto almost seven years. Done some bad things, took money I shouldn't have. Maybe this is my chance to get out, go home where I belong."

Helen wrinkled her nose. "There aren't many good-paying jobs in Leamington, Doyle."

True that, but Doyle said he'd land on his feet, maybe catch on at the ketchup plant, Heinz. He knew someone in the union, or at least Dad used to. Even though Dad was dead a long time now—heart attack—maybe the guy'd still want to do right by the old man. Or maybe Doyle could get his old job back at Point Pelee National Park, junior assistant to the assistant warden.

"A what?"

"Helping with the animals, passing out flyers on protected areas, plants, species. And tours sometimes. I'd always take 'em to the hop tree. Tell 'em the Point is home to it, the northernmost naturally occurring citrus plant. Everyone always got a kick out of that, simple."

"Sounds like a job for children." Helen leaned in, smiling without showing teeth. "Besides, if you testify, it is not going to work out that way, Doyle, simple."

He chin-nodded to her phone, reminding her again. They had him calling Jean-Max personally just before twenty-nine classic cars disappeared in Doyle's territory over the past seven months alone. He'd been so stupid, bank records showing $500, less gas money and the odd cheap thrill, going into savings shortly thereafter exactly twenty-nine times.

That was aiding and abetting, profiting, some other frauds Doyle couldn't remember, as well as conduct unbecoming of a parking enforcement associate. He read the papers, and there were going to be more charges all around.

The hell did Doyle want to be a green hornet for anyway? Right, left, refreshingly non-partisan—it didn't matter—they all hated his uniform, the drab-green work pants that didn't quite match the olive shirts. Legit handicapped drivers who couldn't find spaces didn't like him any more than able-bodied people with wheelchair plates. Even Mom giving it to him, something about getting dinged for parking on the wrong side of the street on the first day of December, happy fucking holidays. No wonder Doyle was corrupt. He was a green hornet. Job was being phased out anyway with new openings taken over by police services. Attrition. That's why there were only three green hornets left. The rest were cops now, almost, blue hornets, or parking enforcement officers. Doyle, he could never be an officer because of a pot conviction from his last year of high school, 1988, fucking Mounties, and it was still costing him here in 2001.

"Last chance," Helen said. "Whatever your Cecil promised, I am your lawyer, and I advise you to—"

Slamming a fist on her hundred-year-old maple, Doyle put an end to it. "I'm continuing to cooperate while there's still a window, now. I'll call Cecil myself, call him at home."

Helen looked over her bifocals. What with the stress of clientele Jean-Max brought, she'd packed on some pounds and could feel the tightness of her charcoal Versace, so she made a mental note to get back on the elliptical, asking herself where she was going to get a size 14 in a dress that says you're out of order. She had to get rid of this extra weight.

"I am sorry to hear that, Doyle."

"Call the crown. Do it. Tell him, officially."

Helen took off her glasses, raised them like a white flag. "I'll do what you like."

"And you'll do it now."

She consulted the grandfather clock—newish but built to look old—in the corner. Said it was Friday, almost eight. She would call Monday, first thing, urging Doyle to use the time in between to partake in some sober second thought.

Standing, throwing on a distressed pleather bomber—imitation-suede arms, cowhide-like vest section—Doyle did the snaps with his left. "Just please do what I say. Call me right after."

Out of her chair, Helen rounded the desk. Doyle watched her walk to him, her eyes black marbles in the soft light. Stacked like that hot old girl in *The Graduate*—the live version coming soon to the Canon Theatre—Kathleen Turner, Doyle had never looked at Helen like this. But wow, now that he was calming, feeling he'd made a good decision, he couldn't help but check her out, dress snug, and think maybe heaven really did hold a place for those who pray.

She shook his hand earnestly, calling him Mr. Allenby. Mister? Doyle was twenty-nine, so what the hey? Softly taking his arm, leading him to the door, she did it again, saying, "I'll call you Monday, Mr. Allenby."

Doyle said thanks, walking out, looking back with uncertainty, waving from the elevator before turning to press the down button.

Helen shut the door, studying a large frame of tiny black-and-white pictures, University of Western Ontario Faculty of Law, 1984. Briefly wondering what her classmates would do in a situation like this, she told herself her classmates would never find themselves in a situation like this and removed a cigarette from her tarnished case, killing the lights, striking a match, hitting the tobacco, inhaling, unhitching the new-fashioned window, April biting cold as the seal cracked. Careful to exhale outside—it was a $5,000 fine—she saw Doyle's car parked on Pembroke near Gerrard. How had he described the color again? Right, Cream gold No. 3. Well, Cream gold No. 3 looked like those golf balls her ex used in the '80s, almost optic-green, garish.

Feeling a mild buzz, she couldn't understand what Doyle was thinking, testifying against Jean-Max. And why was he telling her? Sure, Helen had promised Doyle it didn't matter who was paying, that she was bound by oath to represent Doyle to her fullest. But he had to know even lawyers think about who's paying. Whatever, taking another drag, she reluctantly sent the signal—Doyle was taking the deal no matter what she said—flicking her cigarette, watching the ember tumble three floors, sparking the moment it hit the sidewalk. She shut the blinds when she saw Doyle hug the rail, jogging down the wheelchair ramp.

Doyle noticed the cigarette's glow on the pavement, wondering where it came from. It had been thirteen days since he'd had so much as a puff. He'd quit drinking, too, giving up all vice, and he could see that he was trying to do too much all at once. Maybe he ought to treat himself to a burger, some meat, and a beer. Even that advice battle-ax from the paper would've said g'head, for today Doyle was taking responsibility for one set of actions. He wanted to g'head and do what the battle-ax advised tomorrow, too, except Cecil had specifically said no long walks, time being.

Glancing north and south, clear, he picked up the hot butt, sucking until his head rushed. He looked at his Ford Elite, fuzzy around the edges, remembering how Jean-Max arranged for that garage on Eastern Avenue to paint it, special, for the cost of paint. Thinking how Jean-Max wouldn't make a move until the trial was over, too obvious, Doyle was planning to be long gone by then, back home where he'd get the car repainted, when he heard them come.

"Check out the efficient little whistle-blower, already having his last cigarette."

Who was that? From behind, one of them had his hair in

hand, another a gun to his head, pushing him across Pembroke Street. He dropped his secondhand cigarette when he felt someone groping for keys in the pockets of his dungarees, ramrodding him up against the Elite's hood. As soon as they had him upright, he smelled it, gas. A tire was around his shoulders, tight. And Jesus H. Christ, the gas was on the Michelin, soaked in. Unable to force both him and the tire past the steering column, they gruffly ushered him around to the passenger side.

The grease monkey who painted the Elite, he was there. What was his name again? Reggie, that was it. Now this Reggie was running ahead, fiddling with the lock. After opening the passenger side, he turned to help the two others push Doyle in, sitting him down.

Doyle turned his head, said he'd never hurt Jean-Max, watching a beefy guy wearing clunky glasses and a Commie T-shirt—what did it say?—step forward and shove something at Doyle, between his lips. "Have a brand-new cigarette, whistle-blower." The others laughed, watching the T-shirt guy swish his Zippo open—a gold plus sign italicized, the Chevy logo—then work the metal wheel with his thumb, scratching the flint and holding the flame forward. "Now how about a light?"

Everyone except Doyle seemed to get a kick out of that.

"I was just telling Helen, no deal." He smelled burning rubber, talking fast. "Please, don't. I'm not going to say anything."

"That's right," the third guy said. "Nothing." Holstering his gun, doing up his inside button of his dark double-breasted suit. "Now how about a nice cold glass of water? Would you like that?"

"Maybe it's bottled the whistle-blower wants, Evian," the T-shirt guy said. "Know what Evian spells backwards, Doyle?"

It was almost over already, the men backing off as Doyle screamed from deep within his own private hell. If the fire didn't do it, the ensuing explosion would. Even if he lived through all that, a hospital drama had taught him that his body wouldn't be able to keep the bacteria out.

"Any last words?"

Black smoke all around, Doyle could only see them in his head now, connecting the voice to a face, the T-shirt guy, and shouting, "Write in Dick Gregory for president!"

Everyone except Doyle seemed to get a kick out of that, too.

TWO

Cecil Bolan planted a kiss on his wife Freida then threw a ten and a five over the Diamond taxi's front seat. Told the cabbie to take Freida straight home, Bleecker Street, to see that she got safely inside, keep the change. Seeing as how they'd been picked up at the Tender Trap in St. James Town, the driver was saying he wasn't sure there was going to be any change when Cecil opened the door before the car came to a complete stop. Taking three or four stumble steps, he fell into a jog at what he saw on the other side of the black-on-yellow police tape.

Alex Johnson noticed Cecil right away, legs pumping, Alex breaking into a run of his own. Cutting Cecil off well behind the news crews—Jojo Chintoh from City TV looking into the camera, explaining the crude art of necklacing—Alex grabbed the arm of Cecil's suit jacket, pulling him near, holding him on the spot. "You don't want to see this, junior. Don't need to be here." Easing his grip on the navy material, looking around. "Alex gonna take you on home, get some of those Nova Scotia pale ales into you, settle you."

"Doyle." Cecil looked over Alex's shoulder. "He dead?"

Alex's brain flashed to the crime scene, the image of what was behind him. Doyle's butt-ugly Ford Elite charred so bad you couldn't tell how butt ugly it was, hazmat-wearing paramedics standing around, wondering how to extricate the body while it's still hot. And here's Cecil asking, is Doyle dead? "Going to need to compare dental records." Alex stopped. He didn't want to explain it this way, knowing Cecil was going to hear it anyway. "But it looks like that, yes, Doyle."

"Renaldo did this." Cecil felt dizzy, bringing a hand to his head, easing himself down, sitting. "Jean-Max Renaldo."

"We don't know that yet." Unbuttoning the jacket of his gray knock-off Brooks Brothers number—three button, cut tight, Italian style—Alex felt the ground with his hand, dry, then joined his young partner. "I'm sorry. I know you and Doyle came up together, school." Stopping, searching for something meaningful to say, anything.

Ahh, Alex said he was less than a year from retirement, so much experience. Yet the words still escaped him in situations like this, probably because he was what an expert at the annual retreat called desensitized—did Cecil remember that seminar?—on account of having seen he didn't know how many dead people. So there was that. Plus, as a cop, Cecil had heard it all before, meaning Alex didn't have anything particularly new to share. He was just so sorry.

"Thanks, pards, means a lot, you showing emotion, almost," Cecil said. "And yeah, I remember the seminar, you vets pissing and moaning about how you don't feel anymore. Wish I couldn't feel anything. Sounds like a deal." Clasping his hands behind his head. "We got something, anything?"

Alex licked his lips, said, "Not much. Couple residents heard someone mocking Doyle, asking, does he want a light?" Taking a deep breath, letting it out. "And then, would he like some water? Also, they allegedly asked if he knew what Evian spelled backwards."

"Naïve." Cecil narrowed his eyes, open hand reaching out to the crime scene. "What kind of sick thrill-kill shit is that, does he want water? They burned him. I told him he should take the deal, spoke to the crown on his behalf, and they burned him because of it, me."

"Look, son, it's not on account of you." Alex put his hand on Cecil's shoulder, leaning in. "Can't guilt yourself for doing your job first."

"You saying it's Doyle's fault?" Cecil shook Alex's hand off. "Blaming the victim?"

"I'm not blaming anyone. No one's fault, other than those responsible, the culprits, on account of this is some deeply pagan shit to be doing over black-market auto parts, fraud."

"Never mind that." Cecil looked sideways at Alex. "Just tell me, do we have anything else? Anything useful?"

"Was talking to one of Sheff Dubois' boys, Hermosa. You know a Hermosa?"

"Si." Cecil spat in the grass. "I know a Hermosa, and if it's the same guy, what I know of him is he's an uppity spic being racist. I was up there last year to see a training video he was charged with showing on gay Dutch cops, diversity. He couldn't make it work on the computer, couldn't close a document using control shortcuts, so I tried to help him. Next thing I know, German porn pops up, the worst, and he's yelling, calling me gringo in front of other people, saying a bunch of other shit I no comprende."

Alex smoothed his closely cropped whitewalls. "I know you're in shock, Cecil, grieving, but you could clean some of what you say up, just a little, on account of—"

Cecil cut Alex off. "You going to have the same conversation with Hermosa, tell him no calling me gringo and other shit I no comprende?"

Alex hesitated, said no.

"Then don't tell me what to call Hermosa."

Alex shook his head, looking away. "What I'm trying to say is the only other thing I heard came from Hermosa. He was just here—got called out to some other nasty business that may or may not be related—so you need to learn to work with him if you want this resolved. Anyway, Hermosa says some winehead done claimed he heard someone shout, 'Write in Dick Gregory for president.'"

"Dick Gregory?"

"Probably means nothing," Alex said. "Like I told you, just some winehead perchance reliving the sixties, doesn't remember anything about Dick Gregory, save for he ran on a freak-and-love ticket against Richard Nixon way back, 1968, but actually ended up helping elect Tricky Dicky by siphoning too many votes from Hubert Humphrey."

"The fuck was Doyle doing here anyway, this part of town?" Cecil looked up at the corner, Filmores Hotel marking turf as the original bump & grind. "Given he's a possible target of Hells

Angels and maybe, probably Para-Dice Riders, I hope he wasn't here for the girlfriend experience. I specifically said no long walks, time being, so I would've assumed he knew I also meant don't go to places where biker kin congregate."

"Didn't you say he was talking to his expensive white-girl lawyer?" Alex pointed at an old three-story building with burnt-orange bricks and a newfangled wheelchair ramp. "Because Helen Tyndall's office is right in there, top floor."

"Doyle was supposed to tell her he's taking the deal," Cecil said. "Said he'd be meeting her later. I didn't know her office was here, that he'd be seeing her at night, so what? You're saying they got him coming out of his lawyer's?"

"Looks like it."

"How much you wanna bet this expensive white-girl lawyer turns out also to be Jean-Max's lawyer?" Cecil let his hands fall, rested them on his knees. "Or at least in his employ."

Alex said Jean-Max himself had been repped by Castonguay and Associates for some time. Yeah, well Cecil didn't see how Doyle was swinging an expensive white-girl lawyer, what with his accounts froze. Alex said hmm, that he'd pass that on to Hermosa.

"What are you two? Some sort of secret society, the ineffectuals?" Cecil raised his head then dropped it quickly, avoiding something else. "And looky-loo, perfect. Here comes Teddy going to tell me how it is."

"Okay." Alex looked, fighting off a smile. "Only stop calling him Teddy. Man's still wrapped tight on account of how you did the Fido employee so as he would release those cell records. Can't just go pushing, slapping, saying give me the evidence. You've got to finesse it."

"Barely touched him."

"I'm telling you, despite what you've seen in the movies, there's no hitting, being a cop." Shaking his head some more, Alex went on. "On top of which, Theodore doesn't like it when you say Teddy on account of he thinks you're making fun, disrespecting him, a senior officer, your boss. My boss."

"We're adults. What am I supposed to call him, mister? I'm supposed to call another grown man mister?"

"Call him Chief Inspector Almano, what he likes, what he is."

Theodore Almano was almost there when Cecil shielded his eyes from the TV lights, saying, "Teddy."

Biting the inside of his cheek, Theodore said he was sorry. That he knew how hard it was for Cecil to bust his old friend, Cecil showing even the veterans something, loyalty to the blue wall first. But this—this wasn't Cecil's fault. And again, Theodore was sorry, so sorry. Looking at Alex, Theodore was about to say something else when the theme from Hockey Night in Canada began playing in his pants.

Retrieving his cellphone, reading the call display, he said, "Apologies, boys, have to take this." Hitting the talk button. "You have reached the cellphone of Chief Fraud Inspector Theodore Almano. This is Chief Inspector Almano speaking." Nodding. "Yeah, I know it's you, Hermosa, what?" Listening, holding his hand out, stop, like Hermosa could see. "Say again." Taking a few steps from Alex and Cecil. "You sure it's her?" Listening, closing his eyes. "Dental records. Okay, I know we've got a cruiser outside Pam Jenkins' place already, but I want to build on that presence like it's the War Measures Act. Tell Sheff she's a potential witness and I said to get as many more people as you can over there. I want the area blanketed with uniforms, paddy wagons, guys slapping their palms with batons, a show of force. . . And yes, I've got Johnson and Bolan with me, will see that you get their files. Tell Sheff I said call me as soon as there's something, anything. I'll do likewise."

Without saying bye, Theodore held the phone out and hit the end button, looking at his detectives. Alex said, "What?" When Theodore didn't answer right away, Cecil repeated the question, calling the chief inspector Teddy.

"More bad news." Theodore scrunched his lips together. "They got your other witness, too. Same tools of production."

Cecil squinted. "They burned Mrs. Sabo? She's got kids, Christ sakes, a single mother."

"Sacred cow," Theodore said. "Even most of the other side agrees, code, no going after single women raising kids."

"They burned her and Doyle. We gotta... You know Jean-Max Renaldo did this, or at least had it done. We gotta..."

By the time Alex tried to stop Cecil, it was too late. No longer so cordial, Theodore was saying they don't gotta do fuck all. This was a homicide matter now, and Cecil was fraud. So if Cecil thought he was going to find some ambiguous region between the two departments and figure out a way of involving himself, he'd be reduced to chasing able-bodied people using handicap plates to park in cripple spaces, no matter where his loyalties fell.

"Yeah, yeah, yeah." Cecil swung his hand back and forth. "This is my friend we're talking, Teddy. You can't expect me to stay out of it."

Theodore stroked his militant chevron moustache, thinking he wasn't sorry at all anymore, Cecil calling him Teddy again, and giving him, chief inspector, the yeah, yeah, yeah. "That's another reason why you're staying out of it, because you are his friend. Last thing I need is some young punk on my squad going half-cocked on anyone he thinks might've had something to do with it, while at the same time operating under an obvious and gross conflict of interest. Aside from all that, this is homicide's case, as I already told you, and you know why?"

"On account of homicide does homicide," Alex said, picking up the beat.

Sour, Cecil looked at Alex. "I can't believe you."

Alex, his arms held high, looked at Theodore, back at Cecil. "What?"

"What?" Cecil nodded to Theodore. "Kissing Teddy's ass, openly."

Alex said nothing, watching Theodore point back at him, then Cecil. "Whatever happens next, you, Alex, are responsible for him, Cecil."

aturday morning, Antoine Côté pulled his tan '87 Mitsubishi Starion up to Port Credit Marina and used an electronic security card to let himself into the lot. Parking in spot 28, as per Jean-Max's instructions, next to Jean-Max's snot-green '79 MGB in 27, Antoine headed to the dock with a Tim Hortons cup in hand. About seventy meters away, he saw Jean-Max sitting in a chair out on his boat, wearing aviators, multicolor flannel, and denim. When their eyes locked, Jean-Max used a remote to summon his stereo, an elegant piano ballad that Antoine vaguely recognized floating over the marina. He knew the voice, that fat guy from the '70s who made an issue of his fatness with his name—Meat Loaf—was singing this beautiful ballad.

Antoine knew most of the words. Inside, he searched the archives of his mind for the song title, the refrain. And what did Jean-Max mean by playing it now? It came to Antoine just as he arrived in front of Jean-Max. The song title and Jean-Max's message being dramatically delivered: "Two Out of Three Ain't Bad."

Thinking at least it was better than that Québécois teenybopper shit Jean-Max usually listened to, Antoine stepped aboard the *Dine A Shore*, handing Jean-Max the to-go cup. "I know what you're going to tell me, Jean-Max. But by the time they got to Pam Jenkins' house, half the cops in Toronto were already there, waiting. They couldn't do it, couldn't get to her. It was no longer a viable plausibility."

"A viable plausibility?" Jean-Max looked away. Meat Loaf was lamenting a girl packing her bags when Jean-Max aimed the remote down below and killed the volume, turning to Antoine. "I paid for an extermination of green hornets, three. Leaving one behind is better than three. Sure, okay. But this Pam Jenkins can cut a deal of her own now, too, talk. She's the crown attorney's last hope, so he's liable to give her anything and everything she wants." Gesturing south. "A condo in Honolulu."

Antoine didn't think they'd give her a condo in Honolulu but knew enough not to mention it. Instead, he said he understood what Jean-Max was talking about, no question, and that Art and Gervais had in fact been paid to take out all three green hornets, fair enough. But before they did something reckless, Jean-Max had to remember that Pam Jenkins had refused to take a deal at every turn, refused to cooperate. Pam Jenkins was never the bad actor here, so why was Jean-Max so concerned about her?

"Because now she's the last of the green hornets, the only person who can hurt me. They can still get me on a little of this, a little of that, but without a green hornet in the witness chair, Helen, the new lawyer, says there's no chance to put me away, not worth their while. So now that the other two are gone, the crown will offer Pam Jenkins the stars, the sun, and the moon." Gesturing south again. "If she wants, they'll put her in a Hawaiian condo, fish for life."

Antoine couldn't ignore it this time. "They're not putting her in a Hawaiian condo, fish for life."

"They'll put her somewhere nice. Buy her treats."

"Alright." Antoine grimaced. "I'll see that Art and Gervais get the message, tell them to finish the job."

"See that you do." Jean-Max held a finger up. "And like last night, I want the victim spoken to bad, very bad, mocked. Also, what's the name of Art's bum boy again?"

"You mean his mechanic? Reggie?"

"Him." Jean-Max pointed at Antoine. "Make sure Reggie gets the message, too, that they know they are all three on the hook. Tell them we should never discuss this again, other than arranging for final payment once the contract is satisfied. Just talking about it is risky." Glancing to every corner of the marina. "Eyes and ears everywhere. Part of the reason why you pay guys half in advance is so you don't have to deal with adversities when it takes more time than their original estimate. Art and Gervais and Reggie have their advance money. They're not being paid by the hour, just a fixed fee to do a clearly defined job like any contractor, and I don't want to have to continue to renegotiate. Once I come to an understanding, that's it—it's understood."

Glancing around the harbor, boats bobbing as a cruise ship passed, Jean-Max felt his stubble, made a mental note to grab a shave, and went on. "Probably, while all this is in motion, I'm going to take a trip—maybe Vegas, maybe Myrtle Beach—and lay low for a couple or a few weeks, be off at an obscure scurvy bar when it happens. But Art and Gervais and Reggie have a job to do here, making sure Pam Jenkins stays shut up, and they need to go ahead and do that job without you or I holding their hands." Pointing at his deck. "I never want to hear about this again. I never want to discuss it again. I just want it done, now." Pointing in the direction of downtown Toronto. "Make sure they understand. I don't want them phoning me for clarification or anything else, not even on the burners."

Fine, Antoine would pass it along to Art and Gervais and Reggie, ensure they understood.

"Without prejudice," Jean-Max added.

Antoine didn't know what Jean-Max meant there, but fine, he'd pass that along, too. "Without prejudice."

Jean-Max removed the lid of his cup, blew at the steam, took a sip, and held his double-double up like a toast. "Nice." Looking out to Lake Ontario, white caps, he was about to be rewarded with more forgiving climes and boat chicks, but when? So far, it had been a cold, damp, lonely April aboard the *Dine A Shore*— just like the Anglo prairie stories they made him read in school— and Jean-Max wasn't very happy about it being cold and damp, which is why he was dreaming about warmer places where no one knew his name. For now, he just wanted to get rid of Antoine and go down below where everything was heated, maybe listen to some René Simard. Yeah.

"Last thing." Jean-Max reached into his shirt pocket. "I need you to call the new lawyer." Handing over a business card.

"Yes, why do we have a new one?" Antoine took Helen Tyndall's card, glancing at her contact information. "Why leave Castonguay?"

"Castonguay and Associates remains on retainer, but Helen is lead on everything and they are to use their considerable resources to assist her."

"So Castonguay works for her now?"

"Not in so many words." Jean-Max looked at his gray-and-orange Vans on the wood deck. "They report to her, take on some of the research, present her with options, serve as co-council. She is lead. That is how we are to say it, her orders."

"Why is she lead?"

"Because I can trust her completely."

"Why so much?"

"Because she is compromised. Had a gold-digging ex kept coming for more, so she approached me a few months back, when you were off, asked me to discretely resolve the situation. I told Art to tell his bum boy, what's his name again?"

"Reggie."

"Right, Reggie. I told Art to tell Reggie to elbow-cap the ex, mock him for being a layabout, without mentioning Helen. No. Instead, I told Art to tell Reggie to tell the ex to generally focus on being an honorable, hard-working man so he wouldn't get kneecapped next time. See, first his elbow, then, if he doesn't fly right, his knee." Jean-Max was trying to smile, but Antoine could see in his eyes that he wasn't entirely satisfied. "I mean, I offered to resolve the issue permanently, but Helen said it hadn't come to that, yet, so Reggie just elbow-capped him. Since, Helen's been invaluable vis-à-vis three of our new Para-Dice Rider brothers, who are indebted, loyal, after she got their extortion charges stayed because of lack of credible surviving witnesses. She's brilliant. Looks good for a girl her age, too. Experienced at being a lawyer and experienced at being a woman."

Antoine pocketed the business card in the jacket of his black Adidas tracksuit. "So why am I calling her?"

"To tell her I have a new client for her. Have her call Gordon Sung. Tell her to take care of him, bill me."

"Gordon Sung?" Antoine said. "You mean the crime reporter for *Eye*?"

Jean-Max nodded once. "The same."

"What is he anyway, ethnically, with a name like that, Gordon Sung?"

"Scottish Asian, I guess."

"Funny, he doesn't look Asian," Antoine said. "Looks like a regular guy, European."

"Yeah, well, whatever he looks like, he's looking at his second DWI. Get this. He was at a police bar, The Cruiser, cops buying him beers while he brags about his story catching the unit commander of 54 Division collecting crime stats by race. Poor Gordon, he didn't drive a block before one of those pigs pulled him over. Complete set-up. Make sure you tell Helen when you talk to her, how it was a complete set-up."

"Okay, but why do you care to help Gordon Sung? That piece he wrote last year, late fall. He may as well have out and said you had people in the police, some in police officialdom, in your pocket. Accurate, yes, but he's never been a fan of you."

"Well, he is now."

Confused, Antoine shook his head. "But why?"

Jean-Max sipped his coffee, said, "He's vulnerable, looking at the possibility of jail time, loss of his car, his job, maybe his apartment. Gordon needs to beat this thing, and he probably will with Helen's help. Once he does, he'll be indebted, like our Para-Dice Rider brothers. Valuable as a mouthpiece. Don't you see? I'll be able to get things I want into Gordon's paper while relying on him as a private source of police information."

Antoine figured *Eye* was more of a magazine than a paper. Now that he thought of it, *Eye* wasn't even a magazine, more of a bar rag. But sure, okay, Antoine could see the value in owning a crime reporter, whatever the medium. And yes, he'd let this Helen know.

"See that you do." Jean-Max handed over another business card. "I want Gordon resting assured that someone's taking care of him." Thumb-pointing at himself. "Me. Tell Helen to call him, let's say Tuesday before nine. That way, you can tell Gordon when to expect the call, put him at ease. Know what that's worth, Antoine, putting a man in control of information at ease?"

"A lot," Antoine said, looking at Gordon's card, back and front, pocketing it. And no problem. He'd call Helen Monday, first thing, tell her to call Gordon Tuesday, before nine, to bill Jean-Max. After, Antoine would call Gordon, brief him.

"Also, Art and Reggie and Gervais." Jean-Max pointed downtown again. "They need to get with the program and get their work done. Tell them exactly what I said. I never want to hear about Pam Jenkins again, other than reading in the papers that the last of the green hornets has been exterminated by necklacing, avec mocking. That is what I am paying for, necklacing, avec mocking."

"Roger that," Antoine said. "But listen, Jean-Max, they're going to have to wait until the cops get tired of watching out for her. I can tell Art whatever you want, but this isn't going to happen before lunch. They cannot get to her right now. You know that, right?"

Yeah, Jean-Max knew. He just wanted it done in good time, very good time. Then, like he'd been saying, he never wanted to hear about it again, no phone calls. On a lighter note, something else occurred. "And hey, thanks for those tickets last night."

"Were those outfield seats okay? That's all I could get on short notice."

"Perfect alibi." Jean-Max looked straight ahead, smiling pleasantly as if posing for the company website, click, then making eye contact. "We were on top of the Blue Jays' bullpen. When Billy Koch started warming up, I climbed up his ass, chirping about his control issues. I told him, sure kiddo, you can throw it a hundred miles an hour, but where's it going? You don't know. He proceeds to fire one over the bullpen catcher's head, glares back like it's my fault. He gets into the game, Jays up by one, does the same, runner on first jogs to second. After that, he gives up a short single, runners on first and third. Then John Flaherty comes up. That should've been it, game over. Flaherty's not a lousy hitter, but he's more of a defensive catcher, works well with pitchers. So what does Billy do? Throws it down the pipe—any major leaguer should hit that at any speed—and Flaherty lines a double. Jays lose 4-3. Great game."

"Great game?" Antoine half sat on the edge of the starboard ledge, hands at his side, palms down, holding his posture. He was confused again. "You wanted the Jays to lose?"

"Of course," Jean-Max said. "You know where I'm from. You, too."

"Me, too, what?"

"You, too, are from Quebec, and if you're a Quebecer, you must be for the Expos." Jean-Max made a face. "Otherwise, what's the point?"

Pondering the question, Antoine wanted to note that he wasn't actually from Quebec, that he was from Nova Scotia. He'd only moved to Montreal in '97 to escape a youthful indiscretion involving a Halifax police officer's wife and Reddi-wip, which was how he ended up working for Jean-Max, street cred. And sure, being bilingual made it easy to blend. But lots of people in Canada spoke French. It was a bilingual country, so why did Antoine ever have to explain, no, he was not related to Alain Côté who played for the Nordiques, that the name Côté was common.

Fucking Jean-Max, always looking to make Antoine of unmixed stock. Now that they were in Toronto, more opportunity, it bothered Antoine that Jean-Max was still trying to recruit him into the gang that put being Francophone on higher ground than being Canadian. Antoine figured assholes like Jean-Max were breaking up the country, dividing it between English and French when both had bigger problems. More than anything, it was just another reason to find a way out of Jean-Max's organization, if you could call it that. For now, Antoine deemed it prudent to concede Jean-Max's point. He was on about his burner phone system next, swapping in a new one for Antoine's old one, reminding Antoine that he, Jean-Max, would always answer with a bonjour, never a hello. That if someone ever answered one of

Jean-Max's burners hello, it was not Jean-Max and for Antoine to properly dispose of his phone immediately.

"Being lazy with the cellphones is how we almost got in trouble in the first place," Jean-Max said. "So let's not be lazy with the cellphones, the burners."

FOUR

Cecil spent the weekend watching and re-watching the 1988 Southwestern Ontario Secondary School Basketball Championship on VHS. Wow, he could relive that deciding game forever. Doyle throwing a screen as Milky Way Jones made that three-pointer at the buzzer. With Freida feeling bad for him, doting, prancing around in short-shorts and a threadbare Kim Mitchell shirt, serving another Keith's, Cecil said thanks, gulping, watching his younger self and Doyle hoist Milky so he could cut the net down with scissors. None of them, it seemed, realized that their days of meaningful basketball were over. Cecil was still chewing on that part Monday morning, so much bitter in his sweet, when Alex pulled up to Cecil's townhouse on Bleecker Street. Cecil saw the metallic 1995 Mercury Cougar right away, smoothing his sharkskin Sean John in the mirror, tugging on his blow-dried bangs, kissing Freida, and running out to the car. Alex told Cecil his lawn wasn't going to cut itself. Cecil shot Alex a look, silently watching him drive to the morgue where they picked up the ashes, as arranged, before starting Doyle's last journey home.

Alex felt bad for thinking it, but the trip was a mind-numbing drag. Cecil didn't want to talk. Normally, Alex would've put that in the plus column, only Cecil broke his silence to make inappropriate old-people comments, something about Depends, when Alex stopped near Woodstock for a pee. Worse, Cecil didn't want to listen to the radio or Alex's Pucho & His Latin Soul Brothers tape, either. So Alex just drove west on Highway 401 through on-and-off rains, passing field after field, the odd homemade sign declaring Farmers Feed Cities along with billboards pushing whatever honky-tonk tourist trap they were about to pass. Alex noted that there were a fair number of mini putts, like absolutely everyone had to pull off the road to knock a red golf ball through a windmill, and how was that going to make things better?

It wouldn't, he thought, finally hitting the Comber Side Road exit, taking it to Erie, the main drag of Cecil's hometown, Leamington. As they approached Russell Street, Cecil spoke for the first time since his inappropriate old-people remarks. "Take a right here. You'll see Reid Funeral Home on the left."

Alex followed Cecil's directions, pulling in, parking, thinking this Doyle didn't have many friends. Turning to Cecil, Alex said, "You ready?"

"No." Cecil reached into the back for Doyle's plain brown box, pulling it to his lap. "But I guess I really don't have a choice, do I?"

"You always have a choice, junior." Alex put his hand on Cecil's thigh. "What I'm saying is that this is a work-related matter. Nothing wrong with stepping away, professional. I can run the ashes in for you, run back, restart this car, and drive us home to Toronto. Take you bowling, or whatever it is you rural people do."

"You rural people? You know what they called me in high school?"

Alex bit his lip, waiting for Cecil to answer his own damn question.

"Toblerone." Cecil opened the door. "Because I was so good at basketball, I retired a champion. They used to say, 'Make it snow, Toblerone.' So don't be talking to me about you people when I was so deeply immersed in the black arts of African brown ball."

Alex remembered how basketball was actually invented by a white Canadian, James Naismith, then thought he better let everything slide, for today. Watching Cecil step out holding Doyle's box, Alex followed. And Goddammit if they took ten steps before some tall skinny brother, right about Cecil's age, almost thirty, came jogging over in his Sunday best, giving Cecil the secret Leamington handshake, saying, "Hey now... Hey now, Toblerone."

Cecil let go of the young man's hand, looking at Alex while he, Cecil, spoke. "And why would you call me that, Toblerone?"

The young man, perplexed, looked at Alex, then Cecil. "Because you were so good at basketball you retired a champion."

"Thank you." Cecil winked, shot Alex a look. "What'd I tell you?"

After some small talk about how Cecil, as Toblerone, used to make it snow—swoosh, nothing but net—Cecil introduced Alex to the young man, who went by Milky Way Jones because he could make a three-pointer from anywhere in the universe, just about. When they got around to the reason they were here, Alex watched both well up, holding each other without saying anything, tears running down Milky Way's face.

Releasing, doing the secret Leamington handshake again, they went inside, catching Mrs. Allenby on her way out of the Ladies'. Cecil held the box out as he walked to her, saying how sorry he was, that her son was a good man at heart. When he was done, she looked at the box and said, "May I assume that's Doyle?" Waiting for Cecil to nod, yes, she gently took the container, looked at it, and passed it off to her sister, who shuffled away. That's when Mrs. Allenby took hold of Cecil's black tie, saying, "I need to talk to you." Nodding over her shoulder. "In private."

"The Ladies'?" Cecil looked over her shoulder. "I can't go to the Ladies', trespassing."

"It's okay," she said. "There's no one in there, hopefully."

Cecil looked at Alex, who nodded, go ahead, and so Cecil followed Mrs. Allenby into the Ladies'. Alex thought this would be his last chance to tinkle without worrying about Cecil counting and providing inappropriate old-people commentary, so Alex ducked into the Mens' next door. Finding the place empty, downright luxurious with fine, fine cloth washcloths, he unzipped and positioned himself in front of a urinal. Midstream, ahh, he felt bad about missing church again yesterday. Then again, being Jehovah, he was thinking how he could make it up tomorrow, Tuesday, when he realized he could hear the conversation in the Ladies', at least parts. Cecil was talking but Alex couldn't make out the words. Then Mrs. Allenby started speaking, louder, mad, and Alex clearly heard her telling Cecil it was him who told Doyle to take the deal. Next thing anybody knew, Doyle was dead, probably killed by the same reprobates he was going to testify against. Then it sounded like a slap, another, another...

Yes, Mrs. Allenby was hitting Cecil, screaming who was he to tell her son to testify against animals like that? Slap. Slap. Slap. She hoped at least Cecil was getting a promotion out of this, and wouldn't he be proud, getting a raise for getting Doyle killed. Did Cecil remember his *Macbeth* from Leamington Secondary? Good, because Mrs. Allenby could only hope there would be enough soap and water in Hogtown for Cecil to wash Doyle's blood off his hands.

Alex finished his toilet dance, zipping, washing up while Mrs. Allenby told Cecil it was his responsibility to find the aforementioned reprobates and do them just like Doyle got done. And fuck it, by the time Alex was drying his hands, Cecil was saying okay, okay, okay, agreeing to whatever Mrs. Allenby wanted, but enough with the hitting already.

Out in the hall, Alex was still drying his hands, getting between his fingers with one of the fine, fine washcloths when Mrs. Allenby emerged from the Ladies', Cecil in tow, face red. She turned and glared. Cecil held his hands out, asked, "What now?"

"What now?" Mrs. Allenby pointed east. "Go back to Toronto and find them and get them." When Cecil didn't say anything, she pointed at the door. "That's what now."

Cecil dropped his head and left the building. Alex handed his washcloth to an employee, following Cecil to the Cougar where he fumbled for a cigarette, lit one, shaking, sweating.

"It's okay," Alex said. "You can smoke in the car today. Just crack a window. Let's get you out of here."

Cecil nodded, thank you. He was about to step inside when he heard running footsteps, turning to see Milky Way Jones slowing in front of him. Glancing at Alex, back to Cecil, Milky said, "May I speak with you before you go?" Cecil turned to Alex, saying give us a minute, putting his arm on Milky's shoulder for balance as much as love, and walked out of earshot while Alex crouched into the car. Behind a custom van with flying saucers and hot green alien chicks, Cecil dragged his cigarette, hand trembling.

"I heard what Mrs. Allenby said, some of it," Milky said. "And you know that's not okay. She's grieving. She'll come around, will regret what she said and did."

"Thank you." Cecil exhaled a plume. "I appreciate you saying that."

"But," Milky added, "if you do intend to do anything about it, I am here, if, you, you know, need a man from out of town."

"Let me ask." Cecil hit his cigarette, biting the filter, exhaling. "You still work at the marina?"

"Yeah, so?"

"So, you know how to drive a boat, right? Any kind of boat, you can drive it?"

"Pretty much," Milky said. Except for some extreme high-tech jobs at the military level, if it was on fresh water, Milky had probably helmed it. Why? What did Cecil have in mind?

"Nothing yet." Cecil hit his cigarette again. "I have to prove some things to myself. Need to be sure. Just keep yourself ready, available. You, an athlete, know how to do that."

"Will do. So when you get sure, call if you need a guy from out of town can helm most fresh-water boats." Milky held out a fist. "And you know, Cecil, a black man can do other things."

"I will at that, call you." Cecil made a fist, tapping Milky's championship ring with his own. "And yeah, I know blacks can do other things." Winking. "Like hit a three-pointer from anywhere in the universe, just about."

Cecil dropped his cigarette in a puddle before one more man hug and secret Leamington handshake. Then, back in the car, sitting on the passenger side, he lit another Export 'A' and cracked the window as Alex retraced his route, bringing them back the same way they came. Taking 401 east, Alex said, "What'd Snickers there have to say?"

"It's Milky Way," Cecil said. "Milky Way Jones, and it was personal."

"Personal, huh? Now I don't want to go making Mrs. Allenby

wrong, but I heard her through the wall, and that's not fair and just, what she said."

"How's that?" Cecil stared into his reflection in the windshield, eyes hazy. "I told Doyle I was doing him a solid. Now he's dead, in a bad way. And you know this is connected to Jean-Max Renaldo."

"Maybe, maybe not. But this is for Hermosa to figure out."

"Hermosa couldn't find ice in Iceland," Cecil said. "Fuck him."

"Look man, you have got to step back, and you certainly can't go doing people the way Doyle got done, even if you think you're respecting Mrs. Allenby's wishes." Alex waited for Cecil to say something. Getting no reply, Alex said, "Cecil?"

Cecil, snapping back, said, "What?"

"This is not our case anymore. Means we've got to step away, let Hermosa do his job. Tell me you understand."

"Yeah, yeah, yeah." Cecil waved Alex off. "I get it. Don't worry, I understand."

Cecil chain-smoked the rest of the way, regaining some sense of himself by the time they passed Cambridge. Wondering what an African lion safari was doing out here, nowhere, Cecil said he understood that Mrs. Allenby was in shock, and felt it prudent to tell Alex there was no way in hell that he, Cecil, was going to do what she was asking. Much as Cecil also understood her knee-jerk desire to lash out, he agreed that this was better off in homicide's hands, someone who could objectively prove Jean-Max did this in court. Hopefully, they'd fuck him up bad during the arrest. Speaking of which, Cecil said Alex was old, had been around forever, so could he please talk to his friends in homicide—even Hermosa, if need be—and make sure they fucked Jean-Max up when they arrested him?

Officially no, Alex said. Unofficially, he would try to discretely pull someone's coat next time he ran into Sheff Dubois' people at Fran's.

Closer to home, the CN Tower coming into sight, Cecil said he was calling it a day, that he wasn't going back to headquarters.

27

Alex said that wasn't a bad idea. He'd take Cecil home where maybe he could work out his ya-yas mowing his lawn. Forget the grass, Cecil said, take him to Kensington Market, drop him off. Alex said okay, but why did Cecil want to go to the market? If he needed groceries, Alex could wait in the Cougar while Cecil shopped, then take him home. No, Cecil said he just wanted to go to The Greek's and get good and drunk and numb his guilt. Alex said drinking wasn't any way to cope. And, by the way, did Cecil remember the seminar at the annual retreat where the leader said there were but two kinds of guilt?

"Sort of," Cecil said. "Hum me a few bars."

Okay, to summarize, Alex said true guilt is when we knowingly do something unrighteous, like when Cecil used excessive force busting Killean Jones, too much pepper spray, while false guilt is taking on blame for something that's not our fault, like Doyle's criminality. As such, Alex said the guilt Cecil was feeling was false, so he needn't feel any at all. And maybe, circumstances considered, Cecil should consider the Employee Assistance Program. No shame in that. Cecil said thanks, but he didn't care which kind of guilt he was feeling. He was going to numb it his way. Okay, Alex said, but The Greek's? Why did Cecil want to go there? It wasn't anything but alkies and druggies and whores and pimps, pagans.

Yeah, well that's who Cecil wanted to drink with. At least they wouldn't judge. And just in case Alex wanted to be any more helpful, Cecil made it clear that he wanted to fly solo. All that was fine by Alex. He didn't want to hang with alkies and druggies and whores and pimps anyway, so he was going back to headquarters, hopefully to meet Theodore and get their new assignment. Maybe even catch up on some paperwork. Otherwise, Alex would meet Cecil at 8 a.m. sharp tomorrow at the Jet Fuel Coffee Shop.

FIVE

Antoine Côté had dealt with the easy jobs earlier that Monday. He'd already used his landline—no reason to waste a burner—to call Jean-Max's new lawyer and got through right away, introducing himself and advising Helen Tyndall that Jean-Max wanted her to rep Gordon Sung on his DWI, briefing her on how it was a set-up, and kindly directing her to call Gordon early Tuesday, before nine, to touch base. Antoine gave her Gordon's work cell. And yes, in terms of clarity, Helen was to bill Jean-Max. Antoine then switched to his burner to call and introduce himself to Gordon, telling him when to expect Helen's call, to be free.

With that said and done, Antoine left his apartment to take care of some premediated banking, withdrawing $60,000 cash from his money-market account, leaving another twenty-plus to accumulate interest, assuming he could return to it, disappointed that was all he had to show for four years of dedication to Jean-Max. It didn't matter. The 60K was now hidden in some zip-up pillowcases, ready to go, and six of his seven Adidas tracksuits had been laundered. All Antoine had to do was get Jean-Max on his way to Vegas or wherever, without pissing him off. If Antoine could do that, he could come up with all sorts of reasons for fleeing after the fact. Of utmost importance, however, Antoine figured he had to follow Jean-Max's directives to a T until such a time. There could be no doubt about Antoine's loyalty, questions about him planning to run, doing calculated things without Jean-Max's knowledge. No, Antoine's getting-out-of-Dodge routine had to be seen as a last-minute dash for survival.

All that made perfect sense. Running like hell wasn't much of a plan, but the best Antoine could come up with as Jean-Max's situation disintegrated. And what was with the mocking? Once that started, Antoine knew it was time to giddy. Killing someone and getting away was difficult enough without standing around trying to be ironic when you know the cops are on their way. It was an unneeded degree of difficulty, gratuitous, and too much to ask of inexperienced hitmen like Art and Gervais and Reggie. That's why Antoine was more than a little conflicted about what he had to do next and spent most of the rest of the day sitting in his living room with his burner next to him on the couch and the utilitarian-tan dial phone in his lap, wondering how he was going to send Jean-Max's message to Art, without prejudice, whatever Jean-Max was talking about there.

Antoine was putting it off, knowing that Pam Jenkins would still be impossible—or at least extremely difficult—to eliminate. Nonetheless, that was the message Jean-Max wanted sent, so what the hell? Antoine kept telling himself he wouldn't have any-thing to do with the actual killing, as always. He just had to deliv-er the message advising Art that Jean-Max said to get on with it.

Telling himself the rest wasn't his problem when his burner buzzed, Antoine ignored it, taking a breath, waiting for the land-line to ring in his lap, which it did moments later. He pretty much knew who was calling both times, but gingerly placed the landline on the couch and jogged into the kitchen anyway to consult the call-display feature on his main landline. And yeah, it was Jean-Max, likely wanting to confirm that his message had been sent.

Knowing he had nothing to report, not even the slightest ef-fort, Antoine let the call ring through to his answering machine. After hearing a click, then a beep followed by his own voice invit-ing the caller to leave a message, Jean-Max spoke.

"Bonjour. Listen, I need a live update on that thing. I need closure before I leave, so give me closure. Please, I just want to know that the message has been delivered, you know, without prejudice. So call, let me know it's been delivered as dictated. And hey, you better not be screening. I reach out to an on-call employee, I expect you to answer unless you're laying pipe. Get back. I want this actioned, off my plate."

Hearing the click, Jean-Max hanging up, Antoine returned to the living room, sitting on the couch, putting the dial phone on his lap, and getting back to where he was physically and mentally before Jean-Max called. Wondering how the hell he was going to tell Art to do the Pam Jenkins job in such short order, Antoine chided himself, thinking he'd done this how many times? He knew how to deliver a message, deadpan, particularly on behalf of Jean-Max, so he told himself to buck up, punching numbers on his burner, listening to the landline on the other end ring nine or ten times—probably to allow Reggie to run into Art's office from the shop and pick up, if he so chose—before hearing a click, then Art's recorded voice.

"Hello, classic car drivers. You've reached Harwood's Select Auto Service. Reggie and I are on the shop floor right now, putting the finishing touches on another vintage vehicle and restoring it to factory specs. Please leave your name, number, and message at the beep."

Antoine hung up, thinking Art Harwood was so seldom on the shop floor. In fact, every time Antoine had seen Art, he was wearing a business suit. So he was probably doing the same thing to Antoine that Antoine was doing to Jean-Max, all of them avoiding each other's calls.

***

Alex dropped Cecil off at the corner of Baldwin and Kensington outside the Coffee Cup, eight or so doors short of The Greek's. Stealth, Cecil walked the rest of the way, opening the door, throwing daylight at the dark bar, and the chatter went silent. Cecil looked about, sure he smelled the faint taint of plumbing issues, everyone watching as he made an announcement. "I don't want any of you alkies and druggies and whores and pimps worrying about a thing this one time." Holding his hands high. "No busting your ass until tomorrow."

"Do you mean tomorrow after midnight?" said a call girl going by Venus de Milo. "Or tomorrow, as in not until morning proper?"

"Morning." Cecil pointed at her. "And don't push it next time someone cuts you slack."

"Don't you point at me." Venus took a sip of her house red.

"And why do I need slack? I haven't done anything."

"Yeah, right." Cecil looked her over, dramatic makeup, blue eye shadow. Her leather jacket was fully zipped, but the way she was sitting on the barstool, skirt almost covering her fishnet-clad ass, it was clear she was working. "Then why're you suited and booted?"

Venus took another sip, said she was hoping for a date.

"What kind?" Cecil said. "Prom?"

"Something like that."

Cecil said he should bust Venus for corrupting a minor. Venus said she didn't do anyone under eighteen. While she didn't mind breaking in virgins, she'd even ask for ID to be sure. Why was a fraud cop interested in busting her anyway? Cecil told Venus he wasn't busting anyone tonight, like he said. But, leaning in closer, lowering his voice, he said he could use a little company. Venus made a face, cross. Was Cecil looking for a freebie? No, Cecil wasn't looking for a freebie. When Venus began quoting prices, Cecil held her hands together and said it wasn't sex he was seeking, just a little conversation, and yeah, he'd make it worth her while.

Venus said alright, leading Cecil to a table near the back. When Robert brought over a Keith's for Cecil and another red for Venus, Cecil went to his inside pocket. Robert put a hand on Cecil's arm, said it was on the house all night for Toronto's finest, so long as Cecil made good on his word. Cecil confirmed he wasn't here to bust ass and Robert headed back behind the bar. Cecil turned to Venus, remembering she was younger than she looked under all that war paint. "You're a smart girl, an actual girl, why don't you get out, go home?"

"Because this is better." She was focused on the TV over the bar, sound off. Toronto pitcher John Frascatore was in a jam, bases loaded. "At home, I'm nothing. Here, I'm the female answer to Chris Kattan's Mango character on *Saturday Night Live*. Everybody loves me."

Cecil sighed, said alright.

"Alright, what?"

"Alright, I need some help, and I'm thinking maybe you can fucking help me, okay?"

"Sure." Venus was pleased this was moving along. "I'll help you, but you have to help me, too."

"I will," Cecil said. "Maybe we can help each other."

"Maybe we can. What do you want?"

Cecil looked around, the other alkies and druggies and whores and pimps off in their own little worlds of vice, grooving to Ella Fitzgerald and Louis Armstrong calling the whole thing off. "You know anything about what happened last week? The necklacings?"

"Like I said, I thought you were fraud." Venus felt her throat. Realizing, she returned her hand to her wine. "I can't help with that. Even if I could, I wouldn't. You see what happens to whoever crosses those people."

Cecil held his chin, amused. "Those people?"

"You know," Venus said. "Those people. People involved in those kinds of things."

"What kinds of things?"

"Things that are ultraviolent, necklacings."

Cecil looked at her, uncomfortable, said, "Know who I think does ultraviolent things?"

"Who?"

"Car people." Cecil slapped the table. "Vintage car people trading in hard-to-find parts."

Yeah, well Venus knew what she read in the paper, like everyone else, so Cecil wasn't batshit for drawing that conclusion. Just the same, she didn't know.

"Thing is," Cecil said, "I have to know. I need to know."

"Again, you're fraud. That tells me this isn't your case, so why do you need to know?"

Cecil saw something move on the table, flicked it, saying both deceased in this case were his witnesses, that he couldn't let that happen to his witnesses. If he did, word would get out that he couldn't protect witnesses and he'd have trouble securing them in the future. But it was more than that. He told her about Doyle, how they played basketball together. How they lost touch until Doyle turned up during this investigation, Operation Cooperation, that Cecil helped Doyle get a plea deal, but that's probably what got him killed. All that being so, Cecil felt a certain obligation to Doyle's mother to make sure his necklacing didn't go unpunished.

"For his mother?" Venus looked at Cecil, her voice climbing. "You want me to risk my neck, literally, by helping someone's mother get Jean-Max Renaldo?" As soon as his name escaped her mouth, she covered it, looking around. Again, nobody seemed to be paying attention. "Even talking to you about this is going to get me in trouble."

"You aren't going to get in trouble," Cecil said. "Nobody will know."

"How's nobody going to know? Soon as I find something out, you're going to want me to testify like you wanted your friend to testify."

"You won't need to testify. It's not like that." Cecil held his hands out to her. "You just get the info." Bringing his hands to his chest. "Then give it to me. After that, you're done."

"Done?"

Cecil chopped his right hand twice. "Done-done."

Venus asked if Cecil could make it so she wouldn't be busted, ever. Cecil couldn't do that, but he'd look out for Venus. Okay, but Venus said he'd have to look out for her for real. She was smiling a little when she said she could probably do it, for this Doyle's mother. At least Venus could try. There was this crime reporter for one of the alt-weeklies, *Eye*, she had coffee with most mornings at the corner. She said the guy had long ago crossed the line so far as drink and drugs were concerned, but still had a shaky little finger on the pulse of everything law and order. Cecil said Gordon Sung? Yeah, Venus said, Gordon. How'd Cecil know? Only two crime reporters at *Eye*, Cecil said, and the other, Schmidt, was a choir boy. Worst they had on Schmidt was a jaywalking, boring. As for Gordon Sung, it was well known that he was facing his second DWI, so it was just a matter of time before something gave with his job. Until it did, Cecil told Venus to handle the matter delicately, that Gordon was rumored to be in hock to bad people—some of them rogue cops—and not to give him anything of value in trade.

"Don't worry." Venus held up a hand. "I've been doing this a long time now."

"How long?" Cecil said. "You're my age, twenty-nine."

She reached across the table, pushed Cecil's shoulder. "How do you know?"

"I looked you up two or three times ago after I was here." Cecil drew his chin in, smiling. "Penelope Pinkus."

Venus reached across the table with a closed fist this time, punching Cecil's shoulder. "You snooped." Punching some more. "And don't ever call me that again."

"I didn't snoop." Cecil rubbed his shoulder. "I'm a cop, have a duty to investigate denizens of the criminal underground."

"I've got nothing worse than a loitering citation."

"They don't call it a citation. But yeah, I know that, too."

"What right do you have investigating me?"

"Gut instinct," Cecil said. "Also, you're a known prostitute. Makes you a criminal."

Venus leaned away, put her hands on her hips. "Being a sex worker is not a crime."

"Maybe not." Cecil was trying, really trying, to put this delicately. "But everything around it is, which is why you run with Gordon Sung, who is buyable, probably."

"Alright." Venus didn't have a handy argument for that. "So I'm going to get some info from my buyable friend. It'll be easy. He loves talking about what's in the paper when he's high on Percs and caffeine. Says he was born for it, news. But if I do that—pry info out of my buyable friend—what are you going to do for me, specifically?"

Cecil patted his breast pocket. "Hire you."

"Hire me? Motherfucker, I put myself out there for this Doyle's mom, and you're going to repay me by letting me suck and fuck you?"

"I'm happily married."

"Lots of my guys are, seventy-five percent, more."

"Yeah, well I'm not one of them." Cecil took a slug of his pale ale, swallowed. "Not saying I'm perfect, mostly, but I don't fool around, ever."

Venus checked Cecil's left hand, ring finger. "Where's your wedding band?"

"I don't wear it on the job so as not to invite fraudsters into my personal life."

Venus shot her eyes at the gaudy bauble mounting what appeared to be a crimson cubic zirconia on his right hand, middle finger. "Why do you wear that?"

Cecil twisted his championship ring. "It's different."

"Sure is. So what do you want then? What do you want me to do? You want a handy?"

"Hold me." Cecil scanned the room, lowering his voice. "I want you to hold me."

"You're happily married. Why don't you get your wife to hold you?"

Cecil didn't hesitate. He just out and said he didn't want to get any of this on his wife. When Venus asked why it was okay to get any of this on her, Cecil said it was already on Venus. That she pretty much knew who did Doyle. Sure, but that was just putting two and two together from the news. Now Venus actually had to talk to Gordon about it. That had to be worth more than Cecil's going to look out. If Venus was going to subject herself to that, and hold Cecil, it was going to cost the same as a suck and a fuck. So how about it? Would Cecil pay for a suck and a fuck even though he was just getting held? Yeah, Cecil said, so long as Venus held him all night. First, he needed a drink, twirling his index until Robert caught it, another round. With that in progress, Cecil checked the Accu.2 watch Freida bought

36

him for making detective, same make as endorsed by pornstar Shai "the Toolmaster" Shahar. Seeing it stuck on seconds, Cecil excused himself, saying he had to make a quick call. Okay, while Cecil was phoning his wife, Venus wanted to check in on the ball game. And fasten your seatbelt. It looked like Buck Martinez was bringing in Billy Koch.

***

Antoine used his landline this time, dialing, waiting nine or ten rings, then getting the answering machine at Harwood's Select Auto Service, again. Okay, it was official, Art was avoiding him. The prick was always there late Mondays overseeing rush jobs for kids who dented Daddy's classic car over the weekend, trying to get it fixed before Daddy came home and displaced his dookie. Hearing Art's half-witted greeting, Antoine thought about leaving a message, maybe telling Art that he, Antoine, would call back at a set time, and for Art to answer because they had to talk.

Thinking better of it, patience, Antoine hung up, resting the phone unit in his lap and looking across his living room at an unsigned painting of an old man in a tiny boat trying to land an enormous sailfish. In that moment, Antoine decided nothing was impossible. Well, maybe some things were impossible, like this thing Jean-Max wanted done. But again, all Antoine had to do was deliver the message. Reminding himself, okay, at least his part was doable, Antoine imagined the old man trying to land that sailfish. The thing was bigger than the old man's boat, so how was he going to do it? Antoine was just telling himself maybe Art's part in this wasn't possible when the burner buzzed again. Antoine readied himself, took a breath and hit the talk button, holding the cellphone to the right side of his face, hello.

"Bonjour," Jean-Max said. "Where have you been?"

"Out for a walk, a hike. I was about to call."

"Sure thing." Jean-Max waited, hoping the silence would force Antoine to divulge what he'd really been up to. When it didn't, Jean-Max said, "Have you delivered the message?"

"I have phoned Art, twice." Antoine closed his eyes. "But I only received his answering system, machine, whatever he's using."

"So did you leave a message, without prejudice?"

"No."

"Why?" Jean-Max said. "Why not?"

"For fear it might be incriminating, a voice recording."

"Oh." That sort of stopped Jean-Max. "Okay, so are you going to drive out there? Tell him face-to-face?"

Antoine waited a beat, said no.

"Why not?"

"Possible surveillance. Also incriminating."

"Okay," Jean-Max said. "Alright. I'm down with avoiding the incriminations, bad, but what are you going to do?"

"Sooner or later, he has to answer." Antoine placed the land-line on his couch, standing, crossing the room, speaking into his burner. "If he's stupid enough to be avoiding my number—I even tried once from my landline so he could see it was me—I will call him from a payphone. He's in business, takes calls from people using payphones who've been in accidents, so he has to answer payphones or customers will simply phone another garage with their last quarter. I will get your message through, without prejudice."

"See that you do. And fast. We don't have a lot of time. Tell him."

"I plan to," Antoine said. "What about you?"

"What about me, what?"

"Are you leaving soon?"

"Planning on it," Jean-Max said. "Some loose ends to tie then I'm gone."

"Will you be calling?" Antoine wanted a clean break, so he figured he'd better scare Jean-Max, ensuring that he wouldn't call for a good long while. "It's probably a bad idea."

"Oh yeah? Why so bad?"

Antoine was ready for this. "The fewer phone calls we have at this time, the fewer incriminations."

Again with the incriminations. But alright, Jean-Max wouldn't call unless he had to. Otherwise, he'd touch base before returning from wherever he was going. Just one more thing. Had Antoine talked to Helen about representing Gordon on the DWI? Yes, Antoine said it was all set. And yes again, Helen had Gordon's number and she would be phoning Gordon first thing tomorrow before she went to court. Perfect, Jean-Max said, confirming that Antoine had phoned Gordon, too, so that he would be expecting the call. Sorry, but Jean-Max had made a lot of arrangements here, so the last thing he needed was for Gordon to miss Helen.

SIX

Early Tuesday, Gordon Sung sat inside the Coffee Cup stirring sugar into black java from Peru as he looked about to see if anyone was watching. Clear, he reached under his untucked lemon polo into the fifth pocket of his skinny jeans and hooked a half Percodan with his index nail, faking a yawn, bringing it to his mouth, scooping it with his tongue, washing it down.

Wondering what the Peruvians did to make their coffee so good, he grooved on the bossa nova mix pouring out of the overhead speakers. Gordon didn't know any of the artists and he didn't care. The only matter of importance was that the mellow tunes went just right with the rest of his morning stimuli, so he sat there sipping his coffee while the Perc kicked in.

One by one, he waited for customers to leave their newspapers behind. First, the young hipster in a dark suit abandoned the *Globe and Mail*, which was okay. Gordon had to admit it was the best Toronto paper, hands down, but it was only so valuable to him as a local crime resource, what with its Canada-wide focus. After that, he got his hands on a *National Post*, same national issues, then a *Toronto Sun*, and finally, the mothership, the *Toronto Star*.

The *Star* owned Gordon's lefty bar rag, *Eye*, which was forever losing money, something for which the mothership was running out of patience. Essentially, at least so far as Gordon could surmise, the original business plan aimed to dilute the ad market for *NOW Magazine*, the established lefty bar rag, and hopefully force it under. Gordon figured *Eye* was doing fine advertising for prostitutes, dominatrixes, massage parlors, bathhouses, raves, and leather parties. Beyond sundry peccadillos, Gordon didn't see how *Eye* was having much impact on *NOW's* revenue stream, never mind forcing it under.

Editorially, *Eye* had been competitive since it launched in 1991, largely because the mothership could afford to bankroll some decent journalism. And time was, Gordon had been a pretty solid reporter, breaking a national a story on narcotics officers raiding safe-injection sites and skimming seizures to sell back to dealers. Pretty solid—Gordon wasn't ever going to be great, but he was such a damn good reporter that the deputy news editor had talked to him now and again about the possibility of being called up to One Yonge Street, the *Star*.

The more Gordy got drunky however—and not just drunk, but seen yelling at people in front of the liquor store—the more that talk faded, until, finally, he was stopped driving away from that all-male cop bar, The Cruiser, almost three weeks ago. He'd been so stupid, playing watchdog with the flatfeet, asking difficult questions, and writing hard-nosed, old-school news stories that often wormed their ways into the national dailies and generally pissed off a lot of people in the law-and-order community. So what did Gordon do in the thick of all that? He made himself vulnerable, again, went to their cop bar, drank their cop beer, free, shot his mouth off about catching the unit commander of 54 Division collecting crime stats by race, and proceeded to stumble to his car, get in, hit the ignition, and drive. It was like shooting fish in a barrel for the uniform who pulled Gordon over less than a block into his second DWI, Gordon asking, do you know who I am?

Oh yeah, the uniform knew. He most definitely knew.

Career-wise, Gordon could've survived his rookie DWI a couple years back. He'd taken the appropriate actions, checking into rehab and pleading guilty with a fistful of letters from fellow *Eye* staffers about how he did a valuable community service every day. Gordon was the workhorse, the watchdog, and maybe being the workhorse and watchdog drove him to drink, the deputy news editor, himself a bit boozy, wrote at the time. It was common in journalism—the stress, the hours, the psychological violence—so no wonder Gordon turned to drink.

It just wasn't so bad, so unheard of, for a reporter to wind up on a beer beef, and Gordon had enjoyed a reprieve, sort of, getting off with a one-year license suspension plus six months' probation, and what did that matter? Being in Toronto, he could get by on a combination of transit and cabs, so he sucked it up, staying clean and sober that whole time, returning to the glory of his early days at *Eye* and becoming a damn good reporter again, at least until he was done with that bitchy probie.

First came Gordon's return to drink, falling down after last call in front of the Bovine Sex Club, breaking his wrist, claiming he did it rollerblading. The emergency doctor prescribed enough painkillers to kill all kinds of hurt. Then Gordon was hooked on those, too. Luckily, the cops didn't bother with a blood test three weeks ago, relying only on his breathalyzer reading, .081, which was bad enough. That made him not just a bona fide boozer, but a known bona fide boozer inside the small world of Toronto journalism.

Now here he was, higher than the CN Tower in the morning, reading secondhand news, and relying on lowlifes like Jean-Max Renaldo to keep him out of jail. Did that make Gordon lowlife? Probably, but Gordon figured that, as a reporter, he wasn't objective enough to make that determination, that he needed to ask somebody else for comment. But who? And did he even want to know?

Noticing the waitress from Last Temptation, Pauline, walk south on Kensington Avenue, he thought maybe she was the one to take him in her arms and make all this go away, if only for a while. Once she faded from view, Gordon refocused on the savant from the fruit shop across the street with that asinine message scrawled across the back of his flannel shirt, You're Not the Boss of Me. The singer from Bunchafuckinggoofs, Steve Goof, walked into the picture wearing a mohawk a foot tall, said something, then You're Not the Boss of Me threw something at Steve. It appeared to be an apple. Steve grabbed it out of the air and started eating it, enraging You're Not the Boss of Me. Arms flailing, he was yelling, really giving it to Steve, when, behind them, Gordon noticed his part-time drug buddy, Venus, walk out of her building in a pair of army shorts and a Teenage Head hoody, and who was that wet-haired dude in a sharkskin suit with her?

"Cecil Bolan," Gordon whispered to himself.

Gordon knew Cecil from that big E bust Cecil initiated at the raves last year. That was also Gordon's story. He was all over it, with plenty of quotage from members of the rave community on how they were overpoliced, and, for the first time, the marketing department was loving Gordon, given how much advertising rave promoters were buying at *Eye*. Gordon broke the story wide open before the dailies even heard about it, so he recognized Cecil right away. On and off since, Cecil had made his way into the news, sometimes for the wrong reasons, like when he found himself the victim of a pretty girl's bank-machine scam. "The Gimmick" they called it. Every crime reporter in Toronto dined out on that one, Gordon included. But what was Cecil Bolan doing now, freshly showered, leaving Venus de Milo's apartment building with her?

Glancing at the wall clock, almost eight, Gordon determined that Cecil had probably been there all night. He was facing Venus, saying something. They didn't embrace or do anything intimate, just shook hands, so Gordon was thinking maybe, just maybe, the detective wasn't actually shagging her, but why else would a man spend the night with Venus?

Seeing them part, Venus making for the Coffee Cup, Gordon buried his head in the *Star's* local section, not reading, but listening intently as Venus opened the door, ordering her usual, coffee of the day with cream, then walking toward the window, noticing Gordon and sidling up, saying she was hoping to see him and could he spare a Perc?

Gordon considered saying he was fresh out, but Venus had shared more than he reciprocated. Besides, he figured she'd be increasingly likely to tell him what she was up to if she, too, was as high as the CN Tower, so he said sure, hooking his last half Perc out of his fifth pocket, sliding it to her. She dropped it into her mouth by faking a cough, washing it down with coffee. Gordon was tempted to just out and ask what was up with Cecil Bolan walking out of her place with wet hair but figured the less he talked, the better. It was an interview technique Gordon learned at Centennial College, journalism school, to just stand mute as much as possible, that the discomfort of dead air would often be enough to get the subject talking, blurting out important information.

"So," Venus said, "are you in like deep thought?"

"Naw." Gordon looked down at his lap, denim. "Just stoned."

"A little early, isn't it?"

"Give yourself a few minutes. You'll be same as me."

Venus said okay, waiting for the melt-in-your-mouth massage, blinking slowly. "What are you working on these days?"

"Filed this week's story yesterday. News feature on police corruption hinging on allegations by Malcolm Tate, city councilor, Ward 45, that a 52 Division cop dropped a dirty gun at a scene where he shot an American Samoan, unarmed, here on a human rights mission."

Venus had heard about Tate's allegation on the radio, but what sort of human rights mission was the Samoan on? Venus didn't remember that part.

"He's forging ties with Canadian Aboriginals," Gordon said. "Identifying common issues they can work on together, treaty and water rights." Chin-pointing at the *Eye* rack near the door, some dude in a Victorian wig sticking his tongue out on cover. "For now, I've got my nose to the ground for next week, sniffing for something, anything. Waiting for something to happen."

Venus pulled the *Toronto Sun* in front of her, flipping pages until she saw the headline, POLICE SEEK WITNESSES IN NECKLACING INCIDENTS, pushing the paper in front of Gordon. "I bet your bosses would be interested in something fresh on this." Venus waited for Gordon to bite. When he didn't, she said, "If you had an idea where it came from, who might've done it, I bet your editors would want your readers to know."

"I bet they would." Gordon avoided eye contact. He considered challenging Venus, asking if she had a theory, but decided to leave it there. "I bet they would."

The two sat in silence, the drug bringing Venus to the height of the high. Gordon was tempted to change the subject, just to be kind, then decided getting to the bottom of it might be useful. He sat patiently until Venus looked around with relaxed eyes, lowering her voice, saying she read the papers, too. Like everyone in Toronto, she knew it had something to do with that green hornet play on classic cars, so the list of suspects would, probably, be, you know, short. That's when Gordon pounced, asking Venus who would make her list?

"It's just everyone's talking about it." She thought she should've been taken aback, and she was a little, Gordon piping up so abruptly. But he couldn't know what she was up to, so she decided to play along. "I know what I think. I'm curious to know what you think."

"I'm not paid for what I think. I'm paid for what I know, what I can find out, prove. So if you can help me prove something, that really would be a community service. Not to mention a bit of redemption for people like us, part-time drug buddies."

Venus laughed, said yeah, sipping her coffee. "That would sure be something."

"So can you?"

"What?"

"Help me prove something here."

"Oh God, no." Venus felt her throat, pulling her hand away. "I'm just interested."

"Why so interested?"

"It's just, you know." Venus motioned out the window, You're Not the Boss of Me yelling at a poor old lady now. "A girl in my line of work has enough to worry about, now this."

"So you think this has something to do with the sex trade?"

"No, no. It's probably just the car people, like they said in the papers."

"Well, they didn't out and say it was the car people in the papers."

"It was between the lines, car people, and you know who's

in charge of that." Venus was on the cusp of letting the name Jean-Max Renaldo escape her lips but stopped herself, waiting for Gordon to say something. When he didn't, she said, "I hope they get 'em, is all."

"Get who?"

Venus passed a hand over everything and nothing. "They, them, him." Stopping, pointing at Gordon. "You know it was a man who did this, men. And I think you know it was the man in the boat who sent those men, maybe."

"I don't know," Gordon said. "I really don't."

He thought about pushing harder, but he didn't need to. Besides, the last thing Gordon wanted was proof that Jean-Max had those people lit up, because that would have only further compromised him, Gordon. No, it was enough to know that Venus walked out of an all-nighter with Cecil Bolan then made a beeline for Gordon, asking who did those necklacings. Clearly, Gordon thought, she was trying to get something out of him to bring back to Cecil Bolan, and that would be enough of a morsel to feed the man in the boat for now.

Wondering why Gordon was so cagey—he had to have an idea, probably protecting his sources, his story—Venus changed the subject, asking did Gordon have a heart attack every time Buck Martinez brought in Billy Koch? Even when Billy did save a game, there was drama. A wild pitch. A hit batter. Sometimes, like last night, Billy would plunk two in a row.

Baseball? Gordon didn't follow sports. Venus knew that, so why was she talking to him about baseball? Gordon had heard the name, Billy Koch, yes, but he didn't care.

Finally, after finishing most of her coffee, Venus said she had to get cleaned up for an early riser, standing, kissing Gordon on the top of his head, thanking him for the Perc. She left her cup at the counter, heading out the door, back to her building. Seeing her disappear inside, Gordon was startled when his work cell rang. He didn't recognize the number, but one of Jean-Max's people, a guy that went by Antoine, had called last night to tell

Gordon that a lawyer, Helen, would be calling early today, so you bet Gordon answered, hello.

"Gordon, this is Helen Tyndall. My understanding is that you're expecting my call?"

"Yes." Gordon was relieved. "Good to hear from you, Ms. Tyndall."

"Helen's fine. Listen, just to get through formalities, I also understand you're good to go with me being your legal representative."

"Yes, thank you. And my understanding is that your fees—"

Helen cut Gordon off, said he had a very, very good friend taking care of that.

Gordon thanked her again, waiting for the rest.

"Okay," she said. "I'm chasing your paperwork, so this call is just to touch base and get us set up."

"Can I really go to jail over this?"

Helen paused, said, "Theoretically, but it's too soon to go there. Let's wait until I get eyes on the paperwork, see if the arresting officer made any mistakes, broke protocol. Also..." Pausing again, the sound of notes being shuffled. "It's my understanding you were at a police bar, drinking free police-bar beer, before a member of the police pulled you, a police reporter, over."

"All true," Gordon said. "In fact, I'd just broken a story catching unit commander of 54 Division collecting crime stats by race."

"See? That's three potential conflicts of interest right there. I already have something to work with. So listen, Gordon, let's wait on your paperwork and set a phone meeting for a week today, Tuesday, 11:40 a.m.-ish, and go from here. Sound good?"

Gordon's outlook had improved, so yes, that sounded great. They would talk again on Tuesday, May 1st, at 11:40 a.m.-ish. He was just writing it down. Thank you again. Bye now.

Clicking off, depositing the work cell in his backpack, Gordon sat back, thinking of what this was going to be worth in legal fees, ten grand, probably more. Remembering Helen's words, Gordon thought, yes. He did have a very, very good friend in Jean-Max. It wasn't unconditional love. Not even close. Any affection would always revolve around Gordon's ability to pay some sort of ethically challenged dividend, so it wasn't going to end well. But for the here and now, there was one person, just one, who was doing something to save him from losing his license, job, his home, and maybe his freedom. So you're damn right Gordon was reaching into his pack for that burner Jean-Max sent over, avec instructions on how to call Jean-Max's burner, and punching in the number. What was it that Jean-Max had told Gordon to listen for? Right, Jean-Max said he always answered bonjour, never hello. If someone answered hello, it was not Jean-Max, but maybe a cop, someone who had taken the phone. In that case, if someone answered hello or anything other than bonjour, Gordon was to dismantle, destroy, and dispose of the phone.

nside the Jet Fuel Coffee Shop, Alex sat alone at a round table for three minding his latte as well as one he bought Cecil. The Jonathan Richman playlist was running off the Mac behind the counter, Jonathan urging patrons to give Paris one more chance while Cecil, hair almost dry, pushed through the throng clamoring for lattes, Americanos, and expressos. Cecil told the owner, Johnny Jet Fuel, he ought to start serving normal coffee, in addition to that metrosexual shit. Johnny told Cecil all drinks here were expresso-based, so he should fuck off for good this time, that Johnny would even pay Cecil's tab at Tim Hortons if he promised to stay there.

Cecil told Johnny he'd bust his ass sometime out on Parliament Street. Then Cecil made eyes at Kim the Cougar, saying he loved her Elvis purse, making her smile. But Cecil couldn't leave it there. Always had to be some kind of slap and tickle with Kim, probably because Cecil was kind of turned on by her penchant for younger men. He'd seen her around, snuggling with dudes in his age range—late twenties, early thirties—so Cecil liked to make a point of getting her attention. Stopping next to her, he said, "Hey Kim, I think you should meet this pal of mine on the force. You two'd be perfect."

"Oh yeah?" Kim straightened Cecil's lapels, flirty. "Why'd we be so perfect?"

"He's tired of romancing cougars. Now he's desperately seeking a saber-toothed tiger."

"Is that an old-person joke?" Kim was mad at herself, letting Cecil make her the punch line, again. "If that's an old-person joke, I'll shove my cane up your narc ass."

Pleased to be under her skin, Cecil said he wasn't a narc and Kim didn't have a cane, that she wasn't that old, yet. Pushing along, he told some bike couriers to get in their lanes, nudging them out of the way. The place wasn't at capacity, but every table

49

had at least someone sitting there, so it took some actual detective work before Cecil located Alex near the stairs and sat down in front of the untouched latte, taking a sip, looking up with a milk moustache. "It's cold."

"It was hot at eight o'clock, which was when you were supposed to be here, as agreed." Alex looked at the wall clock. "It's cold because you're more than twenty-five minutes late."

Sweaty from his walk from the market, Cecil held out his watch, said it wasn't his fault. His watch was stuck on seconds. Over his shoulder, Alex noticed Michael Ondaatje wander through the room looking for a place to sit and narrowing in on the open seat between Alex and Cecil, who was mumbling about time being a social construct when Michael tapped him, Cecil, on the shoulder, politely asking if he could join the table. Alex held a hand to the open chair, about to say please do when Cecil said fuck no. They were discussing official police business, and that was no place for an unkempt bearded guy who looked like an ethnic Nick Nolte on a bender. At that, Michael backed away and scooted up to the next level, out the back.

"Cecil," Alex said. "You done just told Michael Ondaatje to fuck off."

"Didn't say that." Cecil looked around for the unkempt bearded guy who looked like an ethnic Nick Nolte on a bender. "And he's Michael who?"

"Ondaatje. Author of *The English Patient*."

Cecil snapped his fingers. Said Freida made him watch the movie, buzzkill, so Cecil didn't bother reading the book.

"No doubt," Alex said. "No doubt. Anyway, it looks like we're going shopping today."

Cecil showed teeth. "Shopping?"

"Shopping." Alex picked up his latte, finished it. "Theodore has us staking out the Eaton Centre where there's been a rash of identity thefts." Standing, smoothing his indigo Perry Ellis suit, slim fit and machine washable. Nodding to the front door. "Will brief you en route."

As they walked through the throng, Cecil sucking back most of his latte and slamming the glass on the counter, Kim took a final shot, saying Cecil couldn't excite himself. Cecil looked ahead, smiling, pleased he had Kim's attention. It was a good morning so far.

Out on Parliament, sitting in the Mercury Cougar, Cecil was making a figurative connection between the car and Kim when Alex keyed the ignition, Pucho & His Latin Soul Brothers hitting the speakers with a spicy instrumental, "Descarga On Las Palmas." Cecil hit stop on the cassette, playing with the radio. Alex killed the volume, slapping Cecil's hand away.

"The fuck?" Cecil said. "I'm not your little brother."

Alex said that was for Goddamn sure. Putting the car in drive, he pulled a U-turn, took a right on Carlton. When Cecil started back in with the radio, Alex slapped his hand again.

"How come I can't at least sometimes pick the music?"

Alex stopped for a red at Sherbourne, saying, in his experience, allowing Cecil to DJ had previously resulted in him turning the volume too loud and singing along—shouting, actually—to Ricky Martin doing "Livin' La Vida Loca." Conduct unbecoming.

As Alex took the green, Cecil said at least Ricky was a real Latin, more than Cecil could say for Pucho and his so-called Latin Soul Brothers. Their singer, this Pucho, was really named Henry Brown, as Alex previously admitted. Also, Cecil said playing Ricky was a compromise because Alex was always wanting to listen to world music, Latins in particular, and that Ricky, as a former member of Menudo, was a fine representation of world music. Alex said Ricky solo was so over produced that he was not world music, that Menudo was a boy band, so playing Ricky was not a compromise, making it unfair to compare Pucho to Ricky. Cecil partly agreed, saying Ricky sold more records so he had to be better. When Alex said sales were not always an indicator of quality—Eddie Murphy's debut music LP, terrible, went gold on the strength of that Rick James produced gibberish, "Party All the Time"—Cecil said he should be able to pick the music at least some of the time, irregardless of all that.

Hanging a left on Yonge, Alex said Cecil would never, ever be allowed to pick the music in this here vehicle. And why's that? Cecil wanted to know. That wasn't very democratic. Alex said he didn't need to be democratic because this was his car, his rules.

"Not really," Cecil said. "It's now your second ex-wife's car— the angry Yugoslavian girl with hairy armpits and with no neck— and she only lets you use it because it's your work vehicle, your way of milking mileage, paying alimony."

Alex said it was still more his car than Cecil's, and that Svetlana had a fine neck when he helped her immigrate in '94. Since, Alex said, she'd been eating a lot of stress over the world she left behind. Yeah, Cecil said, she'd also been eating a lot of ćevapi, apparently.

Pulling up to the Eaton Centre parking kiosk, Alex pretended he didn't hear that and flashed his shield at the girl inside. Sent into the spiral, driving up two levels before finding a spot on P3, he was about to start briefing Cecil on why they were here when he noticed something. Wasn't Cecil wearing the same suit as yesterday, the sharkskin Sean John? Cecil said it was the cleanest thing in the hamper, that at least he showered. But maybe, probably, he should pick up some fresh socks and unders while they were at the mall, change here.

Alex said yuck, briefing Cecil.

As Alex mentioned at the Jet Fuel, identity theft was fast becoming an issue at the Eaton Centre, where customers were most recently targeted at The Bay. In particular, they were on the lookout for a young couple who appeared to be awfully good at it.

Their play revolved around scamming customers using credit cards to pay for big-ticket items. The woman, posing as a floorwalker, would stand lookout while the man used a cellphone to call the cashier. Passing himself off as a customer service rep, he would instruct the cashier to casually update said shopper's address, social insurance, driver's license, and credit card data. The cashier would usually comply and share by repeating the information into the phone. The couple would then use the information to obtain credit, buying top-shelf merchandise—clothing, food, liquor, golf equipment, elegant ladies unmentionables, that type of thing. Alex told Cecil they had taste, sense of color, probably a nice place.

"How lovely for them." Cecil shook a cigarette out of his pack. "It's a crime, sure. But I resent it's a police matter. Department stores and credit card companies ought to put their heads together, deal with it themselves. They're the ones throwing all this info around. So why do the police, us, have to clean it up when the wrong people get a handle on it?"

"I see your point, but please consider what Eaton Centre stores pay in taxes, our salaries. We're just foot soldiers, sent in where we're needed, following Theodore's orders." Alex watched Cecil light a cigarette. "And what are you doing smoking in my car?"

"You said it was okay." Cecil took another hit, holding it until he could crack the window, blowing smoke through the gap. "You said I could smoke in the car."

"That was yesterday. Back when I was still trying to see you as an empathetic character."

Cecil frowned, held his hands out. "What changed?"

"What changed is that ever since you walked through the door of the coffee shop, late, you've been pissing off every person you come in contact with, including Johnny Jet Fuel, Kim the Cougar, Michael Ondaatje, the bike couriers, and me." Alex was mad he had to explain it, Cecil's audacity. "What changed? Young motherfucker, straight outta buttfuck, telling me this is not my car, insulting my second ex-wife, buggering with my stereo, schooling me on Pucho & His Latin Soul Brothers being race impersonators, that Ricky Martin's better. You're basically a trainee, Cecil."

"I'm somewhat new at being a detective, yes." Cecil lifted his shoulders, let them fall. "So what?"

"So what? So what is it's time for you to take the lesson."

"And what lesson would that be, pards?"

Alex burned inside, the way Cecil was wearing yesterday's Sean John, wanting clean underwear and socks, hungover, and up to

God knows what last night, probably freelancing. "The lesson is we're at work, and work isn't always what you want it to be."

Inside the Eaton Centre, after a quick washroom break, Cecil wanted to buy his fresh boxers and socks, so they hit the Gap. Paying, Cecil asked to use the change room so he could get into his new pineapple skivvies. The clerk made a face, but it wasn't like this was her first weirdo, so she pointed Cecil to the back and took the next customer, a speedy Jack Kerouac wannabe buying khakis and talking in run-on sentences. Minutes later, Cecil was feeling fresh, yeah, walking through the mall.

Alex, reaching into his pocket, handed over a grainy security print of what he said were the perpetrators. Cecil couldn't see a girl anywhere, but if this was the guy, he had dark hair, bone straight. Easy to style, Alex said. Wearing a ritzy outfit, too, Cecil added—a black sports jacket with a white-shirt-and-black-tie combo, gold details on the collar and sleeves, likely proceeds of crime. All that was important, but Alex said the key point here was that the guy was making a cell call from ladies' underwear, panties everywhere, and that was probably his comfort zone.

"He's a sissy, is what you're saying?" Cecil said. "Likes to play dress-up?"

"He likes to commit fraud, is what I'm saying. Feels like panties is a good place from which to operate." Alex pointed at the photo. "Has a good view of the store, the cashier."

"Can I hang onto this?"

Alex said sure, slowing then stopping at the walkway to The Bay. "Now let's go over it again. This couple, if they're here, will be looking to obtain shoppers' personal information. According to Theodore, what we're looking for is a woman posing as a floor-walker. She's, as I say, actually standing lookout while her guy—he plays the customer service role—uses a cell to call the cashier and steal their data. All the cashiers, particularly those in ladies' underwear, know police will be here, so they've been instructed to comply. Once the perpetrators have extracted the info, and only then, do we move in, make the collar."

"That's so stupid," Cecil said.

"Well, it's Theodore's plan, due respect. So, according to you, why's it so stupid?"

"What if that happens, but we're in the wrong part of the store? Bay's a big place, six floors, so more customers are likely going to get ripped off and inconvenienced before we solve this. Teddy's using customers as bait."

Alex thought on it, said Cecil had a point, no doubt, but that was Theodore's plan so they were just going to follow directives. If more customers got ripped off that'd be on Theodore, not Alex and Cecil. Their job was simply to follow orders, stop the fraud, and arrest the perpetrators. That settled, they inserted their earpieces, activated their mics, tested them, and proceeded to ladies' underwear on the second floor. Looking around, no one about other than a salesgirl moving in a rack of pastel bras, Alex said, "Let me have that picture for a bit."

Cecil reached into his jacket, handed it over. "What are you going to do with it?"

"Take a look around. See if I might find them in that summer western collection, How the West Was Worn, over yonder. Maybe get myself a hat in the deal."

"What am I supposed to do?"

"You have the important job, surveilling ladies' underwear."

"And what if someone asks what I'm doing surveilling ladies' underwear?"

"Just tell them you're with Operation Panty Raid."

"Serious?"

Alex nodded. "Theodore said staff here have been briefed, that they know."

"Okay," Cecil said carefully, studying Alex's old-people eyes and looking for a hint of smile. "Operation Panty Raid."

Alex told Cecil he'd see him in a bit and headed yonder.

Cecil wandered, checking out garters and stockings when a saleslady came over, making nice, asking if Cecil knew his partner's size. Cecil pointed off in the direction of How the West

Was Worn, said Alex was probably an XL. Saleslady was slightly confused. But then girls were named Alex, too, so she went with it, pointing out garters available in XL when Cecil interrupted, saying he wasn't here to buy Alex a fucking garter.

"Then what are you here for?"

Cecil winked exaggeratingly. "Operation Panty Raid."

The woman nodded, ah-ha, backing away, telling Cecil to take his time.

He lingered, shuffling from aisle to aisle, checking out silk robes when an actual floorwalker confronted him.

"Sir?" The floorwalker pointed at the saleslady glancing at them from behind the cash register. "Did you just tell that girl you're here for a panty raid?"

Cecil put his left hand on his pepper spray. "Operation Panty Raid."

"What's that? Some hazing ritual. Some seniors put you up to this?"

"I'm twenty-nine," Cecil said, "done with school."

The floorwalker made the come-here gesture with his index, advising Cecil to follow. Fuck that, Cecil went for his shield, flashing it. Telling the prick his place was under surveillance, that he was supposed to be briefed. The floorwalker put his hands up, said he didn't know. But fine, Cecil was a cop, and sorry, officer. Cecil said he wasn't just an officer, but a detective, and for the floorwalker to make himself scarce before he fricked up the investigation and Cecil slapped him with some obscure interference charge that would take years to work through the system.

As the floorwalker sputtered off, Cecil pressed his talk button, asking Alex where he was, another bathroom break? Alex said yeah, he had to go, all that coffee. He was in bedding now, checking out zebra sheets that felt like cotton, that his new girl Sondra would be all over this. Yeah, well Cecil said Alex better fly back to panties before Cecil started busting staff solo. Alex told Cecil not to bust staff solo, that he, Alex, would be over soon. He just wanted to see if they had the same brand in leopard, that maybe he'd do a little mixing and matching on account of how much Sondra loved safari themes.

"This for your bedroom?"

"Of course, Cecil. Sheets are for beds, why?"

"Sounds like maybe you're going for the massage parlor look, sleaze. Somewhere to bang your bitch."

"You can't call Sondra that. Do I ever call Freida that?"

No, Cecil said, but then Freida wasn't into safari themes. Also, Freida was Cecil's wife, not some bitch he banged.

That settled, Cecil lingered, waiting. But Alex wasn't coming right over. No, he was still in bedding, screwing around with pillowcases. Apparently, they had a bed skirt in giraffe, same brand, on sale, 40 percent off. Alex was arranging all the different things together when Cecil said he was pretty sure he saw the perpetrator from the picture, the guy.

"Like I already said, fly the fuck back, and bring that photo."

"Why? What do you see?"

"The guy in the picture, I think. He's over poking around in granny panties."

"What does he look like?"

"He looks like the guy in the picture."

"Describe him," Alex said. "I'm about to make my purchases after picking all these fine things out. Want to make sure it's worth my while before walking away from my purchases."

Cecil was pissed, telling Alex the guy had dark hair, bone straight. And he appeared to be wearing the same outfit—black sports jacket and white-shirt-and-black-tie combo, gold details.

"Do you see his partner anywhere? A woman?"

Cecil scanned as far as his eyes could see. "Negative."

"Well, Theodore said they work together, so just keep one eye on him and another looking for her. I'm going to make these purchases then come right over, help you."

"Thanks," Cecil said. "Thanks, pards."

While Alex was presumably making his purchases, Cecil saw the guy go for his phone. He thought about radioing Alex again but a fuck of a lot of good that was going to do. Help? Cecil had asked twice now. He was alone, loitering in women's underwear, tired of listening to Alex play Jehovah. And looky-loo. As soon as the guy stopped pressing numbers on his cell, the phone at the cash rang. That was all the evidence Cecil needed to nip this shit in the bud and save a lot of people a lot of grief. On his own, he IDed himself, police, crossing the floor, making a beeline for the guy, turning him around and telling him to kiss the carpet. When the guy didn't comply, Cecil could only surmise he was resisting and proceeded to take his phone and use it as an instrument to beat him to the carpet, which he'd explicitly been told to kiss. About that time, Alex showed carrying three shopping bags as he said, "What the fuck, Cecil?"

"I'm subduing the suspect, rendering him nonviolent."

Alex let his bags fall, hurrying over, holding Cecil's arms, telling him to drop the phone. That's not the suspect, Alex said. Cecil dropped the phone, let the guy go, turning to Alex, the two of them holding each other, eyes locked when Cecil asked who was it then? Alex pushed Cecil away, saying that was the city councilor for Ward 45.

EIGHT

After Gordon used his burner to call Jean-Max's burner, Jean-Max used another burner to call Antoine's burner, telling him get to the *Dine A Shore* tout fucking suite. That said, Antoine picked up a double-double and drove out to Port Credit Marina, going through the security ritual, waiting on some asshole in a Para-Dice Riders jacket to pull his Harley out of spot 28, then parking his Starion next to the MGB, walking out to the boat and handing Jean-Max the Tim Hortons to-go cup. He took the lid off, blew at the steam, had a sip, savoring, swallowing, merci.

"You're welcome." Antoine figured he'd cut to the chase. "And look, if this is about Pam Jenkins, I've been calling Art and—"

Jean-Max raised his hand, stop, telling Antoine to tell Art that him and Gervais and Reggie still had to deal with that Pam Jenkins job, but to prioritize it as Job B. Jean-Max said he had something more pressing, declaring his relationship with Gordon Sung to already be paying dividends, information-wise. So, the new Job A was that Art and Gervais and Reggie now needed to deal with a call girl in Kensington Market the same way, necklacing avec mocking.

"And get this," Jean-Max said, lowering himself into his deck chair. "She goes by Venus de Milo."

"Of course she does." Antoine closed his eyes, worrying what this would be about. "But why? Why do you need to do this now?"

"That Cecil Bolan who, with his bamboula partner, was investigating all of us—you, too—he's sleeping with this Venus."

"Sleeping with her?" Antoine felt he had to at least try to talk Jean-Max down. "We're killing a hooker for sleeping with a cop? I mean, we can do it, sure. But if we kill every hooker sleeping with a cop, we might as well go ahead and kill all the hookers. That's what cops do to deal with their stress over dealing with people

59

like us. They sleep with hookers."

"Not killing her for sleeping with a cop." Jean-Max slapped at air. "We're killing her because Bolan has this bitch of his working as his snitch, his mole, investigating me like a double agent, getting her to ask Gordon, could the necklacings be a result of me?"

"Specifically," Antoine said, putting a hand on the starboard rail. "Did she mention you? Say your name?"

"May as well. She told Gordon it was probably the man in the boat who did it, the necklacings, and what did Gordon think about that?"

Antoine thought the man in the boat was a reference to a woman's clitoris, that maybe Venus was carefully soliciting Gordon by using a metaphor, but Antoine figured mentioning it would only muddy the waters further, so he watched and listened as Jean-Max looked at Toronto in the distance. "Anyone in that city commissioning covert investigations against me, telling people to dig dirt from reporters, that city isn't big enough for both of us. So I want this Venus gone, too. She's an informant against this organization, our organization, and I want it done now while everybody is looking out for Pam Jenkins."

"Sure." Antoine nodded, holding a hand out. "But can't they just shoot her, bang-bang?"

Jean-Max said no. What kind of message did bang-bang send? That could be a drug deal gone wrong, a dispute over services rendered, leaving a guy with blue balls, crotch crickets, anything. Jean-Max wanted this done the same way it happened to the green hornets, necklacing avec mocking. That would send a message everybody involved could comprehend. After, Art and Gervais and Reggie had to figure out the Pam Jenkins job and get it done, too, sending another message. Perhaps they could deal with that priority, Job B, when most of homicide ended up in Kensington Market in the aftermath of Venus, Job A, surprised to be in the wrong part of town.

"Fine," Antoine said. "I will deliver that message."

"See that you do." Jean-Max picked up one of his burners,

brandishing it. "And no more phones. Tell Art I don't want to hear from him. I want you to drive out to Art's garage and deliver this message in person." Pointing at his deck. "I want the message delivered now." Pointing harder. "And I want Job A to be done first thing tomorrow morning, very first thing. Gordon says this Venus informant has her morning routine every day at the Coffee Cup in Kensington Market. So, what I'm saying is, I want her dealt with tomorrow morning between seven and nine, and that you have to deliver the message not now, but right now."

That was enough nows and tomorrows, so Antoine understood. Was there anything else?

Jean-Max thought about it, nodding. "Yes, given the state of things, urban espionage, there is no laundering, no processing of stolen cars, or anything sketchy going through Renaldo's Auto Body. At this time, my shop is doing mainstream work only, operating at a loss, and will remain doing so until this blows over. Until then, any illegitimate work and or laundering or processing is to go through Art's shop, since they aren't looking at him, I'm pretty sure. In particular, Art is to chop and shop Gervais' Nomad." Jean-Max wiggled in his chair, digging into the pockets of his jeans, coming up with a Chevy keychain and handing it to Antoine. "Here's the extra set of keys to Gervais' car and Club. Give them to Art so he can pick up Gervais' car. And tell Art to tell Gervais, I don't want any calls from Gervais, either. Tell Art to coordinate with Gervais and Reggie on that, work it out. Gervais is scheduled to report it stolen next Tuesday, a week today. He's going to leave it near the House on Parliament overnight."

When Antoine pocketed the keys in his powder-blue Adidas tracksuit, same style as his black outfit, confirming he'd deliver that message, too, Jean-Max took another sip and looked at Antoine earnestly. "I want you to remember something when you are dealing with these jobbers, Art and Gervais and Reggie. They are not like you and I."

Antoine said, "How so?"

"They are not Quebecers."

"What about Gervais? His name is French. He smokes French cigarettes."

Jean-Max shook his head. "Gervais is a poseur. Doesn't speak a word. He is from Burlington." Holding his right thumb and index an inch apart. "These dolts can't even remember a little high school French. Ignorant. Makes you wonder how they graduated. Or did they?"

***

Theodore Almano was livid. Bad enough he had to be pulled out of a meeting with Sheff Dubois over these necklacings. When Theodore found out it was because Cecil beat the city councilor from Ward 45 with his own phone, he was double livid. Worse, Theodore had to hightail it to the mall to straighten things out. And worse again, the city's police reporters had been tipped off—likely by the councilor's media savvy staff—and were gleefully arranging in ladies' underwear to document the toils of a detective who needed more seasoning.

With the truth makers cordoned off near tangas, Theodore had Alex and Cecil up against nightgowns. And man, in all his years of police work, thirty-one, Theodore had never seen two detectives crash and burn like this. He didn't even want to hear from Cecil. No, Theodore was looking at Alex, asking didn't he, Theodore, make it clear that Alex was responsible for Cecil?

"Yes." Alex looked over Theodore's shoulder at the cameras and notetakers. "But with due respect, Chief Inspector, I can't hardly be with Cecil 24/7/365."

"Wasn't asking you to be with him 24/7/365. I just asked you to watch him on the job during normal work hours." Theodore rubbed his hands together. "Now, where were you when young guns here started beating on an elected official?"

When Alex looked down at his black brogue elevens, saying nothing, Theodore turned to Cecil. "Where was he when you did that?"

Cecil looked at Alex. "You gonna tell Teddy or should I?"

Theodore looked at Alex. "Tell Teddy what?" Back to Cecil.

"And this isn't a real good time to be calling me Teddy. You know I can have you chasing able-bodied people parking in handicap spaces all summer. Better, I can bust you back to being a plain old cop, traffic duty."

That didn't faze Cecil. He looked at Theodore and said, "That's unlikely, Teddy."

Theodore couldn't believe it, the insolence, the insubordination. Cecil, in all this trouble, and still calling him Teddy. "How's it unlikely I can bust you down, bury you?"

"Because then," Cecil said, "you'd have to explain to Chief Vogel why you couldn't turn his star officer into an effective detective. You know how that'd look, like you lost the room."

Theodore would've drilled Cecil right then if it wasn't for the reporters. Instead, Theodore pinched the bridge of his nose, silently weighing his options until deciding on the path of least resistance.

"Look, Cecil I could take your gun and shield pending investigation and the chief would have to live with that as me doing my due diligence. But then, if I did that to you, I'd have to do the same to Alex here. Mad as I am at him, too—leaving you without a minder—I'm not going to do that to a man I came up with here in the autumn of our careers."

Alex looked down at his elevens some more, thinking they needed a shine. "Thank you, Chief Inspector."

"Don't thank me yet, Johnson." Theodore followed Alex's line of sight, white paper bags at Alex's feet. "Were you shopping when all this went on? Is that what this is about?"

When Alex didn't say anything, Cecil said, "Go ahead. Tell Teddy where you were."

Theodore told Cecil that if he called him Teddy one more time, he was gonna... He was gonna...

Cecil interjected, "Gonna do what, Teddy?" Pointing. "You're gonna do fuck all, that's what you're gonna do."

Theodore bit the inside of his mouth, saying he was gonna put Cecil in the sensitivity training with the two-hundred-pound rockabilly girl says don't ornamentalize her. For now, Theodore was simply telling his only two-tone team to take seven days off. Theodore wouldn't protect Alex and Cecil from whatever investigation was called to cover everyone's asses, maybe the Special Investigations Unit, but there would be no discipline from him. None. Instead, Theodore told Alex and Cecil he needed a little breaky-break from them, that a week might suffice, so long as Cecil humbled up. In addition, and this was just an advance on a pending memo, Theodore said their return day would be May 1st, the new casual day, Casual Tuesdays, and to please dress accordingly without turning it into Halloween. Did Cecil understand all that?

Cecil's first instinct was to call the chief inspector Teddy yet again. But the more he thought on it, he figured he could use the time to get a little proof together on Jean-Max Renaldo and decide what to do from there. Plus, he could kind of use a week off. Since Doyle's death, Cecil had largely been running on fumes, and now, as he stood there, hungover, being disciplined, he didn't think a paid week off was going to exactly suck.

"I said no more calling me Teddy. Do you understand?"

"Yes, Chief Inspector." Cecil said he understood, and thanked Theodore for his lenience, addressing him as Chief Inspector a second time.

Theodore stood in shock at Cecil's sudden contrition. Rather than question his good fortune, Theodore looked at the reporters setting up then back to Cecil. "And there'll be no commenting, pending investigations and litigations, no matter what the scribblers say. You're not to discuss this with anyone." When Cecil nodded, okay, Theodore beckoned the floorwalker. "How do we get out of here without having to walk through them, the media?"

The floorwalker pointed over his shoulder. "Take the staff elevator down to B1, then, to throw everyone off, enter the stairwell and climb one floor up to the EXIT. That leads you right outside onto Yonge, lots of foot traffic to camouflage you."

"Please." Theodore opened his hand. "Take us now."

As the floorwalker led, reporters started firing questions. Would the SIU be called in? Was there an update on the medical condition of the city councilor? By the time they made the elevator, Theodore hitting the down button, Cecil heard Gordon Sung shouting out a long question about this attack potentially being politically motivated, as the city councilor was a longtime police critic, alleging more corrupt police activity as late as last week, a dirty gun. The doors to the staff elevator opened. Alex and Cecil walked in. Theodore straight-armed the floorwalker, letting him know that he, Theodore, would take it from here.

Stepping inside himself, Theodore pressed B1, the box descending, looking down at Alex's bags. "I have to know, what were you shopping for?"

"Bedding." Alex looked to his right. "Just a couple or few sections over."

Theodore chin-nodded to the bags. "What'd you get?"

Alex picked up his bag of pillowcases, opening it. "Leopard."

"Nice." Theodore took the bag, fondling the material. "Cotton?"

"Feels like cotton," Alex said. "A new ultra-fine fiber they say is just as good, better."

"Better, right." Cecil sniffed. "Nothing's better than cotton. And what's an ultra-fine? Probably from China, made of their dead."

Theodore shot Cecil a look. Cecil said what? He hadn't called the chief inspector Teddy, so why was Teddy eyeballing him like that? Theodore couldn't remember the first reason he was eyeballing Cecil, he was so mad, but he was eyeballing Cecil now because he was still coming up with creative reasons to say Teddy. So, from here forward, Cecil was to refrain from saying Teddy, period. To keep the name out of his dirty little mouthy-mouth.

The elevator opened into a concrete corridor, the three men stepping out. Cecil said sure, he could pretty much drop Teddy from his vocab. Except, what was Cecil supposed to do when he came across a guy, other than the chief inspector, actually named Teddy?

The chief inspector said to call him Theodore. Time being, he didn't otherwise want to hear Cecil say shit. Handing the bag back to Alex, Theodore nodded at the other two bags, asking what else Alex had? Pinning the first bag under his arm, Alex opened the others to show off the sheets and bed skirt.

"Zebra and giraffe," Theodore said. "Nice mix with the leopard, very animale. If you don't mind my asking, what'd you pay, all in?"

"In total, $93.87."

Not bad, Theodore said he might pick up a similar set at that price. He was sure Sondra would be dazzled. But again, for seven days Theodore didn't want to hear from Cecil and Alex. He didn't want to hear about them, nor did he want to hear about people in Cecil's demographic. And he most certainly didn't want them buggering up anything else while they were off. They were to simply take a time-out and do normal people things. After this breaky-break, Theodore expected them to come back focused, refreshed, and—looking at Cecil—respectful of the chain of command. But for now, there was to be no police work whatsoever. None.

Still looking at Cecil, softening, Theodore said he could handle Chief Vogel and the media. One other reason Theodore hadn't busted Cecil down was because he knew what Cecil was going through, sort of, and that Theodore, too, had lost people relative to the line of service. For Cecil to use the time to mourn, not to go messin' into whoever killed Doyle. And did Cecil understand? No freelancing. When Cecil agreed, no freelancing, Theodore assured him homicide was on it. That Hermosa would get them, whoever they were, in court. Theodore further stressed the importance of doing this right, free of conflicts of interest, so that whatever they ended up charging the guilty parties with would actually stick.

Cecil was about to say the guilty parties were Jean-Max Renaldo et al. but swallowed his skepticism and said Hermosa had his complete trust, his ball.

"Good to hear." Theodore shoved a hand in his pocket, playing with change. "See you gentlemen one week today, next Tuesday morning, at your desks. We'll take it from there."

"Thank you," Alex said.

"Yes," Cecil added, watching Theodore start off. "Thank you..." Whispering, "Teddy."

"I heard that." Theodore didn't hesitate, pivoting and running at Cecil. Alex reacted slowly but was able to get himself between the two men, holding up his shopping bags as a buffer. Theodore, eyes bulging, saw a hole in Alex's bag shield and threw an overhand right through it, connecting, popping Cecil on his dirty little mouthy-mouth, knocking him down.

Alex and Theodore stepped away while Cecil, on his ass, felt his lip. Spitting blood, he reached into his side jacket pocket, producing yesterday's gray pinstripe boxers, wiping his face as he looked up and said, "Kiss me again, Teddy."

***

From Port Credit, Antoine aimed his Starion downtown and hit the gas, thinking what the shit did Jean-Max want now? It wasn't enough anymore to take someone out honorably, bang-bang. No, Jean-Max wanted it done in an unreasonable way on an unreasonable timeline. Sure, while Antoine was merely delivering messages, if caught, he was going to be facing charges with the word murder attached, and not in a good way, mostly because of the mocking.

Making Eastern Avenue, turning, Antoine told himself this was proof Jean-Max had lost it, way too brash. And what was he thinking having a Para-Dice Rider out to the boat? The whole point of Jean-Max residing at the marina was to create a buffer between church and state, so to speak, avoiding the outward appearance of biker activity while the Canadian Hells Angels sought to quietly and discreetly take over Ontario, as they'd promised their American counterparts, by amalgamating with the Para-Dice Riders. Jean-Max's focus was supposed to be on setting up legitimate businesses, or at least businesses that looked legit—not ordering fucking necklacings—and now he was having bikers park in spot 28? He was projecting as a gangster, just like Maurice "Mom" Boucher, president of the Montreal Hells, who was trying to get away with having those jail guards killed, on his third or fourth court action now, and Antoine could see Jean-Max, lost in his own hubris, making the same mistakes. Briefly, Antoine considered shooting Jean-Max himself, bang-bang. No one had more access, and Antoine had done nothing to leave Jean-Max questioning his trust. So sure, Antoine could shoot Jean-Max, get away. But then Antoine would forever worry about Jean-Max's cronies—who were also Mom Boucher's cronies—doing the math and taking actions of their own. Also, Antoine had to worry about police, who had to be taking a closer look at Jean-Max because of how and why witnesses were being abused, humiliated, and assassinated, none of which the system was going to tolerate from Jean-Max any more than it did Mom Boucher. And the way they were going after Mom, it was just a matter of time before something stuck and they found a way to lock him up for good.

So yeah, the way for Antoine to extricate himself quickly was to make arrangements with his super—who still had another seven months of post-dated cheques—to pick up the mail and toss the restaurant flyers. That's all that was standing now between Antoine putting his pillowcases in the trunk and going for a long drive. He was thinking of Sudbury or maybe North Bay where it would be easy to rent a modest cottage near the water, pay cash, as he pulled up to Harwood's Select Auto Service. Through the doors, inside, he saw Art talking to Reggie on the shop floor and made a beeline.

"Nice outfit." Reggie looked down at Antoine's powder-blue Adidas sneakers, up to his pants and jacket. "Matchy-matchy macho."

Art sharply told Reggie to hush up, turning to Antoine. "If this is about the last of the green hornets, we're still looking for opportunities."

Antoine motioned out back. "I'm sorry to barge in, but we must talk. New messages."

Considering the request like he had a choice, Art led Antoine to the back entrance. The sound of vicious guard dogs exploded as soon as Art cracked the door, causing Antoine to jump a step. Art held a hand up, said, "It's just Reggie's new alarm system. There are no actual animals." Shouting over the noise to Reggie who was popping the hood on a chartreuse microbus. "Hey, could you turn the dog alarm off so it doesn't scare the shit out of us when we come back?"

Reggie wiped his hands with a rag, crossing the floor, picking up a remote, aiming it, killing the vicious sounds.

Relieved, Art continued outside, Antoine following.

"Sorry about that." Art motioned to the door. "Reggie's idea. I mean, it shuts off after the doors close, but it is a little jarring until you get used to it."

"No apology necessary." Antoine shook his head. "I understand. In fact, both Jean-Max and I appreciate you taking security so seriously at this time."

"Also." Art loosened his tie with one hand, pointing at Antoine's outfit. "I'm sorry what Reggie said about your tracksuit. I like it, the original Blue Jays powder blue."

Antoine shook it off, no harm, no foul.

Alright, with the pleasantries commenced, Art started to explain why there was no way to take out Pam Jenkins now, when Antoine interrupted, saying he had good news and bad news.

"What's the good news?"

"The Pam Jenkins job still has to be done, but it is no longer your Job A priority."

Art looked down, relieved, then brought his tired eyes up, re-establishing contact. "So what's the bad news, our new Job A priority?"

"Same drill, avec mocking, Jean-Max says, same means of execution." Antoine chin-pointed northeast. "New target in Kensington Market, far away from Pam Jenkins. Nobody will expect this on Kensington Avenue tomorrow morning between seven and nine. The market is quiet then. Your biggest worry will be vendors bringing in fresh goods, deliveries."

Art didn't love the avec mocking part. In fact, he was tired of the whole thing. Knots in his stomach before, a fair bit of drinking after. But who was Art to say no to Jean-Max?

"Tell me about the target," Art said.

"Hooker, goes by Venus de Milo."

Art managed a laugh, said of course she does. Jinx, Antoine said he had the exact same reaction. Anyway, she had coffee every morning between seven and nine at the Coffee Cup at the corner of Kensington and Baldwin. Except tomorrow, as per Jean-Max's dictate, Venus wouldn't make it to the Coffee Cup. No, the way Jean-Max asked for it to be done was to get her on the way to coffee, fewer people to worry about the earlier it happens.

"Still lots of people around," Art said. "Still downtown Toronto."

"What can I tell you?" Antoine held a hand to his chest. "I am a humble postman delivering the letter. It is not for me to judge. I am additionally charged to tell you that you and Reggie and Gervais can double back on the Pam Jenkins after, when it's safe. Otherwise, I am to ask you if you understand this whole message, without prejudice."

"Without prejudice? What does that mean, without prejudice?"

Antoine said he didn't quite know himself, but was that the message Art wanted sent back to Jean-Max, that Art didn't understand Jean-Max's message? No, Art didn't want that.

"Alrighty then." Antoine patted Art on the shoulder. "Message delivered."

"Sure, sure. But you know what he's asking. You can't talk sense into him?"

Antoine avoided the question, saying there was something else. Jean-Max's shop was too hot at the moment for any illegitimate operations. Until things cooled, Renaldo's Auto Body would be doing legitimate work only, so any and all stolen vehicles needing to be reduced to the sum of their parts would be processed here, and could Antoine tell Jean-Max that Art was okay with all that?

Art thought about his choices, realizing he didn't have any, and said, "Sure."

"Okay then, good." Antoine reached into his pocket, handing over a set of keys. "First thing Jean-Max wants is for you to deal with Gervais' Chevy Nomad, for you to coordinate with Gervais and Reggie to chop it and shop it. Gervais is due to report it stolen Tuesday morning, so Jean-Max says inform Gervais of the change in plans and work together on both matters."

Art reluctantly nodded, agreeing to those conditions, too. When he asked if there could possibly be anything else, Antoine made it clear Jean-Max did not wish to be on the receiving end of phone calls right now so as to avoid incriminations, and that Art was to brief Gervais and Reggie on all of the above.

NINE

Alex was so upset—like, there was no way he was going to church tonight in this state—that he refused to drive Cecil home. No problem. Cecil was used to hoofing it. From the Eaton Centre, he walked to St. James Town, Parliament Street, picked up a case of Keith's at The Beer Store. On the way out, he saw one of those fancy-pants cars, a flamboyant station wagon, probably from Operation Cooperation, pull into a handicap space near the door. The car had wheelchair vanity plates, M'HKN. Yep, this was one of the defrauders. Cecil couldn't recall every detail, but he specifically remembered vanity wheelchair plates on an old-fangled wagon. And talk about disrespect, the bespectacled dumpling inside swung his door open like he didn't have a care, walking breezily toward Cecil in an ironic Bigfoot T-shirt. Apparently, Bigfoot had seen this adult male, whoever he was, probably another legend in his own mind.

"I'd get back in my car, I was you." Cecil held his case with both hands, chin-nodding across the lot. "And park it in a natural-walking-man spot."

"What?" The guy pointed at his bumper. "I've got wheelchair plates."

"Trouble is, you're a natural-walking man."

Tilting his head left, the guy maintained eye contact, looking at Cecil through utilitarian dark-framed glasses. "So, what's it to you?"

That did it. Cecil took a half dozen steps and slammed his case on the hood. Turning, listening to a few bars of the guy complain about what that was going to do to his sea-blue paint, had to be ordered special, Cecil flashed his shield, saying whoa-up when the guy dared take a step forward.

"Sorry, Officer." He held his hands high. "I didn't realize." Nodding to his plates. "And I know how it looks, but I have a right to that space."

"How's that?"

Bringing his hands down, the guy said, "I have an invisible illness."

"Invisible illness, my ass. Let's see your license."

"C'mon," the guy said.

Cecil waved at himself until the guy produced his wallet, removing his driver's permit. Cecil took it, looking at the guy's name, Gervais Garret. Cecil couldn't see as how a dumpling in a Sasquatch shirt had anything to do with Doyle's demise, but memorized the pertinent info anyway, handing the license back. "Thank you, Mr. Garret." Chin-nodding across the lot again. "Now I'm telling you, park that ancient piece of shit—probably gets a kilometer to the gallon—in a natural-walking-man spot before I bust you for being a fraudulently-acquiring-cripple-plates ratbag."

"There's no fraud," Gervais said. "My paperwork checks out."

"But you don't." Cecil pointed at the guy then his car. "Now move it."

Cecil followed Gervais, who stepped into his wagon, keying the ignition. Cecil retrieved his case of Keith's, watching Gervais back out and park in a natural-walking-man spot. Satisfied, Cecil walked a street west to his townhouse on Bleecker, pushing a dozen bottles of Sudbury Springs water to the back of the fridge to make room for his pale ale. Freida was at Jada's workshop with her seamstress group, leaving Cecil the privacy to make a delicate landline call to his union. Upon hearing Cecil's "kiss the carpet" remark, the steward stopped Cecil right there and said this was no biggie, that Cecil followed procedure, pretty much, and to rest assured that the union had Cecil's back. In fact, by the time this was over, the city councilor might find himself facing a resist charge if he didn't reverse course on his BS dirty-gun story.

Breathing a sigh of relief, thanking the steward, Cecil decided he was hungry and headed north to Wellesley, ordering a goat roti at Mr. Jerk, waiting on it, getting caught in a downpour on his return home, where he made a mental note to cut the grass as soon as everything dried. He stripped down to his new boxers, washing his roti down with a cold ginger beer, just the right amount of bite, switching to the real thing and pounding Keith's India pale ale until the wall clock read 6 p.m., picking up the remote, aiming it at the TV. And fuck Cecil. Right away, the anchor was on about that phone-whipped city councilor, throwing to Jojo Chintoh standing in front of headquarters.

"The Special Investigations Unit is investigating after a Toronto fraud cop allegedly beat Ward 45 City Councilor Malcolm Tate with his own cellphone in the women's underwear section at The Bay's Eaton Centre flagship store earlier today. Tate was making a call, checking sizes with his wife, he says, when his phone was stripped from his hand and used as a device to beat him onto the floor, only after, police say, he resisted arrest, but for what?"

Now that Cecil was good and stoned, green Keith's bottles scattered on the coffee table, he was starting to find the whole thing the least bit amusing, especially when Jojo breathlessly spouted on about the city councilor needing three stitches to close his wounds. Jojo actually considered it newsworthy that the councilor needed a few stitches, the malingerer. If Jojo did a story every time a cop needed stitches, he'd be covering that and nothing but.

And no, it wasn't the same deal for police. They were on the frontlines, soldiers, like Alex said, expected to be hurt in the line of duty. This city councilor? He gets a papercut and Jojo wants to recall Parliament. Then Jojo was on about how the city councilor was a frequent critic of police, particularly on the targeting of ravers when all they were doing was hugging. Most recently, the councilor alleged that a cop dropped a gun at the scene of a police shooting. That all being the case, Cecil didn't feel the least bit bad anymore, nor was he worried. He IDed himself, told the city councilor to kiss the carpet, and the sissy failed to comply. Jojo could split what hairs he wanted, but that was resisty enough for the union. So, in the end, it wasn't going to matter how much Jojo wound viewers up. Cecil was going to be cleared, again.

Jojo was saying something about sources telling him that a second detective was shopping for bedding—Goddamn Alex—during the mistaken takedown when Cecil noticed Gordon Sung in the background. Wondering if Venus de Milo had a chance to get to him yet, Cecil thought about phoning her, then decided Venus would've phoned him if she had anything. He was thinking of the way she held him, nothing the least bit sexual but still intimate, when Freida bolted through the front door in a damp red-orange sundress she copied off a Chinatown vendor, pointing at Jojo signing off with a promise to continue updating until City TV got to the bottom of what could be the latest abuse-of-power story to come out of police headquarters.

"Holy fucking shit, Cecil."

Cecil aimed the remote at the TV, killed the power. "Holy fucking shit, what?"

"Holy fucking shit, what? You don't come home last night, then, next time I see you, you're all over the TV, radio, internet, everything." Placing her hands on her hips when she noticed the Keith's bottles. "And hammered, I see. Hammered, again."

Cecil smiled, said, "Me as well."

"Don't be smart. Were you drinking when this happened?"

"It was morning."

"That's not an answer."

"No, I wasn't drinking at all until after I got home and had lunch, Mr. Jerk, ballast to soak up the alcohol. Only then, when I was prepared, did I start drinking."

"And you didn't leave this house wearing pineapple underpanties because you don't own pineapple underpanties, only hula dancers." Freida left one hand on her hip, pointing with the other. "So where'd you get pineapple underpanties?"

"The Gap," Cecil said. "This morning." Pointing across the floor. "Also, I bought new socks but you're not up my ass about that."

Freida had both hands on her hips again. "Where are the underpanties you were wearing when you left the house yesterday?"

Cecil pointed at his wet Sean John piled on the floor. "Jacket pocket."

Freida got on her hands and knees, hanging Cecil's pants over one chair, his jacket over another, locating the gray pinstripe boxers, inspecting them, and asking why there was blood, a fair bit, on the underpanties Cecil left the house wearing?

Cecil pointed a Keith's bottle at his mouth, said, "I cut my lip."

"Okay, okay." Freida kicked off her beat-up Blundstones, falling onto the couch next to Cecil, looking at him, noticing the cut. "So now tell me what happened to your lip."

"I was tying my shoe in the car when Alex slammed on his breaks so as to avoid a cyclist. I kissed the dashboard pretty good." Patting his hip. "I had yesterday's underwear in my pocket, used them to wipe the blood away."

Sighing, she said, "Sure, Cecil." Reaching for the bottle in his hand, taking it, sucking back most of what was left, handing it back. "Just tell me the truth, is there any chance we're getting fired over this?"

"No, no." Cecil brought the bottle to his mouth, finished off the last bit, backwash. "Spoke with my steward, went over everything. The councilor resisted when I told him to kiss the carpet. I didn't know who he was. Made him for a perpetrator. We could've sorted it out from the carpet, but he wanted to be a Kiefer Sutherland cocksucker and got all resisty. Once he does that, gets resisty." Pointing the empty bottle at his chest. "It's my sworn duty to render him nonviolent, which I did." Pointing the bottle at the TV. "Jojo can toss around untruths about abuse of power as much as he wants. I was within my rights, totally. I mean, it might make for some bad press. But mark my words, I'm going to get good press, too. A lot of cops—even some reporters—will toast me tonight. They're going to say the city councilor had it coming, always taking the turnoff to negativeland. The union has my back, believe me. It's no biggie."

"No biggie, right." Freida nodded at the blank telly. "It's not just Jojo." Pointing a thumb over her shoulder. "My seamstress group didn't even talk business today. We just watched news updates, listened to the shock jocks. It's been on talk radio for hours."

"Your seamstress group get a report from *All News, All the Time?*"

Yeah, the seamstresses got a report from *All News, All the Time*, why? Why, because *All News, All the Time* liked Cecil, so he wanted to know how he was portrayed there.

"Same as they said when you busted Killean Jones on the telemarketing scam, pepper sprayed him," Freida said. "That you're tougher than a dozen nights in jail."

"See?" Cecil slapped his knee. "And I know that's how the *Sun* will play it, good on me."

"*All News, All the Time* is right-wing clap trap, same as the *Sun*. They always take the cop's side no matter what, so you better get good play with them. The point is you're getting too much play for a detective, and the whole time I don't know what's going on. I phoned you all day on your work cell."

Cecil crossed the room, reaching into a jacket pocket, retrieving his cell, studying it. "Yep, turned it off."

"But why?"

"Teddy sent Alex and I home." Cecil sat back down on the couch. "Gave us a week off."

"Sounds like he suspended you a week."

"No, no. Just paid time off."

"You mean suspended with pay?"

"Wouldn't have my gun and shield if I was suspended." Cecil pointed his bottle at the coffee table, his service Glock and badge. "It's just a breaky-break, I'm telling you, a time-out."

"A time-out." Freida didn't like it, thought Cecil was being evasive, sort of like last night when he called from that skeezy bar saying he wouldn't be home, that he was on a stakeout. It wasn't that she thought Cecil played around, God no, just that he was trying to protect her from something to do with work. "Don't you get us fired. I'm not going back to Leamington with my tail between my legs. I'm proud my husband is a detective and I want to keep it that way." Looking around the living room, the big-screen Sony, a Pioneer stereo with two-foot speakers, new peach shag from the Rug Gallery, and a fresh coat of eggshell picking up all the colors. "I like our life here. We are city people, Torontonians. That means something."

Cecil put a hand on her knee. "Our life here is secure."

"Then why don't I feel secure?"

"Because you've been consuming enough media to put you in the pistachio place, committed." Cecil scratched the back of his neck. "We're fine. Just one thing."

"Here we go."

"Here we go what?"

Freida sighed, putting both hands in her dark-ginger hair, wet, pushing it back. "Here we go. You just said our life is secure. Then you said just one thing. My guess is you're about to say something that makes me feel less secure."

Cecil brought his hands into a praying position. "You won't love it, no."

"Alright, just a sec." Freida used Cecil's thigh to push herself up, went to the kitchen, the fridge, grabbing two Keith's, opening them, heading back to the living room, sitting next to Cecil, handing him a bottle. "Okay, tell me."

"May I ask, could you please stay with your sewing friend Jada for a week or so?"

"Again?" Freida took a pull on her beer. "For a week?"

"Or so."

"Why Cecil? What did you do that I have to leave my own house for a week or so?"

"Just doing my rock and roll duty. It's this Doyle thing. I think it's close to being solved, but whoever did this, it probably had something to do with my communication with Doyle, me telling him to take the deal." Cecil held the bottle to his heart. "And you know me. I'm a take all precautions kind of guy."

"You're a hothead." Freida pointed her bottle. "And all this has something to do with you being a hothead." Hesitating. Leaning over to kiss him. "But you're my hothead." Hesitating again. "You're sure this is going to be okay? I appreciate your concern for me, but I worry about you, too. You're going to stay here, alone?"

"I'm armed, all times. And you know me. I'm a hothead." Cecil motioned to his piece on the coffee table. "Anybody—man, woman, child, or beast—enters this domicile who's unwelcome, they're going on a blind date with Dr. Glock." Then he remembered something. "Oh yeah." Taking off his watch, handing it over. "Can you fix it again?"

Freida looked concerned, taking the Accu.2. "What's wrong?"

"It's stuck on seconds."

ondra Brooks woke at 8:53 a.m. on Wednesday. Alex's new sheets felt silky against her bare skin, warm, only where was Alex? He couldn't have gone to work. He said he was suspended. Sure enough, she spotted a note next to her saying he drove to the Jet Fuel for lattes, then the phone rang. Sondra considered answering, but she didn't live here so she let it ring through, listening to ex-wife number two leave a message in her spitty talk saying she needed her car. It was important, very important, and if Alex didn't pick up, she was going to have his black ass tracked and repo the Cougar. *Dovraga,* that was her car now.

Thinking about how she might respond on Alex's behalf, Sondra decided she had him and that would be her revenge on ex-wife number two. Matter settled, she was slipping into the leopard Ralph Lauren robe Alex bought her, likely with alimony money, when ex-wife number one called to leave her own message, something about her cheque, that she'd haul Alex into court if she didn't get it today. Yeah, Sondra wanted to pick up and say something to that bitch, too. It was terrible the way the ex-wives club hounded poor Alex. But again, Sondra had him, so she sank into the couch, grabbing the remote, aiming it at the TV, and flipping channels until she stopped at Eddie Murphy being gently woken by a symphony.

Sondra put the clicker on the coffee table, thinking she was going to help Alex make the most of his suspension, that they'd spend the morning sipping lattes and watching *Coming to America.* After making more of that sweet, sweet love, mayhaps she'd take him to that new BBQ at the corner for lunch. Then they'd go back to his apartment, nap, wake up, make more sweet, sweet love, before repeating a similar drill revolving around dinner and another movie. She was thinking how she was going to make a little vacation out of his suspension, she'd do Alex so good. But when the phone rang again, she didn't care which ex-wife was hounding him about what. She just picked up and said, "Hey bitch, get a job."

There was nothing for a moment, then a male voice. "Sondra?"

"Yeah, and who's this bird-dogging me, phoning here? Something wrong?"

"It's Theodore. Theodore Almano. And hey, how do you like Alex's new safari sheets?"

Sondra took the phone away from her ear, looked at it, put it back. "Why're you phoning here all chummy when you done just suspended poor Alex?"

"Is that what he told you? I just gave him the week off, did him a favor."

"Yeah, well he thinks you disciplined him over something that stupid white boy did."

"It wasn't what Cecil did. It was that Alex was shopping for bedding when he was supposed to be watching Cecil."

"So you are punishing him."

"Not punishing him," Theodore said. "It's a paid vacay, no paperwork, gave him a whole week with you. Figured it'd make you happy."

"It do." Sondra looked at the TV, Eddie's character celebrating his birthday in a pool with naked Egyptian-looking girls. "So why are you bird-dogging him now?"

"Official business. I have to talk to him about some official police business."

"Official business while he's on vacay, huh? Okay, I'll have him call. Just one thing."

"Yeah?"

"Promise you won't unsuspend him."

Theodore laughed. "I won't. I just need to ask him about something."

"Okay. But if he's on vacay, like you say, make it snappy and happy. It's not going to feel like vacay if you stress him."

Theodore promised he'd keep it snappy and happy, saying he only wanted Alex's expertise, that this wasn't his case to stress over. It'd take a few minutes, tops, then Alex would be all Sondra's. She was thanking Theodore, saying she hardly got enough Alex time, ever, when she heard her man keying the lock. He walked in wearing double denim, holding two lattes in a cardboard tray.

"What are you doing on my phone?"

Sondra ignored the question, speaking into the mouthpiece. "He here now." Holding the phone out to Alex. "It's Theodore. He say you're on vacay, not suspended, but that he need your expertise. Says it'll take but a few minutes, tops."

Alex placed the lattes on the counter, glaring at Sondra, taking the phone, telling her not to answer it until they had an exclusive arrangement. Sondra said if she was sleeping over, Alex should already assume they had an exclusive arrangement, and that if other women were sleeping on his safari sheets, including either of the ex-wives, she was going to expose Alex to something truly biblical.

"Just don't answer my phone," he said, bringing it to his face. "Chief Inspector?"

"Yeah, me. That Sondra, she's a pistol. I like her."

"Yeah." Alex shot her a look. "Me, too, especially when she's not answering my phone."

"Anyway, I'm calling about some highly unpleasant matter. Nothing for you to be involved in. I just need everything you know on one Penelope Pinkus who on the street went by Venus de Milo. I've seen her mentioned in Cecil's reports."

"We've nothing of note on her. A call girl, likely a little bit criminal, suspected to have had a minor role posing as a distraction back when someone was picking Richie Rich's pocket in Kensington Market. Street plays like that, but nothing I know of that was worth our while to get her on. Just a minor cog in the criminal community. Goes to that dive bar Cecil hangs at when he goes to his dark place, The Greek's."

"You saying Cecil's maybe doing her, extracting favors? We don't need a repeat of what happened with the drug squad, those jackasses making trans hookers give 'em blowies. *Eye*, what with how they're living off the avails of shemales, was all over it, so please don't tell me I have to worry about that with Cecil, too."

"No, no. But I have been meaning to have a sidebar with you. You know he's straight outta buttfuck." Alex paused, minding his language, thinking how he'd planned this conversation and wanted to put it in a balanced manner so maybe Theodore would deal this time. "He's funny peculiar in that he votes NDP, workers party, wears Sean John, has black friends, consumes Jamaican food and Latin music, and gets along with homosexuals on his street who don't do meth. But there are people close to him, or those he admires, like Ricky Martin, and everyone else in the world. That plays out in the field, creates situations."

"What kind of situations?"

"Slurs. Refers to Hermosa as an uppity spic being racist."

"Look," Theodore said, "I'm no fan boy of Cecil, but Hermosa brought that on. I was there supervising Cecil watching a training video about how Holland has gay cops and it's swell. Cecil was still new, in awe, trying to be helpful when Hermosa couldn't work his end, tech, then Kraut smut starts playing. Hermosa was at fault. He shouldn't be watching water sports at work, so he had no cause to call Cecil gringo. I pulled Sheff aside, told him, control your hombre."

Alex said fine, but Cecil wasn't a normal Torontonian the way he made inappropriate comments about gender, age, and race beyond Hermosa. Cecil counted pees, cracked Depends jokes, and generally operated like the top cop when he didn't know his way north of Bloor.

"Nothing the two-hundred-pound rockabilly girl says don't ornamentalize her can't cure, huh?" Theodore said. "Seriously, it's fun to joke about, threaten Cecil with it, but sensitivity training's not going to do any good unless the other 4,999 cops in this city attend along with him."

"It's not that bad, within the force."

"Really? Well, look in the mirror, Alex, because you're the same kind of asshole you're complaining about with that straight outta buttfuck jive. It's in the regs, no making it about skin, so take heed, you and Cecil. Cut that shit before the trust is gone, man, gone..."

Sweet Jehovah, Alex wished he hadn't pushed because Theodore was giving his speech on how he said the same to all—blacks, whites, mulattos—he didn't want hate dividing their big blue house. But it was here, playing out at headquarters and in the field. Bureaucracy was the same, people winding people up over blood, destabilizing everything. Some days, what with the way everyone was talking, the best Theodore could hope for was that we'd kill each other in such a way so as to not bugger up the rest of the universe. Then he stopped, sighing into the phone, admitting he called Cecil manga in private, so they probably all did it but maybe didn't see it because they were like the seminar leader at the annual retreat said, desensitized. And no, Theodore didn't see how the two-hundred-pound rockabilly girl was going to make any of them sensitive again. Theodore said Alex would get his revenge when Cecil's generation discovered this mess was theirs to sort. Cecil was the future, which was why Theodore had him with Alex, whose last order of business was to make Cecil an effective detective. What Theodore wanted to know, in the here and now, was, did Cecil cheat on his wife with uncompensated pros?

"No way," Alex said. "He doesn't cheat on his Freida at all. Young man's faults are multiple, like I say, racist, ageist tendencies. He just doesn't dick around far as I can tell."

"Good to hear."

"Why ask?"

"There's been another incident," Theodore said. "Just over an hour ago, broad daylight in front of scores of delivery people, fruit vendors, on Kensington Avenue."

Alex covered his eyes with his spare hand. "Necklacing, again?"

"Afraid so. And again with the irony. This time witnesses say they saw and heard three guys singing a Rolling Stones song a cappella, telling this Venus she's playing with fire."

Alex was sorry to hear that, hellacious, but if Theodore was asking, Venus never came up during Operation Cooperation and there was nothing linking her to the suspected players. But—and this was a pretty big but—it was impossible to ignore that she was killed the same as Doyle Allenby and Doris Sabo.

"True that," Theodore said.

Alex asked if Theodore wanted him to come in, go over his notes, make some calls. Theodore said no. Homicide had it handled. He just wanted to be up to date when he met with Sheff Dubois. Meantime, Alex should debrief Cecil, see if he knew more about this girl. That if Cecil did, Alex should call it in, not Cecil. Under no circumstances was Theodore to find himself speaking with Cecil this week. Was that clear?

"Clear," Alex said. "Will call you later either way."

Theodore said no. Alex was not to call either way. Theodore was still mad at him, too. Alex was to phone only if Cecil had some helpful intelligence. Knowing Cecil, that was unlikely.

The fact that Theodore wasn't hoping to hear back put Alex at some ease and he assured Theodore he'd follow the finery of his directives.

"See that you do. And one more thing. Next time Cecil calls me Teddy I am holding you personally responsible. I'm not just talking about him saying it to my face. Next time I hear about it from someone at The Cruiser, or even if I think he's calling me Teddy in his head, I'm going to give it to both of you."

"Okay, I'll see what I can do."

"Don't see what you can do. See to it that he stops."

Fine, Alex would see to it. With that, he bid Theodore adieu, hanging up and looking to Sondra. "Now, I am sorry to interrupt our time, but I have got to go see Cecil."

Sondra nodded to the phone, said Theodore said it was a vacay, that he wouldn't fuck it up, and now Alex was telling her he had to do work shit? Alex said he'd be quick about it, meet Sondra at her condo within the hour. Why, Sondra wanted to know, couldn't she wait here and watch the rest of *Coming to America?* Alex said it was on account of he still didn't want Sondra answering his phone. Sondra said she didn't answer until it was Theodore, but just so Alex knew, both ex-wives called. The second ex-wife phoned first, the angry Yugoslavian bitch with hairy armpits, no neck. Croatian, Alex said, Yugoslavia's no longer a country. Well, whatever kind of pasty bitch she was, Sondra said ex-wife number two was talking all spitty, saying she wanted her car back, that she'd repo it if Alex didn't answer. Then ex-wife number one called saying she wanted a cheque today, that she'd haul Alex into court if he didn't deliver.

Alex said that wasn't going to happen on either count. But how was it Sondra knew all that if she wasn't answering his phone? The machine, Sondra said, nodding to it. Bitches shouted all that into the answering machine, one after the other.

Whatever, Alex absolutely had to see Cecil, so Sondra got dressed. Alex asked where she parked. River Street, she told him, near the Canada Post box. Alex said she was but a few spaces from him, that he'd walk her to her car. However, the spot where Alex parked was empty. Ex-wife number two, apparently, had already repo-ed the Cougar. After some substitute curse words, Alex asked Sondra, polite as he could, to drive him to Cecil's on Bleecker, close. It was somewhat important, urgent.

Sondra said sure, but only if Alex promised to come straight back to her condo right after. He said he would, so they climbed inside her teal Nissan Altima and just about flew to Gerrard Street, Sondra saying she could hardly wait to meet this Cecil.

"Yeah." Alex sipped his latte. "Don't say anything, but he thinks you're just some bitch I bang."

"He said that?"

"Yep."

Sondra ran the yellow, taking a right on Parliament. "What did you say?"

"I said he couldn't call you that. Said I didn't say that about his Freida."

"What'd he say?"

"He said Freida didn't dig safari sheets and she was his wife, not some bitch he banged."

"See? He wouldn't say that about a white woman." Sondra hit the horn at a jaywalker, reaching for her latte in the holder. "Means he's racist."

Yeah, Alex said he was just talking to Theodore about that, and maybe they all were—Cecil, Theodore calling Cecil manga, Alex saying Cecil was straight outta buttfuck. And why was it okay for Sondra to call ex-wife number two a spitty-talking pasty bitch? That right there was racist. Sexist, too. Sondra sipped her latte and said repeating facts was not racist. Fact one, ex-wife number two was spitty-talking and there could be no argument about that. Fact two, she was even pastier than most whites, translucent. Fact three, racism is about power blacks don't have, meaning blacks can't be racist. And fact four, the way ex-wife number two was talking about tracking Alex's black ass—that was racism—please forgive Sondra if she took that bitch for a bitch, so it wasn't sexist, either.

"What was it then?" Alex said.

"Just me," Sondra said, taking a left past the CIBC onto Carlton. "Proving my love."

Lightening up, watching his girl step on it then hang a right, Alex pointed to Cecil's townhouse, which looked like most of the townhouses on Bleecker—lots of clay brick—except Cecil's lawn was going to seed. Parking a few doors down, Sondra asked if Alex wanted her to wait in the car. He said he wasn't sure it was safe. Sondra wanted to know what he meant. Alex looked at her and said, "I've been avoiding this, but what with what Theodore just told me, I don't think it's safe for Cecil and his wife Freida here. I don't think it's safe at my place, either."

"So you took me to Cecil's to break up? You said you were coming back to my condo."

"Not breaking up. In fact, I've been working up the courage to be so bold as to ask, may I please stay at your place all week, is what I'm saying."

"Honey." Sondra put her fingers under Alex's chin. "I'd be happy if you showed for a booty call with a half-empty sixer of Miller Lite."

Relieved, Alex said thank you, that he just had to pick up some clothes, stepping out, leading Sondra to Cecil's, ringing the bell. Listening, hearing no movement inside, Alex used his fist to hammer the door, shouting, "Police. Open up before we ram the entrance and cap your Casper ass." That seemed to raise Cecil, answering in a gray Leamington Lions T-shirt and matching house shorts. Looking at Sondra standing there holding a latte in white boots and a white raincoat splashed with newspaper headlines, he said, "Hi." Asking Alex, "Why's your girlfriend here?"

"It's complicated." Alex pointed his latte past Cecil. "Let's talk."

"Okay." Cecil motioned them in. "But it's not exactly the Waldorf right now."

Sondra stepped inside. Seeing the coffee table covered in Keith's bottles, a gun, an overfilled ashtray, Mr. Jerk wrappers, she turned to Alex. "I thought he has a wife."

"He do." Alex pointed to the wedding photo on the mantel. "Freida."

"Yeah, well no woman lives here presently."

Cecil scratched his stubble, said it's amazing how much he trashed the place since yesterday. He said Freida left this morning. That he sent her to stay with friends, safety purposes. Picking up a Keith's bottle with a few gulps left, he took a swig, said he told Freida to stay until this necklacing business got sorted.

"So you heard?" Alex said.

"Heard?" Cecil looked at Alex, then to Sondra, back to Alex. "Heard what?"

"About Venus de Milo."

Alex didn't have to say it. Cecil took the last swig of piss-warm Keith's and weighed the merits of smashing his little green bottle against the wall. But, of course, that would've set Alex off wondering why Cecil was affected. So no, as much as Cecil wanted to break shit, he steadied himself, sitting on his couch and bringing up a burp, there. "I am sorry to hear that." Flashing a smile at Sondra, looking at Alex, saying no disrespect, but why did Alex bring her to have this conversation? Alex sat next to Cecil and said Theodore just called, told him about Venus and asked Alex to ask Cecil if he had any pertinent-type information from the bar that might connect Venus to the necklacings. Cecil wanted to know if Teddy wanted him, Cecil, to call directly with his information. Alex said no, and that Cecil needed to stop calling Theodore Teddy. Cecil said fine. Was there anything else then? No. Only thing, like Alex said, was that if Cecil had info of value for Alex to phone it into Theodore.

Cecil shot Alex a look. "You sure you just don't want to take credit for my intelligence?"

"No." Alex held his hands high, to-go cup on the right. "Rest assured I don't want that. Why? What you got?"

Cecil thought about sounding everything out, and maybe he would have if Alex hadn't brought a date. Even if Alex was alone, how was Cecil supposed to say he slept with Venus but didn't have relations? Who was going to believe she was just holding him? It wasn't like Alex could leave that tidbit on the QT in a murder situation. And once all that funneled through the head-quarters gossip machine, Serpico would leak it to Gordon Sung who'd end up telling *Eye* readers Cecil was extracting favors. Nope. Sometimes a man had to live alone with what he'd seen or done so as to protect himself and others, and Cecil deemed this to be one of those times.

"She was a call girl who hung out at The Greek's." Cecil held his hands together then opened them. "Nice girl. No real priors, but that doesn't mean she was innocent. Like I told her once, I ran her particulars because she's obviously involved in an occupation that's hardly legal, and, as you know, people involved in one illegal occupation are usually involved in another, more. But I can't imagine what connects her to Jean-Max and the car people. I don't see it from here."

"Me neither." Alex looked at Cecil, the way he spoke almost

articulately, thinking there was hope. Then Alex worried that Cecil actually was thoughtful, that he'd just been acting dumb. "Could even be a copycat. You see her the other night when you were there, The Greek's?"

"I did." Cecil tugged at his bangs. "We had a drink, spoke. I made a joke about not busting her, then carried on, made jokes with other whores and pimps and junkies and alkies."

"You think that's of any value? That I should phone it in to Theodore?"

Cecil lit a cigarette, thinking he didn't want Alex phoning Teddy, but figured protesting the notion of reporting in would be suspicious. "Not sure it's worth much, but if my intelligence is going to Teddy, then from Teddy to homicide, I want it coming directly from my mouth. Sorry, but if a story gets passed so many times, you know what happens, gatekeeping."

Alex figured every tidbit should be reported but doubted Cecil's intel would be of value. Asides, Alex was sure a direct phone call would result in Cecil calling the chief inspector Teddy.

"Okay," Alex told Cecil. "It all stays on the QT, for now."

"It either stays on the QT or it doesn't. We tell him now or never. If we tell him in a week, he's going to say we held out." Cecil pointed at his phone. "I'll phone him, you want."

No Alex didn't want. Just to cover his ass, he was tempted to confirm that Cecil wasn't extracting favors, to look him in the eye and ask. Same time, Alex was pretty sure that wasn't the case and he didn't want to waste time when he could be cooling his heels at Sondra's condo. "Fair enough, Cecil, fair enough. But what are you doing with the rest of your vacation?"

Cecil fluttered a hand over the Keith's bottles covering his coffee table. "I'm doing it."

"So you're not going to be freelancing?"

"Fuck no. They're not getting my free labor. Not after the way Teddy treated us."

Alex thought Theodore had actually done them a solid, removing them from the media glare while still getting them paid, and Alex figured it was just a matter of time, seasoning, if you will, before Cecil came around to seeing things that way, too. For now, Alex had one question.

"You going to be safe here, alone?"

"I'll be fine." Cecil picked up his Glock, brandishing it. "Intruders? Not so much."

Alex wondered if Cecil should have a gun with all that Nova Scotia pale ale in him. But Alex had done what he could do. So long as Cecil confined his circus to his own tent nobody else would get hurt, except for intruders, like Cecil said.

"Good enough." Alex stood, looking at Sondra who had remained standing this whole time—she didn't want to touch anything—then back to Cecil. "See you Tuesday."

Cecil was about to stand, but stopped himself, snapping his fingers. "Hey, have you talked to Hermosa about Doyle's expensive white-girl lawyer, told him to see who's paying?"

By the way Alex dithered, Cecil knew he hadn't, telling him he could get in the game any time now. Then Cecil held an open hand out to Sondra, saying sorry she had to hear that, but sometimes a cop had to kick his lollygagging partner in the ass, tough love. Sondra figured Cecil wouldn't talk like that to a senior white officer. She sipped her latte and said, hmm, was it true that Cecil referred to her as some bitch Alex bangs? That brought Cecil to his feet. No, he said, hitching his shorts, he wasn't speaking about Sondra when he said that. He was talking about Alex's other bitches.

ELEVEN

Last thing Antoine wanted to be doing was driving back to the Port Credit Marina to serve as an audience for Jean-Max, again, especially after Antoine just thought he got rid of Jean-Max, maybe for good. Yet there Antoine was, acting on Jean-Max's every whim, making another stop at Tim Hortons. This time, along with the double-double, Jean-Max wanted a chicken-salad sandwich and a sour-cream donut for dessert. Carrying everything to the boat, Antoine handed the bag to Jean-Max, who placed it on top of a long fish cooler then took the to-go cup, flipping the lid, blowing on the coffee, and taking a sip. Satisfied, he went for his wallet and withdrew a ten, waving it.

"No, no." Antoine waved back. "It is my pleasure to do this for you before you head out."

Jean-Max thought about arguing that Antoine take the money for the sake of it, but he was hungry, wanting to get this over with so he could kick back and eat, listen to the live René Simard CD that came in today's mail, maybe get into that new bottle of bourbon. "I want to tell you how pleased I am that Art and Gervais and Reggie cleaned up our market mess, while also sending a message to others who might consider abusing their own freedom of speech. Moreover, I thought that was excellent use of 'Playing with Fire' by The Rolling Stones, so I give them full style points, a perfect ten." Pointing downtown. "Tell them."

Antoine was pleased Jean-Max was pleased but knew Jean-Max didn't call him out to the *Dine A Shore*, again, to dole out compliments. So Antoine nodded in acknowledgment, polite, waiting for the rest of it while Jean-Max took another sip.

"I also want you to tell Art and Gervais and Reggie that I love them, that I respect them." Jean-Max paused to collect his thoughts, sitting on his deck chair. "But if the Pam Jenkins job isn't done, avec mocking, by the time I get back, Art and Gervais and Reggie will be the ones getting necklaced." Pointing at Antoine.

"You are to send the message like that." Pointing at himself. "That said, I have considered your reservations about this being a plausibility of some kind."

"A viable plausibility," Antoine said.

"Yes, a viable plausibility." Jean-Max nodded quickly. "And I want to thank you for that input, because it made me think how I should bend over backwards to be a reasonable man. So give them the weekend to relax on one job well done, time to rejuvenate, then deliver the message I have just dictated promptly on Tuesday morning. By then, the cops will be letting their guard down on Pam Jenkins, which, in turn, should make Art and Gervais and Reggie more receptive to the message you'll be delivering." Clapping his hands once. "And oh yes. I have a special request this time. In terms of satisfying the avec mocking part, please tell them to sing 'We Didn't Start the Fire' by Billy Joel, the three of them a cappella again."

Antoine thought about trying to talk some sense into Jean-Max. The cops weren't going to let their guard down by Tuesday. Even if they did, there was no way Art, Gervais, and Reggie were going to memorize "We Didn't Start the Fire" and still have the wherewithal to get to Pam Jenkins, necklace her, sing the song, and get away. Fuck it. Antoine decided it was just all too far gone by the time he found himself agreeing to send the message as Jean-Max communicated it. Maybe Antoine could leave for the north, then call the message into Art from the road, if Jean-Max didn't insist on a personal visit. Or maybe Antoine could fake his own death. Whatever way out, Jean-Max had to be under surveillance, again, which of course meant Antoine was under surveillance. With Jean-Max pissing off so many people for fun, it was clearly time to make a break. That said, Antoine felt that maybe he had to figure out a more graceful exit. He still couldn't be seen crossing the man. Batshit crazy as he was, disorganized in businesses and thought, Jean-Max remained undiminished as a threat.

"Meantime." Jean-Max thumbed his chest. "I am going to get

gone. I need to be seen in other places while this next thing is happening."

"Where are you going?" Antoine said. "And for how long?"

"What do you care?"

"Well, because Art and Reggie and Gervais will want to know how long they have."

"As of Tuesday, the day you inform them, they have not much time. Tell them they need to act." Jean-Max sized Antoine up, the way he leaned on the starboard rail for balance, a bit awkward. "So that answers why you need to know how long I'll be gone, but why are you asking where I'm going? Wouldn't you knowing be a self-incrimination?"

Antoine wasn't sure that Jean-Max was using self-incrimination properly, but didn't say anything, partly because Antoine recognized it as another sign that their relationship was ending. Whatever Jean-Max was saying, Antoine understood, more or less. In his mind, he was just picking Jean-Max apart like his last girlfriend, finding the way she wiggled her toes grating. Likewise, pretty much everything Jean-Max had to say was getting under Antoine's skin now, so yes, there was a temptation to lash out and pettily break down the difference between incrimination and self-incrimination. But the last homme to correct Jean-Max's English ended up with a depressed skull, courtesy of his new Para-Dice Rider buddies who didn't seem to have any interest in mainstream business. No, all the Riders were bringing to the table was more drug dealing, more gambling, more extortion, more guns, more robberies, and more flamboyant executions, avec mocking—all Jean-Max specialties—while American Angels became increasingly restless, sparking rumors about not just Mom Boucher's leadership, but Jean-Max's as well. Fuck this indeed. Antoine just needed to go through the motions and deliver this last message on Tuesday morning, hopefully from another area code. First, he had to get Jean-Max on his way, for real this time.

"I want you to be safe." Antoine extended his right hand. "Wherever you go, I want that place to be safe."

Jean-Max stood and shook Antoine's hand, saying thank you, that he would be cutting off contact, meaning Antoine wouldn't hear from Jean-Max until just before his return. Nothing personal, as Antoine would understand. It was all about avoiding incriminations. That's why Jean-Max went below and returned with a fresh burner, swapping it out with the one Antoine had been using.

***

Sondra and Alex couldn't have been twenty minutes gone when Cecil pep-stepped to Becker's on Wellesley, bought a disposable phone. Back home, he had the device working right away, calling his old basketball buddy. Milky answered halfway through the second ring.

"Leamington Marina. Jimmy speaking."

"Hey," Cecil said. "Hey now. Are you Milky Way Jones, point guard for the '87–88 Leamington Lions?"

"Toblerone. What's shaking, man?"

"I'm going to need you to drive that boat."

"Understood," Milky said without hesitation. "How soon?"

"Earlier the better."

Milky said he was off for two days as of 6 p.m.—Thursdays and Fridays were basically his scheduled weekends—so he could be on his way shortly thereafter.

"Here's what you need to do," Cecil said. "It's a three-hour drive, so leave after dark, nine. Wear your seatbelt and keep to the limit. We don't need a record of you being pulled over. That puts you at my place around midnight. We'll do our rock and roll duty and have you back home for coffee tomorrow morning at your usual time."

"Alright," Milky said. "See you around midnight."

Before they hung up, Cecil told Milky to buy a disposable phone at a truck stop, to call at this number, if he had to. Also, Milky was to tell no one. The people of Leamington should never know Milky was anywhere other than his bed tonight. Milky said aye, aye.

Clicking off, Cecil looked around and said fuck this shit. He grabbed a half-full Keith's and went to the kitchen, pouring it out before putting on some coffee. As it brewed, he collected the rest of his Keith's bottles, emptying anything left, placing them in their case. His coffee was ready, so he poured a cup, black, tapping out a cigarette and lighting up. Out in the living room, on the couch, he sipped his joe and hit his Export 'A,' exhaling, asking himself if he was having another knee-jerk reaction and going off half-cocked, again.

After all, the fact that Venus de Milo ended up necklaced, same as Doyle, right after Cecil asked her to look into Jean-Max Renaldo, wasn't going to get Jean-Max convicted in a court of law. Mostly, judges ruled that evidence such as this was circumstantial, that it was proof of something, maybe, but not proof enough to convict.

All that was fine, to a point. Cecil himself had been the beneficiary of proof beyond a reasonable doubt, including the way he seemed to be getting away with working over the city councilor. Deep down, Cecil wanted due process to work. He wanted Jean-Max to have a fair trial because his rights were connected to Cecil's rights, and Cecil had come to appreciate his rights whenever scurrilous, mostly, allegations were mounted against him in the line of duty.

Besides, Alex always told Cecil that working within the system was the best way to protect one's own self. But working within the system also got Doyle killed. Same as Doris Sabo and Venus de Milo. So if Cecil kept working within the system and allowed homicide to lollygag along until Hermosa hopefully stumbled onto something, another human was going to be necklaced, maybe Pam Jenkins, while Cecil sat around listening to Alex play Jehovah. With all his teachable moments, Alex still hadn't talked to Hermosa about who was paying Doyle's expensive white-girl lawyer, something Cecil saw as key. But even if Alex had shared the intel, fucking Hermosa really couldn't find ice in Iceland. So if Hermosa was lead, Cecil decided he was right to take matters into his own hands.

It wasn't just systems of law and order, police forces big and small. There were instances of failure throughout institutions Cecil was brought up to trust, with a belief that governments were working to protect their people first, last, and always. Not far from Cecil's hometown, communities endured decades of boil-water advisories, which was why Freida was in the habit of keeping the fridge filled with bottled. Cecil didn't see that as a solution, the problem being what to do with all that plastic. The food supply wasn't safe—salmonella, listeria, and some other creepy crawlies Cecil couldn't pronounce. Once you started pissing out shits, healthcare wasn't operating properly, waiting lists for people dying. Every other week, some politician or another with power over police was on TV for peddling influence while terrorists formed sleeper cells that were reportedly waking up with increased "chatter" on the fringes of the internet, just one more thing to worry about. In the States there were shootings in schools—even here in Canada sometimes—and everyone, it seemed, was giving everyone else hell for their ancestors while the media separated into partisan camps. Jean-Max wasn't exactly playing by the rules, either. So how, in the midst of all that impurity, was Cecil himself supposed to be pure?

Sure, the great buildings of the world were still standing. But something was coming of all this instability. Cecil could see it happening. He could feel it and smell it and taste it.

Figuring he was just doing a community service for an unfit community, he decided, yes, he'd done right calling Milky in, that they needed to go through with it. Butting out his cigarette, Cecil went to the stereo, located Ricky Martin's self-titled English debut, deposited the CD, and hit play. Moments later, Cecil was "Livin' la Vida Loca," singing along about black cats and voodoo dolls. By time Ricky got to the refrain, Cecil was in full maid mode. The living room didn't seem so bad twenty minutes later when Madonna joined Ricky on "Be Careful (Cuidado Con Mi Corazón)." It still wasn't the Waldorf, no, but it didn't look like some celebrity's drug den in the *National Enquirer*, either.

Satisfied it'd be good enough for Milky, Cecil grabbed his keys and went down to his tickle trunk in the basement. Unlocking it, he checked his unmarked weaponry, first the Smith & Wesson Model 10 then the Firestar M45. The Model 10 was fully loaded, so Cecil, as the experienced shooter, would carry it. The Firestar had four bullets left. Cecil put it aside for Milky. Cecil also had a small bag of weed and loose papers in there. He picked up the bag, sniffed it, thinking maybe later, and put it back. After removing two ski masks and two pairs of yellow dish gloves and placing them with the guns, he rooted around, coming up with a Velcro restraint system he was going to use to hogtie Jean-Max and ball-gag his mouth. Figuring he'd need such a system one day, Cecil had the foresight to pay cash for it at the Folsom Fair North two years ago, so there'd be no record of his purchase.

Wondering whether he'd ever find a use for the blue feather boa, Cecil locked the trunk, re-checking the guns and placing them in a shopping bag with the gloves, ski masks, and restraint system. For a moment, Cecil worried about Jean-Max thinking maybe Cecil wanted to cornhole him once the hogtie system was introduced. Then Cecil thought, what the hell? That would only subject Jean-Max to further horrors, and maybe, just maybe, Cecil could use such intimidation to get the names of everyone involved. So yeah, after thinking it through, Cecil was glad that Jean-Max would be worried about getting cornholed.

Chuckling at the scenario, Cecil stopped when he noticed Freida's work area, her 1967 Pfaff sewing machine folded shut and resembling an odd desk with various sheets of material neatly stacked along with tins containing needles and thread. Upon Freida's arrival in Toronto, Cecil paid to have the wood refinished, the moving parts serviced, and motor rebuilt based on specs from the Pfaff manual. That was something of which Cecil had been proud. The original owner of the machine was Freida's mother. Now that she had passed—aneurysm—it pleased Freida to be putting together a decent industry as a seamstress on her mother's machine, and that pleased Cecil, the innocence. But, seeing it now, realizing its proximity to his tickle trunk and all the darkness it contained, he looked away.

Up the stairs, closing the basement door, Cecil returned to the living room with his bag of tricks. He was going to leave it on the coffee table then figured he ought to keep the guns near and brought the bag upstairs, placed it on his nightstand. Thinking he could use a little sleep, he climbed into bed and assumed a fetal position, hugging his extra pillow. Too wired, he pulled the sheet back, had a dry wank imagining he was giving it to Kendra Mann from the Neighborhood Watch Committee, his body releasing hormones. That put Cecil out for almost an hour. Waking at least a little refreshed, he hit the toilet then the shower, had a shave.

Clean and clean-cut, he couldn't find his Drakkar Noir balm, so he went through Freida's things and located moisturizer, rubbing some in until he smelled lavender. Wiping away the excess, he dressed in a heather-gray sweatsuit, finishing it off with a pair of all black Air Jordans. He checked his watch against the clock, 5:58 p.m., went down to the living room, and aimed the remote at the TV, hitting power. First there was a spot for Bad Boy Furniture featuring Mayor Mel Lastman and his son Blayne, then the City TV news jingle jingled. Anne Mroczkowski appeared on screen, throwing to Jojo Chintoh who had just attended a news conference at police headquarters where the city's latest necklacing victim has been identified as Penelope Pinkus, twenty-nine, of Kirkland Lake, Ontario. Cecil huffed a breath out his nose, thinking how Venus would have hated Jojo outing her as a call girl with apparent ties to the Toronto underworld. Yeah, yeah, yeah, Cecil thought. Jojo didn't have much, which is why he was pivoting to some good news, announcing that an investigation into the fraud cop who beat the city councilor for Ward 45 with his own cellphone was already over. Fucking eh.

"The Special Investigations Unit has decided that security footage shows the detective in question clearly telling City Councilor Malcolm Tate to kiss the carpet," Jojo said. "By hesitating or refusing—depending on one's interpretation—the councilor effectively resisted arrest, so the SIU has found that Detective Cecil Bolan followed best practice, somewhat, when he deployed use of force to subdue the city councilor who'd been mistaken for a suspect."

"To clarify, Jojo," Mroczkowski said, "Bolan is cleared of any and all wrongdoing?"

"Not only is Bolan cleared. But, in the wake of these findings, Toronto Police are announcing that a charge of resisting arrest will be instated against the councilor, who has until noon tomorrow to report for processing."

As Tate had been a frequent police critic, Jojo said noises were increasingly being made alleging the situation to be politically motivated, adding insult to injury, and the city councilor would be holding a press conference of his own before attending headquarters.

Cecil laughed, thinking Tate was due all the free speech he wanted. He could complain before, during, and after the processing of his charge. That was his right. It was also the right of every cop in Toronto to celebrate, and Cecil figured they would, mostly. He stopped laughing when he saw Gordon Sung walk into Jojo's shot for a change, shaking out a cigarette.

Drunk or fucked on drugs, it didn't matter. Gordon was intentionally loitering, up to something. It was the way he lit up, blowing smoke as he looked over Jojo's shoulder. Aside from Jojo, Cecil didn't know who the "fuck you" was aimed at, but it was for someone watching from home, maybe even Cecil. The prick was smiling and posing in his two-tone bowling shirt—acting like a gangster, is what he was doing—after a girl he just talked to winds up dead. Cecil picked up the clicker but stopped himself from offing the power when Jojo turned and told Gordon to get out of his shot, man. Gordon said it was a free country, man, and took another drag.

For a moment, Cecil thought about how he might get to Gordon, maybe kill him, too. Then Cecil reminded himself that

Gordon had to be getting something out of all this, probably a free lawyer, probably like Doyle, and that separating Gordon from Jean-Max might be punishment enough. If, for whatever reason, Gordon still beat the DWI, Cecil could always catch up to the double-dealing prick and kill him later.

***

Jean-Max sat alone in his deck chair, finishing the chicken-salad sandwich, wondering where he ought to go. He thought about jumping on his laptop and booking a flight out of Pearson or maybe the island airport, then figured either would leave a trail, making him easy to find, and did Jean-Max want to end up talking to Cuban cops, for instance, about any of this? No, he was just going to untie his boat first thing tomorrow, early, and go. He'd keep it safely on the Canadian side so as to avoid the US Coast Guard, Customs, American scrutiny.

Yeah, Jean-Max had all his IDs, a few different passports, just in case he had to get out of the country, but that hopefully wouldn't be necessary, assuming those imbeciles would be able to get to Pam Jenkins. Weather permitting, Jean-Max decided to head to Port Dalhousie, just sort of drift all the way across the lake, dock at the marina there, pay cash for everything out of his safe bag, figure out the rest on the way.

Best thing, he told himself, would be to keep moving a little every day, slowly getting farther away, docking in obscure scurvy bars that would record his patronage and alibi. Before returning, the only people he'd touch base with would be Antoine and Gordon to make sure he wasn't coming back to a surprise party. In the process, he'd find out which was more trustworthy, loyal. Probably Gordon, Jean-Max thought. Gordon was still at the point of being scared, looking for ways to make himself valuable, so he'd suck Jean-Max's uncircumcised frog dick if he whipped it out. Only problem there was that Gordon was not a Quebecer, and how could Jean-Max trust someone who couldn't empathize and understand that Quebecers had to protect themselves with devices such as French-only sign laws? That's right, Quebec was put in the position by the rest of Canada where it had to force immigrant kids into French schools, too, so as to protect the language and culture of a country within a country, and outsiders could take a Greyhound to Vancouver, where everything was permissible, if they didn't like it.

With the above firm in his mind, Jean-Max ate half the sour-cream donut, washing it down with his now cold coffee, and looking out on the smooth lake. He wondered if maybe he was being too harsh with all this necklacing avec mockery business. Then he took another pull on his coffee, telling himself there had to be consequences for anyone daring to wonder aloud about things that could or would harm him, Jean-Max, just like Quebecers had to beat back the rest of Canada, especially Alberta, consequences be damned.

Deciding he'd chosen not just a career, but a course of action, he placed the half donut on the cooler for later, gathering refuse and walking to the marina's main building, disposing the garbage and returning to his boat. He went down below for another layer, returning in a Carhartt hoodie, and broke the seal on a bottle of Maker's Mark, pouring out a generous shot into a gold-rimmed highball glass, and sitting in a deck chair listening to René Simard's *En Concert* CD with headphones. There was some initial playing to the home crowd, a disco-funk instrumental Jean-Max didn't appreciate, but what the hell? René was live in Japan here, 1974, where he'd received some award from Frank Sinatra, so Jean-Max wasn't going to pinch turds over the glitzy intro.

By "Toute La Pluie," Jean-Max was quietly singing along, sipping bourbon, and thinking about what became of René. Couple years back, he was the star of *Phantom of the Opera* in Toronto, which should've been indignity enough, then René was replaced by Paul Stanley of Kiss. So sure, René had a something of a career. Still, as Jean-Max remembered, switching to English pretty much killed René in terms of Québécois culture. It wasn't enough for him to be a Francophone superstar. No, René had to rule the world, probably a result of something Sinatra advised, leading to René's English debut, *Never Know the Reason Why*, a 1977 flop on London Records. And, of course, by the time René had his come-to-Jacques moment, recording in French again, his voice had changed and so had the Québécois.

So, yes, Jean-Max surmised that switching to English had most definitely put René on the career path to mediocrity, which was too bad because *En Concert* was proving once again to be such a timeless, singular tour de force performance, the hairs standing on Jean-Max's neck during "Ne Coupez Pas Les Roses."

What a waste, Jean-Max thought, a damn waste.

But if René was milquetoast for cozying up to Anglos, or at least trying, then what did Jean-Max make of himself? Now that he thought of it, he spoke in English almost all the time. He even had to tell himself to at least think in French. Other than answering the phone bonjour and taking Angels' calls from back home, Jean-Max figured he was pretty much an English pig himself, drinking Tim Hortons, eating chicken-salad sandwiches, avec mayo, and kissing Para-Dice Rider ass, dirty. Jean-Max even drove that impractical little Pommy car, the snot-colored MGB, so what was assimilation going to cost him now that he'd been co-opted?

The more Jean-Max thought, that was the wrong English word, *co-opted*, for something he was half processing in French, and he couldn't find the right term in either language. See, no one had forced him to live the cushy Anglo life. The Angels merger with the Para-Dice Riders simply provided the opportunity for Jean-Max to be president of his own chapter, without having to wear a vest or even ride. It was the perfect cover, an Angel working out of a boat. And the power. Tabernac, the power to direct people was overwhelming. Even that little Pommy car, Jean-Max took it from a man named Monty who owed him money. So no, the more Jean-Max thought, he hadn't been co-opted. He'd merely been charmed by his lust to run the country, or at least his own territory within the country. And yes, there were times when that lust seemed a fickle mistress. But those times were fleeting, which is why Jean-Max concluded that this, too, shall pass, hitting the Maker's Mark and quietly singing along to René Simard at the absolute height of his powers.

TWELVE

Milky Way Jones arrived ready for action in flat-black utility pants, a matching shirt, and Converse One Stars, everything sun bleached. He knocked on Cecil's door just before 11:30 p.m. Cecil figured Milky had to have been speeding, but didn't mention it, no reason. He was here without incident. They did the secret Leamington handshake at the door, Cecil making way so Milky could enter. Inside, he looked around, turning. "Freida?"

"Staying with one of her sewing friends until this blows over," Cecil said. "We have the place to ourselves."

"Then you've changed, man."

"How's that?"

"You've learned to keep house."

"I have at that." Cecil held a hand to his heart. "Housekeeping cannot be a social construct, Freida says."

"And you smell good, too. What are you now, metrosexual?"

"Couldn't find my Drakkar Noir." Cecil pointed upstairs, smiling, a little embarrassed. "Had to use Freida's lavender moisturizer. Only makes me smell like a metrosexual."

"Glad you only smell like one." Milky wrung his hands. "So, do we have some semblance of a plan?"

"We do. Figured I'd brief you on the way. First, you need anything to eat?" Cecil pointed to the kitchen this time. "And coffee? I just put a fresh pot on."

Milky said he ate on the road, but could he please use the facilities and grab a coffee, two creams, one sugar? Cecil said go ahead and had Milky's joe ready to go by the time he was back. Out the door, in Milky's car, a six-year-old Toyota Camry, beige, almost invisible, Cecil guided Milky to the Gardiner Expressway, west, telling him about Jean-Max Renaldo and his ties to Doyle's death. That Jean-Max lived on a boat, so Cecil genuinely needed Milky because he knew how to drive one.

"That means we're not going to do it right there in the harbor."
Milky glanced in the rearview, nothing but headlights. "You want
to take him out on the water, do it there?"

Cecil nodded, said they were going to put Jean-Max at the
bottom of Lake Ontario. The longer his body sat, the colder the
trail would get. If Cecil and Milky did this right, homicide might
never find the body. That being the case, yeah, Cecil needed Milky
to drive the boat out to the deep. After, they'd return Jean-Max's
vessel to where they found it and quietly make their separate
ways home, no one the wiser. Okay, but wasn't Milky taking Cecil
home first? Hopefully not. Cecil said that would cost Milky an
hour. No. Cecil was going to find a Neon near the marina, hotwire it, drive it downtown, dump it, walk home.

"Why a Neon?" Milky said.

"Easiest car to break into. Easiest to hotwire."

Milky sipped his coffee, thinking about that part of Cecil's
plan and nixing it, saying it was one step too many, that it'd be
better for Milky to drive Cecil home and decompress. After, Milky
would motor himself back to Leamington, no problem.

Cecil thought about arguing, but knew Milky was right, agreeing, telling him to follow the Gardiner to North Service Road in
Mississauga and take exit 136. Milky said yeah okay, but what
were they going to do once they arrived at the yacht club? How
were they getting in? Cecil pulled the wire cutters out of his bag,
said they were cutting their way in. Cecil knew the place, the lay
of the land, or water, in this case, from Operation Cooperation,
and Jean-Max's boat was near the fence. Cecil said they were
going to just climb aboard, confront Jean-Max, and take him out
to the deep cold water.

Both men were quiet after that, the only sound being the hum
of tires until Cecil pointed at a sign. "There's exit 136." Directing
Milky to take Dixie Road, then Lakeshore, to the Lakefront
Promenade. "Now park behind that U-Haul."

Doing as Cecil said, Milky killed the ignition, looking over as
Cecil handed him a ski mask and dish gloves, told him to put

them on. Again, Milky did as Cecil said. But when Cecil handed over a gun he said contained four bullets, Milky felt himself wobble inside.

"Am I really going to need this?"

Cecil cut his eyes, said they were about to sink a biker-type guy, so both Milky and Cecil needed guns. Okay, but Cecil could understand how Milky might assume this might not involve shooting. Ideally it won't, Cecil said, less noise. But if there was one thing he was sure of it was that Jean-Max Renaldo had some sort of weapon or weapons, that he might not be alone, so Milky better be ready to protect himself, all times.

That made sense, so Milky took the gun, hefting it in his dish-glove hand. "Alright, I hear you."

Stepping out of the Camry, Cecil pointed the wire cutters to a bushed-in area. "That shrubbery leads to a fence. We cut it, step through, and Jean-Max's boat, the *Dine A Shore*, is about fifteen paces from there."

"Lead the way," Milky said, locking up and pocketing his keys.

He followed Cecil through the bush, watching Cecil cut the fence, step through, and hold it open. Milky came after, Cecil allowing the fence to quietly close. Drawing his gun, nodding for Milky to do likewise, they tiptoed to the *Dine A Shore*. Jean-Max was out on deck in his chair, sipping bourbon, listening to *En Concert* for the third time, the hairs still standing on his neck while René Simard sang "Ne Coupez Pas Les Roses" to the people of Japan. No question, this was René in his prime.

"Perfect," Cecil whispered. "He can't see or even hear us." Stepping aboard.

Startled by the boat's movement, Jean-Max pulled his headphones down, looking at the gun on him, the guy holding it lifting his mask with his free hand. Yeah, it was that whoremaster dick, Cecil Bolan. Then the other guy, the black, lifted his mask. Was that his partner? No, Jean-Max remembered, Cecil's partner was an old black. This was another black, young, late twenties, early thirties. Looking at Cecil, Jean-Max smiled and said, "Detective."

Pointing over his shoulder toward downtown. "I thought you were suspended."

"See?" Cecil said. "Gordon Sung's already giving you imitation information. I'll have you know I've been cleared—Jojo Chintoh had the story at six—so I'm on vacation and this is how I'm spending it."

"That smell." Jean-Max sniffed thrice, looking at Cecil. "Are you wearing perfume?"

"Wife's moisturizer," Cecil said. "Lavender."

Noticing the half-eaten donut on the cooler, Cecil reached for it, smelled it, and was about to take a bite when Jean-Max slapped it away into the water, saying, "Bad cop, no donut." Placing a hand on his headphones. "You have just intruded on a very personal moment."

Observing the Maker's Mark standing on the deck, Cecil figured there was a lot of courage in that bottle, picking it up, checking the cap, putting the bottle in a holder, calling for Milky to step aboard, then looking at Jean-Max. "We're going for a ride, a talk." Jiggling the gun. "Keys." When Jean-Max didn't react, Cecil stepped forward. Gun in his face, Jean-Max reached in his pocket and produced keys. Cecil passed them to Milky who climbed up to the flybridge and started the boat. Surprised they were this far along—it was happening fast now—Cecil told Milky to train his gun on Jean-Max while he, Cecil, untied the boat. Doing so and re-boarding, they were off. When the gold-rimmed highball glass tipped over, rolling on deck, Cecil picked it up and tossed it overboard, telling Jean-Max he wouldn't be needing it anymore.

"Where are you taking me?" he wanted to know.

"The middle of the lake, the deep."

"But why, Detective?"

"To put you at the bottom of the middle of the lake, the deep."

"C'mon, you're a cop." Jean-Max wasn't taking this seriously, figuring Cecil was going to stress him, call him names, maybe even hit him—all of which would prove invaluable if this situation found its way into court where Helen would have a field day.

"That can't be legal."

"Neither is ordering the execution of Venus de Milo," Cecil said. "But that didn't stop you. No, it didn't stop you from ordering the necklacing of Doris Sabo or Doyle Allenby, either."

"You can't prove any of that."

"Like I need to." Cecil looked over the stern. The marina was miniature in the distance, little boats bobbing on a little dock, not a human in sight, perfect. Shifting his view toward downtown, Cecil turned and focused on Jean-Max. "Here's what I know. I talked to Venus Monday at The Greek's and your name was mentioned. She thought you had Doyle Allenby and Doris Sabo killed, even said so, directly, when pressed. Said she was going to talk to her drug buddy at *Eye*, Gordon Sung, see what he knew. Next thing I know, she's necklaced Wednesday morning." Checking his watch. "Roughly seventeen, maybe eighteen, hours ago."

Jean-Max waved all that away, circumstantial.

Cecil agreed it might well be deemed such in court. That's why they were almost at the middle of the lake, the deep. Out here, Cecil wasn't just the arresting officer. No. Cecil was also the crown attorney, judge, and executioner. He'd already made his argument and rendered his decision, declaring Jean-Max guilty of having three people incinerated, probably others. And it wasn't just killing. No. It was a thrill killing, cruel. Because of that, Cecil had been hit he didn't know how many times by the mother of one of the deceased, which was why, in part, Cecil had to fulfill the executioner role and put Jean-Max at the bottom of the middle of the lake—for the guy's mother. At this point, it was just a matter of how much Jean-Max was going to suffer. The way he was popping off, proud, Cecil was hating on the pretentious prick even more.

"So how about it?" Cecil grabbed the bourbon bottle from the holder. "How about you tell me the other parties involved, the firebugs, and I let you have one last drink, kill you softly?"

When Milky shouted that they were out far enough, deep,

Cecil looked around like he knew something about it and said, okay, here. Milky slowed the boat, letting the engine idle, and came down to join Cecil on deck.

"I'm going to find out anyway," Cecil said. "So who did you contract all this out to, the necklacings?"

Jean-Max looked downtown. Shit le merde, this wasn't some ruse. These guys meant to kill him. And it was all the fault of Gordon, winding Jean-Max up about the hooker this cop was balls deep into. Why did Jean-Max react? He shouldn't have, because even if he did get away with it, legally, her crazy cop boyfriend here was obviously going to make him pay. And no matter what Jean-Max surrendered, he didn't think Cecil would do it in such a way that he, Jean-Max, wouldn't suffer, so why surrender anything?

"You want to kill me, fine. But I'm not giving up associates, *porc*. I admit nothing."

Cecil chuckled at the guy calling him pig, circumstances considered, hearing a familiar song. A party boat was passing and Jean-Max called out to it. "Help. They are killing me. Help." Cecil laughed as it went by playing "Shake Your Bon-Bon" too loud for the partiers to hear Jean-Max. Fucking eh, even Ricky Martin was doing his part, singing a song so ridiculous it was fun. Still, Cecil decided he better keep this moving, sitting on the cooler, patting it.

"What's this for?"

"Fish." Jean-Max held his hands a foot apart. "With cocks this long."

"Must be some pretty big fish you're catching, cocks that big." Cecil looked to Milky. "You know a kind of fish a guy needs a cooler this size for trolling Lake Ontario?"

No, Milky wasn't aware of a good-eating fish that size on this lake. There was the odd hundred-year-old sturgeon or granddaddy cat, sure. But Milky said you release those because they're not good eating, that the cooler was better suited to a big-game ocean operation, so this asshole was probably using it to transport bodies and whatnot, drugs.

Cecil was thinking the same thing as he placed the capped bottle on deck, standing and opening the top of the cooler. He turned to Jean-Max and told him to get in. When Jean-Max said no, he wasn't going to do that, Milky forced him up, pushing him to the edge of the cooler, the bottle tipping over from the motion on deck as Cecil hammered Jean-Max in with a fist, facedown. Laughing while Jean-Max said something about his lawyer, Cecil forced the Velcro restraints around Jean-Max's ankles and wrists, pulling him into the hogtie position.

"I knew you were wearing perfume," Jean-Max said. "What're you doing with this? You trying to breed me?"

"I might at that." Cecil kneeled on the deck, working his gun between Jean-Max's buttocks. "I bet you're a tight little twenty-four-ounce Pepsi, aren't you?"

"Just please," Jean-Max said. "Don't do it like this. Do not shoot me there."

"Okay, I promise not to shoot you there if you tell me two simple things. One, were you paying Doyle's expensive white-girl lawyer?"

Jean-Max thought fast. Divulging as much right here, right now, would be like admitting the whole thing, a confession, so he said no. Cecil increased the pressure on his gun, asking again, was Jean-Max paying Doyle's legal fees? Okay, fine. Jean-Max didn't want a shot up the arse, so he figured there was no way out, that, if he did live, none of this would be admissible anyway, so he said yeah, okay. He was paying Doyle's lawyer fees. And yeah, again, he was paying Gordon Sung's lawyer, too. Same lawyer in both instances. Helen Tyndall.

"Okay," Cecil said, "one last question and I'll let you go, softly. I know you heard back from your people after they killed Doyle. You know what was said, the wittier repartee, because you get off on it, I think. So tell me, sicky, what were Doyle Allenby's last words?"

At that point, Jean-Max knew this was it. Cecil was going to kill him, and not in a nice way, so why should Jean-Max cooper-ate at all? The indignity.

"Why do you want me to say that?"

"Because Doyle's last words are going to be your last words." Cecil backed off, swinging his gun around. "I think it's poetic."

"I'm not going to say it. Those words are not going to be my last words."

"Fine." Cecil rolled his free hand over like Jean-Max could see the non-verbal cue. "What are your last words then?"

Jean-Max thought about the René Simard show he'd been listening to, beautiful turns of phrase in the beautiful language. Why, oh why, did René ever even think about singing in anoth-er tongue? Even the Japanese loved it in French—as evidenced by the reaction on *En Concert*—and they couldn't have known what René was singing about. They could only feel it, René's voice becoming another instrument to their little yellow ears. Still, as much as Jean-Max bowed at the altar of everything René recorded from 1975 and earlier, his words were not going to be Jean-Max's last. No, instead, Jean-Max would quote Charles de Gaulle, who, while not a Quebecer, was at least a true Frenchman supporting Quebec's right to self-determination.

"Get on with it." Cecil rolled his hand faster. "Your last words. What are they?"

Eyes focused on the cooler's interior, Jean-Max said, "Vive le Québec libre."

"How cerebral," Cecil said. "I'm impressed. Very impressed." Reaching in and inserting the ball gag, tightening it. "But then Doyle's last words are going to be the last words you hear. Write in Dick Gregory for president, motherfucker."

Cecil closed the cooler, locked it, and looked at Milky, who said, "What now?"

"We put the cooler in the lake, let it sink."

"You sure it's going to sink?"

"Pretty."

"I don't know, Cecil. It looks buoyant."

"Let's just put it in the water, see."

Both men grabbed a handle. They heard muffled screams from inside as they lifted the cooler over the stern and dropped it in the water, splash. Waiting, watching... It didn't appear to be sinking. Milky said, "Now what?"

"We shoot it." Cecil held his hand out. "Gimme your gun."

"What good's shooting it going to do?"

"Bullet holes will allow it to fill with water. That'll sink it for sure. Gimme your gun."

When Milky handed over his piece, Cecil took aim and fired four shots, emptying the Firestar into the cooler. Sure enough, it started sinking and slowly disappeared. Cecil threw the gun as far as he could, another splash, looked at Milky and said, "Get us the fuck out of here."

"Where are we going?"

"I told you." Cecil pointed a thumb over his shoulder. "Back to the marina, dump his boat where we found it and hoof it back to your heap. We get out cleanly, it'll be weeks before they find him, months. Maybe never."

That sounded good to Milky. He climbed back to the flybridge, put the boat in gear, and pointed it in the direction they came. Meantime, Cecil said he was going to have a looky-loo downstairs to see if he could come up with anything interesting.

THIRTEEN

Alex wanted so badly to just get out of his head and sleep, but he couldn't stop watching the red numbers change on the Yorx clock radio. Sondra sat up in bed next to him, said, "What're you angsting about now?"

"Cecil."

"Let me get this straight." Sondra resisted the urge to check the time, looking at Alex. "You, sleeping with a fit woman does yoga ten years your junior wearing nothing but a leopard slip at her swish condo in the heart of the city paid by three other men's alimonies—twenty-four-hour security, indoor and outdoor pools, hot tubs, tanning beds—and you're thinking about Cecil?"

When Alex didn't say anything, Sondra said maybe Alex should get Cecil to suck his dick, flick the head with his tongue while he looked Alex in the eye. That made Alex laugh, sort of, a little comic relief. And sorry, but he just knew Cecil was freelancing. Dammit, Alex knew it. Freelancing? Sondra said Alex mentioned something about that to Cecil yesterday. Specifically, Sondra wanted to know what Alex meant by that. Freelancing, Alex said, when one detective unilaterally does work, usually subversive, on the sly without informing his partner and/or senior officers about his activities, freelancing.

Oh, Sondra thought freelancing was when you did different jobs for different companies but didn't pay taxes, benefits, union dues, or any other deductions. Alex said that was another kind of freelancing. Yeah, Sondra said Alex was assigning new meanings to old words, which was some Orwellian shit to be pulling in bed, so mayhaps he should drop the copspeak and rap like a civilian, a lover. Also, Sondra didn't see the problem with Cecil getting a little work in. That it was his vacay to do with what he wanted, and he'd probably even have the difficult legwork done on whatever case they were working on by the time Alex went back. Mayhaps, it would even help Cecil keep his mind off his dead friend. And what was so wrong with that?

"You don't understand." Alex pulled Sondra's burgundy-and-black zebra sheet up to his chin. "Cecil's not working on one of our cases to keep his mind off his dead friend."

"Then what's he working on?"

"Something personal," Alex said. "Something to do with whoever made his friend dead."

"Did I miss something yesterday? Did he say that?"

"No."

Sondra crossed her arms, gave Alex the stink eye. "Are you clairvoyant?"

"No again. I am not clairvoyant."

"Then why are you making like you can read that stupid white boy's vacant mind, even when he's not physically present?"

"Experience," Alex said. "Experience combined with gut instinct."

"Fine." Sondra sighed, let her head drop slightly to the right. "Well then, you know, Mr. Expert. But it's still his time, his business. He wants to work on something personal on his vacation, maybe you just let him be and fixate on me."

Alex looked at her. "How you want me to do that?"

"Pull my string." Sondra rolled on her stomach, maintaining eye contact. "Make me talk dirty."

That caught Alex's attention, his eyes wide. "Like last time? You promise to say the same things you said last time?"

Yeah, Sondra would say the same things if that's what Alex wanted. Also, she had some new material. Alex wanted to know where she got the new material. Like, she wasn't freelancing, right?

***

Nearing the Port Credit Marina, Milky brought the boat to an idle and called to Cecil down below. He appeared on deck carrying a gym bag in one hand, Maker's Mark in the other. Taking a slug, notes of vanilla, Cecil studied the marina. He didn't see anyone about, so he told Milky to guide them back into Jean-Max's spot. Within a few minutes, Cecil was dropping the bottle in the water and jumping out with the bag on his shoulder, tying the boat down. In the morning, it would look like the *Dine A Shore* had been there all night. Jean-Max? Not so much.

Milky killed the engine and stepped out holding the keys in a dish-glove hand. "What do I do with these?"

"We don't need 'em," Cecil whispered, taking the keys and throwing them into the harbor, splash. "And neither does Jean-Max." Pointing to the fence. "Let's go."

Crawling through the hole, then the bush, they were back in Milky's Camry.

Both men wanted to break the uncomfortable silence, but, taking the Gardiner back into Toronto proper, they were too worried about getting off the road. Anything could put them in Millhaven now. A burned-out light. A speeding infraction. Failing to come to a complete stop. Even some uniform's gut instinct. Cecil wanted to counsel Milky on what to avoid but figured anything he had to say would make Milky more skittish, and thus, more vulnerable.

Soon enough, they were on Bleecker Street, parking, locking up, keying the townhouse door, and, finally, safely back inside where Cecil dropped the gym bag at the door. All the while, it seemed nobody in greater Toronto, other than Jean-Max of course, had noticed them.

"Pale ale?" Cecil thumb-pointed over his should to the kitchen, the fridge.

"Love one." Milky nodded at the wall clock. "Except I want to be back on the road by four. If I leave then, I'll be at my usual café at my usual time, just after seven, having my usual coffee—two creams, one sugar—chatting up the usual short girls."

Cecil snorted, said nothing unusual about that. He asked if Milky minded if he, Cecil, had a pale ale. Milky said of course not. That he was going to start drinking as soon as he got home from his café, come down. Cecil thought that made sense, secretly throwing back a shot of Absolut while he was in kitchen and returning with a bottle of Keith's and asking, "Do you still have that burner phone?"

Milky patted the front pocket of his utility pants. He did. Cecil asked if he'd used it. Not once, Milky said, sitting down on the recliner. Cecil said good, for Milky to keep it, that if Cecil needed to call, he would use that number, and what was it? Milky pulled out his burner, read out digits while Cecil sat on the edge of his couch and jotted them down. As for Cecil's burner, he'd already used it to call Milky at the Leamington Marina, anonymous. Still, he was going to break and ditch it before he returned to work. Until then, Milky could reach Cecil at that same number, but to call only if he really, really had to. They had to be careful with the phones because that's how Alex and Cecil got to Jean-Max in the first place. Cecil beat a cellphone out of one of his biker buddies, traced it to other burners, Doyle's for instance, then they were able to get some records through this Fido guy Cecil pushed around. So Cecil told Milky they needed to properly dispose of the burners at the end of all this.

"Sure thing," Milky said. "When do you go back to work?"

"Tuesday. But let's avoid contact if we can. Less is more here. Less communication is less evidence. Every time we communicate, we create a popcorn trail, so it's best we're not in touch at all for the next little while. No offence."

"None taken. I don't want to go to Millhaven."

"Bad prison." Cecil pointed a thumb at himself. "Not a good place for a cop." Then an index at Milky. "Not a good place for you, either, by reason of you being, you know, minority."

Yeah, Milky knew.

Okay then, Cecil told Milky to send him a signal once he arrived in Leamington. Milky was to use a payphone to place a collect call from Ricky Martin to Cecil's landline. Cecil would refuse the charges, muttering about it being a crank, but the call would be Milky's signal that he was home without incident. If, on the odd chance, the call ever came up officially, Milky would say sure, he cranked Cecil, good times. Cecil, he didn't know who cranked him, just that he'd been cranked. And who was it?

That was copacetic with Milky. All he wanted was two coffees—two creams, one sugar in each. One for now and one for the road. And would Cecil mind brewing a fresh pot? Mind? After the job Milky just did, it would be an honor.

Returning to the kitchen, Cecil put on a fresh pot of Nabob, downing another vodka shot. Once the coffee finished brewing, he prepared the cup as Milky specified. Serving it out in the living room, both men were quiet again, filled with thoughts of what they'd done, until Milky broke the silence. "You remember the championship, that shot."

Sinking into the couch, Cecil said, "Your three-pointer with no time on the clock?"

"That one." Milky was relieved Cecil remembered so specifically. "Do you also remember what was going on when I took that shot?"

"Other than when I watch it on VHS, pixilated at key moments, I never saw the ball leave your hands." Cecil pointed at an imaginary basket. "I was driving to the net, out of habit, for a rebound. Somewhere inside, I knew there was no time, that we lose if that ball doesn't go in, but instinctually, I was still driving to the net as you shot. Why? What'd I miss?"

"Do you remember Templeton played for General Amherst?"

Oh yeah, Cecil remembered Templeton. Big guy. Huge. Six eight or something. Got a full ride to Ferris State. Last Cecil heard, Templeton was playing professionally in Europe. Good on him. Why? Did Templeton do something while Milky was making that shot?

Milky said yes. Templeton was jumping sideways and Doyle nudged him, without explicitly fouling him, just enough to keep his fingers off the ball. If Doyle didn't nudge Templeton, Milky would've never made that shot.

"We didn't have the best players, just the best team," Cecil said, eyes watery. "We were family." Looking to Milky. "And thanks for telling me that. I do recall Doyle throwing a screen from the tape, but I want to see the body contact. Will look for it, the contact, next time I watch the VHS. Did you ever tell Doyle? Share?"

"I did, that night while we were celebrating with the cheerleaders, ball bunnies, and strippers at the Village Inn."

"Good." Cecil took a pull on his pale ale. "I mean, it's good you said that." Rolling his hand. "Expressed it directly. I assure you, Milky, not a day goes by without me thinking about it." Flashing his championship ring. "Best moment of my life." Noticing his wedding picture on the mantel, pausing. "Except for maybe the day I married Freida." Back to Milky. "But she'll never understand our bond." Flashing his ring again. "When we won that day, we made sure we will dribble together forever. What do you think Doyle's doing right now?"

Milky looked straight ahead, smiling as if it was 1988 all over again. "He's asking Saint Peter, where's the hardwood?"

"You know it," Cecil said. "And sorry I didn't make the funeral. Didn't seem Mrs. Allenby wanted me."

"Don't worry. She didn't want anyone."

Cecil pointed. "You, too."

Yeah, Milky, too. Right after Cecil left on Monday, Jack Rodney from the *Leamington Post* showed up asking questions about Doyle's criminal activities, demanding a picture, so Mrs. Allenby slapped the shit out of Jack, too. That was it. After that, she threw everyone out, closed the service to family and relatives only. Even Tim Hrynewich, who showed to pay respects to a fellow athlete, was turned away.

"She refused Tim?" Cecil held his chin. "He played parts of two seasons with the Penguins. Makes him Leamington hockey royalty. Don't tell me Mrs. Allenby hit him, too."

"Naw." Milky laughed, shaking his head. "Mrs. Allenby didn't hit Tim."

"What about donations? They say where to send donations in lieu of flowers?"

Milky nodded, said Erie Wildlife Rescue. Cecil said right on.

It was getting closer to four, meaning Milky would be leaving.

Cecil was worried about being alone and thought about suggesting that Milky stay, but Cecil still knew it was best that Milky quietly made his way back home before anyone missed him. Instead, the two men relived parts of their championship drive, until finally, Milky said it was time, and could Cecil please set him up with that road coffee?

With a pit in his stomach, Cecil went to the kitchen and made Milky another cup like the last. Milky stood, took it, raised his mug, and said thanks. Cecil pointed at the gym bag at the door. Milky said yeah, he was going to ask about that. Cecil said it was money. He didn't know how much, just a lot. He told Milky to keep $5,000, to anonymously send another $5,000 to Erie Wildlife Rescue, then send the rest to Doyle's mother, also anonymously, in a few months, help her with funeral costs and then some.

Milky looked at the bag, asking Cecil if he was going to take any. Cecil said he thought about it, but it would be a conflict of interest. Milky figured Cecil was beyond worrying about conflicts, but just said thank you. Five K would go a long way. And did Cecil find anything else down below? Just a gun with the serial number filed off and a bunch of burner phones, Cecil said, nothing that should be disturbed.

"I mean, I was tempted to take the burners and track some of the numbers to see if I could turn the same trick twice and find Jean-Max's contractors. But I could also get in a hell of lot of trouble if I was caught with Jean-Max's burners, so I just, you know, left everything as it was."

"Good call," Milky said.

Cecil wanted to walk Milky down to the Camry, but he told Cecil to stay inside, that it'd be best if none of his neighbors saw him mucking around in the night. Cecil said Milky was thinking like a cop and engaged him in a man hug. He asked Milky if he still had his boat, the *Electric Eel*? Milky said he did, that Cecil should come home sometime and Milky would take him walleye fishing. Cecil said he'd take Milky up on that. The two men embraced once more, Milky saying the three of them—Doyle, Cecil, and Milky—would truly dribble together forever now. Cecil and Milky made fists, bumping rings, then Milky, gym bag in one hand, coffee mug in the other, told Cecil to cut his grass before the metrosexuals complained and walked out to his car.

Shutting his front door as Milky drove away, Cecil checked his watch, 4:03 a.m., the timing perfect. So long as Milky wasn't stopped, Cecil was thinking maybe they really were getting away with it. Back to the kitchen, he grabbed the vodka bottle along with a shot glass, put both on the coffee table in the living room and proceeded to drink himself to sleep.

***

Alex had Sondra on all fours. The bottom of her leopard slip was pulled up over her ass—yoga really paying off—and she was talking dirty, filthy, nasty when Alex missed what he thought might've been a key part. "What was that?"

"Gonna cum on your cock." Sondra craned her neck, looking at Alex. "I'm gonna cum on your cock."

"No, after you said that," he said. "After that, you said something else."

"I don't know." Sondra thought about it, pace slowing. "I'm on the edge, man. Gonna cum in like thirty seconds, forty-five now. Let's go."

Alex held up a hand, stop. "Did you mention something about freelancing?"

Sondra pulled away, sitting at the head of the bed between pillows, facing Alex. "Are you kidding?"

"What?"

"What? You, in my bed, making sweet, sweet love in the middle of the night, thinking about your white-boy partner, again. Maybe you really should get him to give you a bro job."

"I'm sorry." Alex turned away. "But when you used the word freelancing, I started thinking about him. That's all it was."

"But I never said freelancing."

"What'd you say then?"

"I was on the edge, like I said, talking all kinds of crazy, exaggerating your skills, your girth. But I never said anything about freelancing." Sondra covered her eyes. "What exactly do you think he's doing, you so worried?"

"I don't know." Alex gathered the sheet in his left fist. "But he's doing it right now." Pointing out the window with his right index. "I know it."

"He's sleeping." Sondra pointed at the clock without looking at it. "I don't want to know the time, but it's been Thursday for hours and I'm telling you he's sleeping, the way he drinks those premium Caucasian ales, probably pissing his wife's cotton sheets. That's why she's not there. He's a big, sweaty, hairy, white piss tank."

"I know Cecil." Alex folded his hands. "He might be drinky, but he ain't sleeping."

"What's he doing then?"

Emphatically, Alex said, "He's freelancing."

"Do you have an Employee Assistance Program?"

"Yeah. But the subject's been broached and Cecil's not buying in."

"Wasn't talking about Cecil," Sondra said.

"Who you talking about?" Alex pointed at his bare chest, salt-and-pepper hair. "Me?"

"Yeah, you."

"Why me?"

"Maybe they can give you some pills to help you forget about Cecil when you got a lady ten years your junior on her hands and knees, bare ass bouncing, telling you she's gonna cum." Sondra nodded in the direction of headquarters a block away. "Go ahead, tell the EAP you were thinking about Cecil when all that was going on. See if they think you need help."

Alex said he didn't need the EAP. He needed to get away from Cecil's misdoings.

"Yeah. Except, you did a misdoing when you misled me about what he said."

"How's that?"

Sondra nodded once. "You said he said I was just some bitch you banged, when it appears he was talking about your other bitches, as he clarified."

"That's how good he is," Alex said. "He made it sound like he wasn't talking about you, putting me under scrutiny. But, in actuality, he took the side door to calling you a bitch again."

Sondra thought about it, running fingers through her processed chestnut hair. Parting it and pushing it back, she said, hmm. Alex was right. But then how come Alex didn't prove his love and intervene? And what other bitches was Cecil talking about?

Alex said he didn't intervene because he hadn't realized Cecil had taken the side door to calling Sondra a bitch again until he sounded it out just now. See, that's what Alex was talking about. Sometimes he didn't realize what Cecil had done until it was too late. And please, between work, church, the demands of two ex-wives, and Sondra, Alex didn't have time for other bitches.

FOURTEEN

Cecil woke on his couch, hungover, landline ringing. He glanced at his watch, stuck on seconds, again, fuck, so he checked the wall clock, a few minutes after seven, answering hello, listening to an automated message: "This is Bell Canada. You have a collect call from (Milky's voice) Ricky Martin. To accept the call, say yes or press one. To decline, say no or press..."

"Fuckin' crank," Cecil shouted into the mouthpiece, smile rising in his voice. "No way. I don't accept. And whoever's doing this, you better hope I don't find you before Bell Canada." Slamming the phone on its cradle.

Okay, Milky was home like he never left, one less thing to worry about. Despite this sliver of good news, Cecil was suffering from post-alcohol-something-something and decided to put that shit off, heading to the kitchen for a Keith's, hair of the dog. Back on his couch, he aimed the remote and City TV came to life with the city councilor bemoaning his resist charge. Mayor Lastman addressed a rise in inner-city violence, the recent rash of necklacings in particular, floating out the idea of calling in the army. Then there was a bit on terrorists making weapons out of common household products. Also, they were telling Canadians not to go to Turkey unless they really, really had to.

Sure, the world was falling apart, more instability. But for now, City TV had nothing concerning gunplay on Lake Ontario or a break-in at a Mississauga marina, more good news.

In between news and sports—Billy Koch getting the save against Texas despite giving up a home run—the host trotted out a group of swimsuit models, every one of them with nip-ons, something Cecil hardly needed in his hungover state. Nonetheless, he remained tuned in, nursing his Keith's, and eventually fell back to sleep until the phone woke him again, Freida checking in.

She said Cecil sounded drunk. He said it was morning and did Freida know him to drink this time of day? Not often, she said.

So okay, maybe Cecil was just hungover and sounded like shit, but was it time for Freida to come home? Jada was being great about all this. She had some leftover material and Freida was using Jada's back-up machine to make something for Cecil, so Freida was having fun, circumstances considered. But she wanted to sleep in her bed, to hold Cecil in her arms, to get fucked-up and fuck around. When would it be safe again to do all that?

"Soon," Cecil said. "Just two or three loose ends."

Okay, Freida said Cecil should get those tightened, because one way or another she was coming home, soon. She told Cecil she loved him. He said he loved her. She told him to take care, again that she loved him, and signed off with a "bye, hun."

Cecil wondered how he could be angry all the time when he had Freida loving him so unconditionally. At first, he thought he was still suffering from post-alcohol-something-something, emotional, then remembered he was actively drunk. What with the stress of being up against the worst of the worst every day, Cecil figured he also had post-something-something-else. He briefly considered what Alex had said about the EAP. And yeah, there were confidentiality clauses, but Cecil couldn't exactly tell the EAP he was stressed over killing some biker capo who killed his friend, so what good was the EAP going to do if Cecil couldn't discuss what he'd done? Point was, Cecil figured that if he was Freida, he would have left himself long ago, the shit he brought back to their little brick-of-the-month club.

What with the massive mortgage they were carrying through the credit union, Cecil and Freida couldn't afford a car, even when her modest seamstress numbers, mostly tax-free cash, were figured into the calculus. They were house poor. That's why Alex was always driving, Cecil getting by on an assortment of free rides, cabs, streetcars, subways, and long walks. It was no life, waiting all the time, relying on others to get from A to B, or hoofing it.

All that might seem normal to a proper Torontonian. To a rural man, it wasn't. Toronto left Cecil in a state of perpetual culture shock, what with its violence and corruption emulating American cities. People here lived on top of each other, jammed into what experts at the bar described as the most densely populated neighborhood in Canada, St. James Town. That lack of space fit Cecil like a pair of shrunk skivvies, so no wonder he was on edge. Too many people in too small a place. But why was he fretting over all that? He'd killed a man last night. And sure, while the dead man was himself a killer, deserved a terrible death, was it really up to Cecil to be the crown attorney, judge, and executioner?

In an ideal world, no, probably not. But if Cecil didn't step up, more people would've died while the system sputtered, as it did during the investigation into thrill killer Paul Bernardo. Cecil heard all about it while earning his Police Foundations (Fast Track) diploma in Chatham. The cops had Bernardo—the sicky bragging he was an upstart hip-hopper—but let him loose because Toronto and Niagara cops weren't sharing intel. Cecil's prof said they were calling each other names, the state of cooperation was so bad. Everyone wanted to make that bust. And what happened in the interim? More young women were kidnapped, defiled, and killed.

So, even from a classroom setting, Cecil could see the system cracking before he arrived in the big smoke. Now that he was here, getting a firsthand view of law enforcement's sausage being made, what was he to do but act alone?

In this case, same as the Bernardo situation, the dissention was unmistakable, only here it ran within a single force. No doubt Teddy had sent Operation Cooperation files to homicide, and he seemed to have a decent working relationship with Sheff Dubois, good start. But did Hermosa make any effort to debrief Cecil? No, not even a courtesy call. While it seemed that Alex had spoken to Hermosa more than once, at last check Alex still hadn't told Hermosa to look into who was paying Doyle's expensive white-girl lawyer. That meant Alex was holding out, gatekeeping not just Cecil, but Hermosa as well, so Cecil thought fuck Alex, the old prick turning everything into a teachable moment when he didn't have a handle on his own end.

Somewhere in there, Cecil figured he was wrong, too, given some of the shit, mostly defensive, coming out of his mouth. He shouldn't have said Hermosa was an uppity spic being racist. But then Hermosa shouldn't have called Cecil gringo. It wasn't Cecil's fault Hermosa was watching piss porn on his work computer. And fuck Alex two times. Cecil knew how Alex felt, openly declaring Cecil straight outta buttfuck, a play on those Cali hip-hoppers sing kill cops. Point remained, however, that Cecil had knowledge of details Alex didn't and Hermosa couldn't, none of which were being considered because cops were busy fighting cops over petty shit. Speaking of which, did Cecil have to ride Theodore, calling him Teddy when it so affected him? Goddamn right, and it was because it so affected Teddy, who was having sidebars with Alex—fuck him a third time—making the job harder for everyone. So who started it? Who snubbed who first? And did it matter? Even if Hermosa found evidence to file charges, Cecil figured the expensive white-girl lawyer would've seen to it that Jean-Max beat the beefs, everything being so circumstantial.

Figuring any evidence against himself would also be circumstantial, Cecil drank through morning, adding up his own little corruptions. He couldn't count how many Keith's he'd accepted at The Greek's, drinking for free so he'd ignore the pimping, whoring, and drug dealing. Cecil was sure Robert was making his own wine and putting it in decoy bottles. There was no way the toilets were up the code, the faint taint everywhere along with evidence of vermin, both kinds. Cecil didn't report any of it so long as he got what he wanted, free information and free Keith's. So, yeah, withholding all that from the appropriate departments—it would've been nothing to make a call, kick it sideways—made Toronto a more unscrupulous place, because all sorts of people in all sorts of departments were failing to kick it sideways. See, the system was serving them. They were all getting what they wanted, money and status and power, which is why the same righteous souls addressed certain imbalances, but not others, such as the fact that Cecil's ward had seventeen halfway houses.

The Bridle Path, not so much, because Bridle Path people bought their elected representatives, meaning none of their politicians were going to attend a ribbon cutting for a halfway house. Cecil's city council rep, Pam McConnell, she would've been right there, going on about how halfway houses enrich the community. May we please have another.

And more or less, Cecil thought, glancing at the wall clock, that's why the grass was literally greener in some parts of town.

At noon, he watched City TV news again, basically a repeat of the morning misinformation without all the nip-ons. Somehow, in this great big world-class city—2.5 million and counting—no one seemed to notice what Cecil and Milky had been up to in the night.

Still, Jean-Max hadn't done Doyle himself. He'd contracted it out to three other players, so far as Cecil could surmise, but who? For a while, Cecil second-guessed himself, thinking he should've spent more time trying to force Jean-Max to name names. Sure, Cecil could've done that. He could've burned Jean-Max's eyes out with Export 'A's all night. That would've for sure elicited a response, made him say something, but would it be true? Maybe, maybe not. Cecil couldn't know and he didn't want to go killing people on Jean-Max's say so. Nor did he have time to screw around. If Cecil really was right and just in doing Jean-Max, Cecil was also right and just in getting Milky the hell off the lake and safely back to Leamington.

Odds-on, Cecil was never going to know who actually did Doyle, and how could he? These guys were pros, probably, guys who killed dozens in diabolical ways. They'd be next to impossible to find. Even if Cecil found them, would it be wise? Bad enough they might kill Cecil. He could live with that, so to speak, but did he want to put Freida in more danger? No way. Cecil had done enough. While his conscience wasn't exactly clear, he was going to let it go now. But then of course, if Cecil didn't find out who actually did the deed, how could he ever believe Freida was safe so long as she was with him?

✱✱

After spending a fair part of the night discussing Cecil's alleged freelancing, then finally, changing the subject and making some of that sweet, sweet love, Alex and Sondra lingered in bed all morning. With Sondra nodding off next to him, Alex decided to slip out to pick up some lattes from the café downstairs. Back up the elevator minutes later, he returned, finding Sondra sitting up in bed with the sheet pulled to her neck, and handing her a latte. She said thank you, baby, took a sip, said it was good, but not good like the Jet Fuel. Not even close, Alex said, but he had no way of getting to the Jet Fuel, what with Svetlana taking the Cougar, so the café downstairs at Wellesley near Bay, The Muffin Foundry—which seemed to be more of muffin specialty shop that made lattes on the side—had to do. Speaking of which, he said he needed Sondra's help on something. She said hmm, looking at him, waiting for the hook of it.

"I need to go get my car back Tuesday morning."

Sondra took another sip, narrowed her eyes. "You need a car so you can go to the Jet Fuel?" Pointing downstairs. "You can borrow mine, if it's to get me a latte."

No, Alex didn't need the Cougar to make trips to the Jet Fuel, though that was a fringe benefit. He needed the car so he could go to work, said he made a hell of a lot extra charging the force mileage, 47.5 cents a kilometer. He even admitted to upping the amount a little every month to get help paying his alimonies.

"Can't you just call the spitty-talking pasty bitch with no neck?" Sondra held her latte out. "Hold your hate and ask nice?"

While Alex made it clear he didn't hate Svetlana, he said there was no talking to her these days, that she was unhappy in Canada, that she blamed him for bringing her here, and where was the culture? Now that the war was over, pretty much, she wanted to return home, Zagreb. Anyway, Alex had been thinking about it, his predicament with her and the car, and figured it'd be best if he acted first and apologized later. He was going to just take it.

Sondra licked a cinnamon sprinkle off her lips, said, "But

wouldn't that be like grand motor carjacking?"

"Gray area." Alex wavered his hand. "Every cop in Toronto, pretty much, knows it as a police vehicle. Worst case, some rookie pulls my coat, says Detective Johnson, you have to sort this shit. No one's going to bust me, charge me, guaranteed. Lotsa cops in this exact situation."

"It's lotsa cops have to steal cars from their spitty-talking ex-wives?"

Alex sighed, said no, just lotsa cops having ex-wife problems, so most empathized.

"Alright." Sondra took another sip. "I'm in solidarity with you blue meanies, empathizing, willing to prove my love. Except, what do I have to do?"

"When the time comes, early Tuesday, just drive me. I'll do the rest. Officially, you're dropping me off so as I can visit with my ex. That's all you know, that I have business with her. What kind? You don't care, didn't ask. Meantime, I'll walk on over to my car like a boss, start the engine, and drive to my work as a police."

"All I have to do is drop you off." Sondra held the coffee to her mouth. "That's it?"

"That's it. Nothing else to it." Alex thumb-pointed over his shoulder, the living room. "You mind if I make a quick work call?"

No, Sondra didn't mind so long as the word quick was operative, and it had better not result in another field trip to Cecil's unclean white-boy cave. Alex promised it wouldn't, that he just had to get a message he'd been forgetting to deliver through to this guy in homicide. Alex had to sort of call and say, hey Hermosa, check this shit out. That was it.

✱✱✱

Cecil spent the rest of Thursday staying drunk and watching City TV while cradling a pillow in the fetal position. Once in a while, Freida would call and he would shuffle to the window, talking, watching the glorious lightning of on-and-off April showers, people holding brollies running by in shubooties. Same thing Friday and Saturday, when Cecil made another trip to The Beer

Store then caught a documentary on Jehovah's Witnesses, fucking cultists, figuring it would give him an upper hand in understanding how Alex ticked. It was dry on Sunday, so Cecil kept his crap in conjunction long enough to mow the lawn. While he didn't have much acreage—the parcel couldn't have been sixty by ninety feet—it really had gone to seed. Given all Cecil had was a reel mower willed to Freida by her grandfather, he had to cut the lawn four times to get a respectable edge. But Cecil got 'er done, rewarding himself with more of everything—Keith's, Mr. Jerk, cigarettes, and TV.

At no time did he hear boo about Jean-Max Renaldo or even vague reports of boating troubles. So far, his luck was holding.

When Monday rolled along, it was almost time to return to reality. Just in case there was any doubt, Alex called, telling Cecil to meet him at headquarters tomorrow, not the Jet Fuel. That Alex had to pick up the Cougar. From where? Alex didn't say. Maybe he was having some work done, a realignment. Also, Alex said they had to meet Theodore to collect their new assignment, likely chasing able-bodied people parking in handicap spaces. And hey, did Cecil manage to get his grass cut? The city was going to ticket him the way it was going to seed. Cecil said yeah, he cut his ugly-ass grass, and at least he had a lawn he could let go to seed, slamming the phone down. There. Getting in the last word.

Cecil's vacation-suspension was almost over, not that said fact cut into his drinking. The place was a crack house again—empty bottles, overfilled ashtrays, and crumpled bags all over. Bad as the place looked, it smelled like butt broth with all the Mr. Jerk he'd been consuming. The windows were locked, Cecil drinking, burping, farting, and smoking the whole week.

It was past dinner now, dark, raining for a change, and Cecil was thinking about how he had to dispose of his burner phone when he heard someone on his steps. Had they come for him? Cecil couldn't be sure if it was someone from Jean-Max's death squad—how could they know already?—or just some poor kid delivering pizza flyers. But when Cecil heard them toying with the lock, he was telling himself that he knew Goddamn well that they would come for him. Sure, it had been quiet. It was always quietest before the storm, and it was actively storming now, rain pelting the roof, so he grabbed his Glock, unhitching the safety, crouching, and assuming the position as the door swung open.

Whoever it was, they were hiding behind a big suit bag, and it didn't seem that they were wearing any pants, just a pair of new Chuck Taylor All Stars, red, and Cecil was curious, having never seen this approach. Who came in ready to kill a cop holding a suit bag, likely containing their pants, in front of them? Whatever the angle, they'd broken into a cop's home, so Cecil would be within his rights to shoot first, ask questions later. The union would back him on this, too, as well as *All News, All the Time*. Still, he figured he better go through the motions of trying to de-escalate the situation, once, as he'd been trained while earning his Police Foundations (Fast Track) diploma.

"Drop that bag before I put a hole right through it and you, too."

The intruder complied, letting the bag fall. It wasn't a dude. It was a girl, dark-ginger bangs and wet curls framing her stunned eyes, and she was just standing there in a DIY sundress covered in butterflies, looking at Cecil. Oh God, it was . . .

"Freida." Cecil still had the gun on her. "What are you doing?"

"What are you doing yourself, Cecil. Get your gun off me."

And so Cecil did, shaking, clicking the safety on, placing the gun on the coffee table, shuffling to her. "I'm sorry. I'm so sorry. I thought . . ."

"I know, I know." She held him, cradling his head in her hands, resting her forehead on his before leaning away and watching his eyes. She could see that he was ornery, agitated.

"And why are you wearing All Stars?" he said. "There's no support."

Freida pushed an errant curl back, saying she blew out her Blundstones today, that she got twelve years out of them. Well, Cecil said, why didn't she just get another pair of Blundstones?

Freida said there was only enough space left on the card for All Stars. Smiling awkwardly, Cecil gave her a thumbs up, bracing himself.

"Now tell me," she said. "I've never known you to be worried about any other man, other than my dad. Never known you to be intimidated by anyone. I mean, it might be a good career move to be just a little afraid of your boss, stop calling him Teddy. But Teddy's not going to shoot you. So tell me, Cecil, who are you worried about? Who has you acting like this in your own home?"

"Can't give details." Cecil turned away, taking a step. "I think the worst is over, but I still don't know all the players, their roles. New excrement has been illuminated." Facing her again. "This is going to take time."

"How much?"

"I don't know. Hours. Days. Weeks. Months."

"Yeah, well I can't stay at Jada's that long. I'm home for good, whatever you're into."

"It's not safe."

"Then hook me up." Freida made a c'mon motion with her fingers. "Get me some guns."

"Can't just get you guns. You have to go through a process, proper channels."

"Proper channels." Freida puffed her chest. "Loan me something from your tickle trunk."

Cecil looked at her, his mouth making a perfect O. He thought about lying, but she'd obviously been snooping. "And how do you know about that?"

"I'm a Capricorn woman, know every inch of my house, and I know you've got guns down there twenty-five feet from my sewing machine. So give me a couple for when you're not home."

Cecil held up his index. "I'll give you one." Pointing at the wet suit bag on the floor. "Whaddaya got?"

"This is what I've been making for you." Freida picked the garment bag up, brushed it off and held it out, still a bit wet on the outside, to Cecil. "Your new detective suit."

"A suit? You made me a suit?"

"Yeah, it was easy. Jada had enough material left over from another project. I had nothing but time over there, access to her back-up sewing machine, and thought what the hell? I'm the one who dresses you. I know your measurements. So I decided I'll make you a suit."

"Huh." Cecil looked at the bag again, all black, but there was a transparent plastic square near the breast allowing him to see the material inside. "It's pink."

"It's not pink." Freida unzipped the bag, pulling the suit out on a wooden hanger. "It's salmon." Hanging the pants on a door-knob, she turned to Cecil, opening the jacket. "And look, I made all these secret pockets for your non-conforming police essentials. There's one for a burner, another for extra handcuffs, another for chemical mace, and yet another for whatever you want—brass knuckles, something like that. I thought about sewing in a pocket for an extra gun, but it would've been obvious, left a bulge."

Cecil looked at the jacket in her hands. The tag read MADE BY FREIDA WITH LOVE and was sized as XK, which stood for Xtra Kisses.

"You don't know how much I love you." Cecil turned backwards and allowed Freida to help him on with the jacket. Straightening his torso, doing up the top button, moving around inside. "It fits." Facing Freida. "How does it look?"

She brushed his shoulders, proud. "Wear your white-on-white shirt-and-tie combo with a white belt, white shoes, you'll look better than Don Johnson and the other guy put together."

"You think?" Cecil said. "Lemme try on the pants."

They were having fun, Cecil handing her the jacket and stripping down to his house shorts. Reaching for the trousers, stepping in, something stopped him. "There's no zipper." He looked up at Freida.

"Buttons," she said. "Jada didn't have any spare zippers, so I made a button fly."

"Where'd you find pink man buttons?"

"They're salmon, Cecil, same as the suit. Jada had them left over from her project."

Thinking what the hell, Cecil did the fly up, wiggling in his pants. "Feels good."

"Looks good," Freida said. "Put the jacket on again so I can see everything together."

As Cecil did like so, she stood back and admired her work. She was about to tell him to run upstairs and try the shirt-and-tie combo, the shoes, but stopped herself, thinking there was no reason to get his fear-and-beer stink on everything. No, she'd dress him in the morning, send him back to work looking top notch. Until then, she said she wanted to get fucked-up, fuck around, so long as Cecil hit the shower. He liked the idea, scratching his ass and asking Freida where they were going to get the pot.

"From downstairs," Freida said. "Your tickle trunk." Crossing her arms. "So where'd you get it? That's the question."

Cecil closed his eyes for a couple seconds, said he made a deal with a dealer.

"What kind of deal?"

"Kind where I seize a quarter ounce, let him keep the rest, tell him to be more discreet going forward. It was a whatchamacal-lit?" Cecil snapped his fingers. "A teachable moment."

FIFTEEN

Early Tuesday, Alex sat in the back of Sondra's Altima, telling her to turn right on Ontario Street. As she hit the indicator, taking the turn, Alex said park in the handicap space on account of it was the only one available. Sondra said wasn't that like a trillion-dollar ticket? Not quite, Alex said, and Sondra wouldn't get a ticket anyway, she'd be parked such a short time. Sondra said it had better be such a short time, pulling in, putting her car into park, and asking what about Cecil? Was Alex picking him up after? And did Cecil know what they were up to?

"No on both counts," Alex said. "Called him yesterday, told him to meet at headquarters on account I have to pick up my car. That's pretty much all I said. Plus, the less time I spend with him today the better. He's still sore, thinks I'm gatekeeping."

Roughly, Sondra knew what Alex was talking about this time—controlling the flow of information, leaving certain parts out—and said, "Are you?"

Alex held his thumb and index an inch apart. "A little."

"Well, a little is a lot." Sondra undid the top button on her tiger-stripe raincoat as she looked at Alex in the rearview. "That's why you and white boy don't work well together. It's part that he's, as you imply, cornfed. But from what I hear—him freelancing, you gatekeeping—you both compromise your relationship, sow the seeds of strife. Once you've got that, too much strife, you can't get it out, like red wine on white-people sheets."

Amused, Alex said, "And how do you know so much about policing?"

"Not policing," Sondra said. "It's just managing relationships, and I think you manage your relationship with Cecil poorly."

"Alright." Alex was displeased, Sondra philosophizing about his work, offering constructive criticism. "Why are you telling me this now?"

Sondra turned, looking directly at Alex. "Because I like you a lot—that's why I'm here, proving my love—and I don't want you to manage our relationship poorly."

"I hear you, and I like you, too." Alex avoided further contact by looking through his binoculars, adjusting them. "Let's talk about this tonight, after I get back from church."

"Okay, fine. Go get your Jehovah jollies passing out pamphlets with Prince. I read he's one now. But it's time you let me answer your phone, so be forewarned what's on tonight's agenda, exclusivity. We're going to talk about our relationship. And I don't want any shit about Christmas. You want to worship the Goddess of Sondra, you celebrate Christmas."

Alex said yeah, okay, he'd celebrate Christmas.

Sondra turned away, looking up the street. "You see your car?"

"Yeah, it's up there, no problem."

"If it's no problem, then who're you bird-doggin' for?"

"Stanislav."

"Stani-who?"

"Svetlana's brother, Stanislav. This is his house."

"You didn't tell me a pasty brother, probably spitty-talking himself, would be involved."

Alex took the binoculars from his face, said there was no way Svetlana could afford even an itty-bitty house like this on his alimony, that she'd moved in with her brother to make ends meet, so Alex had to watch out for Stanislav, too.

"Oh yeah," Sondra said. "What this Stanislav do?"

"Private security contractor," Alex said. "Back in the former Yugoslavia, he was something akin to a Navy SEAL. I forget how they say it proper in Yugoslavian."

"Navy SEAL?" Sondra said. "You didn't say we're boosting a Navy SEAL's car. He's probably the one repo-ed it."

"Not stealing it from a Navy SEAL, just a Navy SEAL's sister, and that's a Navy SEAL in a country that doesn't exist anymore. I don't think Yugoslavia had many boats, maybe three or four, so he can't be all that."

"Yeah, well all that means is that he was one of the best of the best, if they had but three or four boats." Sondra nodded up the street. "He's probably all he can be."

Alex said Sondra had a point, gave her that, but Stanislav was likely asleep.

"Asleep? Aren't those Navy SEALs up every day at five?"

"Six," Alex said. "But that's here in North America. Yugoslavia was a workers' paradise, probably allowed their SEALs to sleep in until seven."

Sondra looked at the clock on her dash. "Yeah, well it's way past seven."

Alex said it was his problem anyway. Besides, even if Stanislav did notice, it'd be too late. Alex had his own key set. By the time he hit the ignition and put the car in gear, Stanislav wouldn't be able to catch up on account of his skills were subaquatic.

Hmm, Sondra didn't like it. There was more to it than Alex originally said. Still, it was an opportunity to prove her love, again, as a prelude to tonight's talk, and well, she'd come this far. Pretty much all she had to do was let Alex out. Okay. But then there was one more thing.

"Just hang back," Alex said. "Stay here, make sure I get out okay."

"And if you don't?"

Alex looked at her over the seat. "If I don't, pretty please come get me." Pointing. "And don't you hit anyone, no matter."

Sondra couldn't hardly see as how it would come to hitting anyone, so, alright, she'd hang, make sure Alex got out. But if she was going to all this, Alex had better not be fretting about Cecil freelancing when he got back to the condo tonight.

Alex promised he wouldn't. Sondra told him to break a leg.

Now, it was good thing it was May 1st, Alex said, because most cars were already correctly parked on the right. Given Stanislav's little house was also on the right, he and Svetlana wouldn't see Alex if he kept crouched below the cars. Worst case, if somebody did come, Alex told Sondra to drive up, lay on the horn, create a distraction. You know, a diversion.

"A diversion?" Sondra crossed her arms. "First you say all I had to do is drive. Then you tell me don't hit anyone. Now you say cause a diversion. Makes me think it's going to be confrontational. That, mayhaps, by the time all is said and done, you're going to put me in a situation where I have to run over pasty people to get you out of here. At least, that's where you seem to be going, the possibility of me having to hit pasties."

"I done told you already, don't hit anybody. Not asking that. I'm just letting you know what to do in a worst-case scenario."

Sondra still didn't like it, but maybe Alex could get going before this Yugoslav sailor woke his workers' paradise ass up. Alex said okay and let himself out. Sondra watched, thinking he wasn't exactly walking over to that car like a boss, as he originally said. No, he was keeping low, wearing that airline jacket like a homeless man fixin' on finding an unlocked car where he could drop the deuce, passing seven or eight vehicles before making it to the metallic Mercury Cougar. From his knees, he keyed the lock, letting himself in and hitting the ignition. It caught on the first try. But then Sondra could see that Alex was in a tight spot, that the Yugoslavs probably planned it this way. For a few valuable seconds, he had to back the car up and forward it before reversing it again, finally freeing the Cougar, heading south.

About that time, Sondra saw a big pasty man, tall—had to be six and a half feet—with an unfortunate hair pattern on his chest. It's like he's wearing a Yugoslavian mankini, she thought, giggling at the hair arranged around his nipples in circles. Whatever they called it in the old country, that man came running around his house in nothing but a pair of black Nike shorts. Barefoot, he raced down Ontario Street after the Cougar. Sondra figured he was moving fast for someone used to working on water, that he going to catch poor Alex, so she jacked her Altima into gear and followed, gaining on Stanislav. Sondra never saw a pasty man run this fast, so she thought, yeah, he had to be some of kind of elite man. And yeah, again, Sondra was going to have to do more than drop Alex off.

Giving the car extra gas, she powered down the window, putting her left hand on the latch and swinging the door open, slamming it into Stanislav as she passed, klunk, knocking him down. Satisfied, she shut the door and glanced in the sideview, shouting out questions. Did that hurt? Did Stanislav think he'd still run like Donovan Bailey tomorrow? What about his sister? Maybe that spitty-talking pasty bitch would have to get a job now, buy her own car.

***

Freida had Cecil all dressed up in her love. Just as she imagined, he was rocking that salmon suit with his white-on-white shirt-and-tie combo, complete with a white belt and a pair of white Florsheims. Checking himself out in the mirror, he spoke to Freida without looking at her.

"You sure this isn't a bit much?" He rolled his right hand. "I mean, for work. My work."

No way, Freida said. Salmon was the new black. Everyone was in salmon this year. That's how Freida got the idea for the suit as soon as she saw Jada's remnants. Okay, for instance, Cecil said, who was in salmon? Well, Freida saw George Clooney in salmon on the cover of one of Jada's magazines. And Clooney, he was as tough as they came.

Actually, Cecil had seen *Out of Sight*. Not only was it subliminal anti-police propaganda, the suggestion that police sleep with criminals, but Cecil thought any guy with abs like Clooney had to be gayer than Ricky Martin. Hands on her hips, Freida told Cecil to bite his tongue. Freida didn't buy the tabloids at No Frills, but she read them in line and they had pictures of Ricky snuggling with this Puerto Rican TV chica, Rebecca de Something, so who was spreading false and malicious rumors?

"Rob Roy," Cecil said. "And he makes a good case."

"Mr. Leatherman Toronto 1979?" Freida pointed south. "The guy from Neighborhood Watch who lives across from Bleecker Street Co-op?"

"The Rob Roy." Cecil nodded once. "He saw Ricky at Out

on the Street last time he was in town—March 2000 when we caught him at SkyDome—and Rob swears Ricky was buying mint-green stretch underwear with a heart hole on the caboose."

Freida looked concerned. "Maybe they were a gift."

"For who? His submissive bottom?"

Freida shuddered. "And you don't care?"

"Why would I?" Cecil said. "Ricky's an entertainer. Rob says lots of entertainers are gay tops, that pussy isn't tight enough for their small cocks. Besides, my experience here is gays who don't do meth make good neighbors, so I don't take it to be a knock. I mean, there's never been a better driving pop-rock song than 'Livin' La Vida Loca'—ever. It's not just a matter of putting Ricky's voice to Desmond Child's composition. Rusty Anderson's guitar solo rules and the rest of the instrumentals are outstanding, so I respect the man as an artist, an arranger. You need to respect he likes pink popsicles. Rob says Ricky'll probably talk about it one day, come out. Rob says it's like in the seventies when no one knew what The Village People were really doing at the Y."

"Yeah." Freida crossed her arms. "Well, 'Livin' La Vida Loca' is about a self-destructive relationship with a hedonistic bitch. The new one, 'She Bangs,' is ardently hetero, too. You see the vid? It's an ethnic festival of scantily clad chicks on him, like we all have a chance, so he's unfairly leaving a lot of women stuck to our seats, teasing us, leading us on."

The way Freida put it, like she had a shot, stung for about a second. Then Cecil remembered Ricky wouldn't covet Freida, lovely as she was, and that was just one more thing that made gays who didn't do meth such good neighbors. Anyway, Cecil's original point was that Ricky always seemed to be dressed in black, never salmon. But Cecil didn't get around to that. He was distracted, starting to really like his new suit, and he loved the secret pockets for his non-conforming police essentials. Turning to Freida, he said, "Now let's get you outfitted."

She looked confused, fanning a hand over her DIY red-paisley yoga outfit she copied out of the Eddie Bauer catalogue. "I look great, too."

"Yes." Cecil laughed at her self-assurance. "You do look great. I want you to look safe."

"What do you mean?"

"The gun." Cecil pointed to the Smith & Wesson on the coffee table, the piece Cecil carried, but did not use, the night he took out Jean-Max. "If you're going to be here, alone, I have come to agree that you should be carrying on your person, all times." He went to the couch, retrieving a black-leather shoulder holster, motioning her over, putting it on her, adjusting it to size. Taking a step back, looking at her, satisfied, he picked the gun up. "This is a lot of hardware, the Model 10, same as cops here used when I came up before upgrading, like most forces, to Glocks."

"Where did you get it, the Model 10?"

"Surplus," Cecil said. "Police surplus."

Freida spat out a laugh. "There's no police surplus store for old cop guns." Looking at the coffee table. "And where's the Firestar M45?"

Cecil was frustrated Freida knew so much, telling her, "You only need one."

"I didn't ask how many I need, Cecil. I asked where is it, the Firestar?"

"Defective. Had to get rid of it."

Freida didn't think it was funny anymore. "Cecil, don't you lie to me. I know you don't cheat. I know that. But you do lie, and I've just about had it with the lying."

"Yeah, well, if I'm lying it's because you're asking about things you can't know, you know?" Cecil securely placed the piece in Freida's holster, stepping back again. "I pity the man comes here looking for trouble. You need a briefing on the Model 10?"

"I grew up on a farm, know my way around a gun." Freida put her hands on her hips, flash drawing with her right, aiming at an imperfection on the wall. "I mean, Christ, Cecil, I'm the one taught you to shoot."

"True that." Cecil looked at his white shoes. "You and your

dad." Then up at Freida. "You know how long it took me to win over your old man?"

"A long time, Cecil, years. What did you expect? You take me out, first date. Dad tells you have me home at midnight, and you bring me home at 3:15. He knew what you'd done."

"What I'd done?" Cecil hitched his pants. "I didn't hear you telling me to take you home." Chin-nodding. "You were having fun, like last night."

Freida felt herself tear up, staring at Cecil's white shoes. "Whatever you do out there, I'll support you, have your back. Just you come home tonight, Cecil."

"I will," he said. "I will."

"See that you do." Freida looked up. "You're a good man, Cecil Bolan."

He looked away. "Don't say that."

She brought her thumb to his trouble spot beneath his chin. "You missed here again shaving. Let me get your razor, clean it up for you."

Cecil pushed her away, said he'd grab a razor at work, clean it up there. But there was one thing she could help with. His watch. It was stuck on seconds, again, and could she please fix it?

***

A week since he'd been suspended, six days since Svetlana repo-ed the car, Alex was back in the saddle, navigating the Cougar west on Carlton. The dash clock had been set to Zagreb time, afternoon already, so Alex made a mental note to fix it later. Otherwise, everything seemed to be in working order.

They'd started repairs on the streetcar tracks. Delayed at Jarvis where a vendor was setting up to hawk T-shirts, Alex reached under his seat for a Pucho & His Latin Soul Brothers compilation while the radio went from Diana Krall to a plea for listener donations.

"What would your day be like if you didn't have this station?" DJ Dwayne said.

"That's a very good question," Alex told the radio. "What

would it be like for ninety percent of WJZZ listeners who don't send you cash money on account of DJ Dwyane has the stones to play some skinny white chick sings standards from a funny mouth and Chrysler's naming a car after her?"

Poor Ryan Flanaghan—man of every news hat at WJZZ—was up when Alex got moving, reporting that police were using dental records to ID a floater discovered on Lake Ontario.

"Some fifty tourists watched as their pleasure charter, *Beautiful Day*, pulled alongside a buoyant cooler late yesterday afternoon. As ordered by the vessel's captain, a mate tried using a gaff to pull the cooler aboard. Instead, he clipped the top open, revealing a bloated body. According to sources, the deceased was hogtied then shot in the face, among other places, through the cooler, apparently, hence the need to use dental records."

Something nice for the folks from out of town, Alex thought. He was about to insert the Pucho tape when Ryan moved on to the next item, and it was about Cecil no less. His beating of the city councilor was still in the news and dammit if the story wasn't turning Cecil's way, mostly on account of the city councilor's wife was now stepping forward to say they'd been separated for almost a year, so there was no way he was buying panties for her. And Cecil, he probably hadn't learned a thing during his timeout. Plus, Alex knew it, he just knew Cecil was going to call the chief inspector Teddy at the first opportunity.

Put that idiot boy out of your head, Alex told himself, find a few minutes of Zen. Inserting the cassette, hitting play, and picking up the lyrics, Alex sang along with Pucho about someone named Sunny easing his pain. By the time the dark days were gone, bright days here, Alex was forgetting himself and shouting how his Sunny shines so sincere. He noticed that the lights were on the fritz at Church Street but kept singing until a uniform in shades punched air, telling Alex to turn it down or roll it up. That his vocals were grounds for a noise pollution charge. Alex passed the constable slowly, flashing his shield. Noise pollution, huh? Another stupid young cop, probably straight outta buttfuck himself, getting off on being a stupid young cop.

At the end of the construction near Maple Leaf Gardens, Alex remembered local boy George Chuvalo going the distance with Muhammad Ali in '66, one of the last Hendrix shows in '69, and an odd Buffalo Braves home game in '74. But his favorite personal memory of the old place was pulling surveillance duty on an alleged matter linking Maple Leafs owner Harold Ballard to ticket scalpers during the deciding game of the Norris semifinals in '87. Alex couldn't recall busting anybody that night, but vividly remembered Motor City Smitty—one of the last helmetless hockey players—scoring the game winner on an end-to-end breakaway to clinch the series. Wasn't that the Leafs were going anywhere that year, the way the Oilers were ruling, just that Motor saved his best for last—the caterpillar becoming the butterfly, columnist from the *Star* wrote. In all his years, sixty-one, Alex never saw anyone bring the house down like that.

Wondering what would become of the Gardens now that the Leafs had moved on to an arena named after the national airline, no taste whatsoever, Alex crossed Yonge, parked near headquarters, taking the stairs to the fifth floor. Thinking Cecil, he paused to catch his breath at the door, walking in with a nod. Sitting, looking across his desk, he fantasized about using his letter opener to hack off the appliance-blown spirals dangling in that manchild's cocksure face.

It was the new casual day, Tuesday. Cecil had responded by throwing his feet up on the desk, crossing them, putting his hands behind his head. Kicking about his spine when Alex started into him. "Your back is wrenched because you don't sit right, exercise, or eat good food."

"What's eating right have to do with it?"

"On account of you don't, your pants is too tight. Clothes don't fit, mess with your back. Otherwise, I just want to say it's casual Tuesday, not disco Tuesday."

Cecil looked down at himself. "What?"

Seriously? Well, first of all, Alex said Cecil's hair looked like that '80s singer killed himself stroking the light fantastic, INXS. Second, Cecil's jacket was lumpy through the chest, tight in the shoulders. And third, what color was that? Pink?

"Salmon," Cecil said, pulling at his lapels, thinking how the old man's smile was slight enough to deny. His old-people eyes were as severe as his cropped whitewalls, tight, but Alex was still smiling alright, probably because he was fit, a guy his age. Probably had some Jehovah's reverence to exertion, taking the stairs, like they mentioned in the documentary. "And it's my clothes you're mad at again?"

"Dammit, Cecil, we're undercover. Like, there's a hidden camera, right? I just know it, we're gonna be on reality TV—*The Stupid, Salmon-suit Wearing Fraud Dick Show*."

"Wait a minute. It's Freida, she's the one that—"

Alex held a fist up, said, "First rule of detection, don't let a woman dress you or you end up trying to blend in a dive bar wearing a salmon suit. Women funny like that, dress you as a man from out of town. Make a mark out of you."

"Easy for you to say." Cecil held his thumb and index like a gun, shooting to emphasize his points. "You're old, too old to have a full-time woman, so old it's—"

"Okay, I'm old."

"Also twice divorced, makes you damaged goods—bang, bang." Cecil shot his imaginary gun twice. "Poor, two times alimony—bang, bang, bang. No CD player, four bangs. And you live in a bachelor near Regent Park—bang, bang, bang, bang, bang. Who'd want to dress you?"

Wondering what Sondra saw in him, Alex ran a hand over his face, finding a rough patch below his jaw on the right side, his blind spot. Opening his top drawer, he located a blue disposable, relieved until he realized the razor was in a slot reserved for the letter opener. Looking up, he said, "You been in my desk?"

"No." Cecil caressed his own trouble spot, smooth. "No, I have not."

Alex picked up the razor with a thumb and forefinger, wet,

dropping it into the waste basket next to his desk. Wiping his fingers on his jeans, he was about to accuse Cecil of stealing the letter opener when he noticed the photocopied clipping stamped Saturday, April 21, 2001.

FRAUD WITNESSES EXECUTED

Two potential star witnesses in negotiations with the Crown to testify against ringleaders of a stolen classic car scam were killed execution-style in separate incidents Friday night.

Parking Enforcement Associate Doyle Allenby is dead after being attacked outside his lawyer's office shortly after 8 pm. Police say his shoulders were fitted with a gasoline-soaked tire before he was pushed into his 1978 Ford Elite near the corner of Pembroke and Gerrard, then set on fire.

Doris Sabo, Allenby's coworker, suffered a similar fate in the parking lot of her residence at Lavoie Housing Cooperative less than forty minutes later.

Both were burned beyond recognition, identifiable only by dental records, prompting police to release descriptions of three suspects described as white, male, and middle age.

"One is said to have been dressed in a dark double-breasted suit," Chief Homicide Insp. Sheff Dubois said. "The second wore coveralls. A third, heavyset, wore a black Rage Against the Machine–type T-shirt, only it did not say Rage Against the Machine. It said something else."

Sources say police were offering Allenby and Sabo immunity in exchange . . .

"What're you looking at?" Cecil said. "In your desk."
"Nothing." Alex closed his drawer. "Just daydreaming."
"About what?"

"Happier times," Alex said. "And before you ask what happier times I was daydreaming about, it was the happier times before Chief Inspector Almano assigned me to you. Telling me to make you an effective detective. How am I supposed to do that when you wear a pink suit?"

Cecil caressed a lapel, said, "It's salmon."

SIXTEEN

As planned, Gervais Garret called traffic shortly before nine, reporting his 1957 Chevy Nomad stolen. It was sea blue on ivory, he told Staff Sergeant Liz Townie, a classic, and they never made a great two-door family sedan again.

"If I had a car like that." Liz stopped herself, under-handing a ballpoint, watching it tumble end over end, catching it. "I'd be parking it in a safe, secure place. Where'd you say it was taken from?"

Gervais hadn't, his answer long, explaining he'd been out late drinking at the House on Parliament. How he only intended to drop in for a quick Guinness. Ended up he stayed longer, watching Billy Koch work himself out of an epic jam on the big screen, wild ride, then it started raining, the final shower of April, a doozy, so Gervais did the responsible thing. Called a cab, arrived alive, all that.

Thinking how she had put out a question and wanted it answered to the nearest intersection, nothing else, Liz bit down hard, jotting down anything sounding like a key point.

"You left a car like that on Parliament Street?" she said. "Overnight?"

Gervais coughed. Excusing himself for a sec, he sipped his greyhound—grapefruit juice splashed with Smirnoff—from a white on red straw. Thinking how he was pushing forty, getting a little old for these shenanigans, feeling lines around his mouth running deeper, he said, "I was drunk and it was a storm. You're advising that I should have driven drunk in a storm? That's not very community minded, and that much about my responsibilities I do know."

"It's just the House on Parliament, Mr. Garret. C'mon, the pub's right near Regent Park, housing projects, old Cabbagetown."

"No, no. Cabbagetown is south of Gerrard, traditionally and officially. Ask Jane Jacobs. Me, I was parked up the street, north, almost Carlton."

"So where does that place you, St. James Town?"

"In between Regent Park and St. James Town, Cabbagetown."

In between, Liz thought. Leave a car like that between Regent Park and St. James Town. Right, those were good neighborhoods. Cabbagetown, too, crack city. "I assume you had a LoJack, something like that?"

Gervais looked into his reflection next to his *Auto Trader* mug on the Pledged pine table. Cradling the phone to his ear on his shoulder, wiggling ten fingers like it was the first time. Yep, he was going to play dumb with her. "Wot dat?"

"Never mind." She picked up the smug in his voice—wot dat?—pursing, telling herself to stay alert. "An alarm, did you have one?"

Gervais pulled back with a yes, ma'am. At least he used to. Damn things kept going off for no reason. He was on his third company when the Palmerston Neighborhood Association closed rank after the holidays, telling him they'd had enough of the false alarms already. Naïve colonizers didn't understand what it was to live in an urban environment—lots of sirens, alarms—and Gervais had letters from two of the association's subcommittees to prove it. Since, he'd been going with the tried and tested mechanism patented as The Club, a red crowbar locked to the steering wheel. And so what if some baddies figured a way to dismantle The Club? What was Gervais supposed to do? If someone wanted his car, they'd get it. That's what the cops on reality TV said.

"No such thing," Liz declared. "It's all scripted, calculated. And it's a 1957 Nomad, you say? Chevy product? Sea blue on ivory?"

"Affirmative on all counts." Gervais pulled his cheat sheet from the upper right corner of his table, voice quaking, affected. "And they never made a great two-door family sedan again."

"Yeah, you said that already. What does it look like?"

"Sporty two-door styling, big chrome details, Ferrari-inspired grill, hood ornament that looks like a rocket, tail fins. Think of a station wagon with a beehive hairdo. Same kind MacGyver drove in the 'Harry's Will' episode." On a roll, sure this would impress.

"Show 111, MacGyver's grandpa wills him a 1957 Nomad. Ends up Abe Vigoda—"

"So now it's Fish you're telling me about from *Barney Miller?*"

"Right, Fish—the one always taking the newspaper to the Mens' on *Barney Miller*—he's the character who blurs the lines between good and bad in this *MacGyver* installment. Abe, he's just out of jail and thinks some big-ass priceless diamond pendant is hidden in the Nomad. So he's stalking MacGyver when Wendy O. Williams shows up on a motor trike. You know her?"

Liz didn't, but she was sure Gervais was frigging going to tell her.

***

From the start, Alex had told Theodore that Cecil needed more seasoning. Told him thrice, at least. Theodore cautiously agreed the first time, admitting Cecil came up from uniform too soon because of that big Ecstasy bust he stumbled onto at the raves. The association called it a "paid-duty" gig. Effectively, that meant rave promoters were mandated to pay off-duty cops $50 an hour for the privilege of being investigated on their own dime. And Cecil had managed to find all that E—about 30K worth of tablets—hidden in one the of speakers after noticing a fair bit of heavy petting near the DJ booth. It was clear, Cecil surmised, that the pettings and drug-doings were going hand in hand, and when that DJ/drug dealer went fucking around with his speaker one too many times, reaching for the drugs to sell to the kids doing all that petting, Cecil found the lion's share and made the news.

However they put it, clamping down on the teen party circuit was one of Mayor Lastman's personal political priorities, his baby. Blissed-out kids hugging each other in dens of drugs and guns. That's what the mayor was on about, the chief, too, and it wasn't just a Toronto concern. Over in the States, a senator from Delaware, Joseph Biden, was just last month pushing the idea of locking up rave promotors and tearing down buildings where raves were held. All over the world, wherever raves took place, everybody in law and order wanted a piece, so Cecil's victory was also a big political win for brass, huge. Chief Vogel sent word personally to get this Cecil Bolan a detective shield of some kind right away. As for the chief's decision-making ability, Theodore would only say maybe Alex would do a better job when he became top cop. Whenever Alex brought the matter up after that, Theodore would say just make Cecil an effective detective, like the chief said.

"How long you been on the job with me now?" Alex said. "Plainclothes, or whatever you call what you got on."

"Seven months," Cecil said.

"That it?"

"Yeah, seven. Started in early October. Almost seven. Why?"

Alex let his head fall, saying he had to keep reminding himself that it only felt longer on account of how much seasoning Cecil needed.

"Look, I'm sorry about last week, the misunderstanding with the city councilor, but he wasn't even buying those panties for his wife. Just some bitch he bangs." Cecil brought his feet down, pointing to the military order of his desk. In particular, he held up a transparent container holding paperclips of various sizes and colors as a symbol of his commitment to order, a beachhead. "So there was no reason for Teddy to talk to us the way he did, take us off the case and pop me with a cheap shot, tell me to take a week off, cool down, just when I'm getting hot."

"That's right." Alex glared, watching Cecil twist his bronze ring. "No reason."

Cecil rolled his eyes, mumbling about his progress—he was the macadamia becoming a shrub—and hey, Frank Williams was a detective at twenty-four. Cecil had been a cop since '93, eight years, so it wasn't like Cecil was a freshie at twenty-nine, you know.

"Frank Williams?" Alex said. "Frank Williams was an *acting* detective back when your average life expectancy was like thirty-seven, Cecil. He was also the first Toronto lawman to die in the line of duty, shot by fur thieves in 1918. Frank Williams gave all, so don't compare yourself to him again." Leaning forward. "And you're not a freshie, huh? If I'm Chief Inspector Almano, I'd make the same moves in the face of that city councilor situation. That's not something to be celebrated, regardless of who the panties were for. You used excessive force, something one should feel true guilt over."

Cecil said no, even according to Alex, true guilt was when you did something illegal or immoral, and the SIU had already ruled that Cecil's actions were above board, so Cecil wasn't feeling any guilt at all over the city councilor—true or false.

Alex thought on that, said, "Well, whatever guilt you're supposed to be feeling, you should feel some. I don't care if you've got to stop eating red meat, start exercising, or take medical candy that makes you happy, but you have got to calm down, I'm telling you again. Times like these, CNN's going to get wind, run with it, Americans touchy about law and order."

"Fuck the Americans." Cecil thumbed his chest. "I know what the boys on the beat think, that I did us all a solid. If an elected official wants to go off like Malcom Tate, making allegations without proof, politicizing issues, and muddying waters in such a way that makes police work more dangerous, some cop is going find an excuse to hold his nose in the wet spot, and the boys on the beat know that cop to be me." Pointing at Alex. "What do the boys on the beat think about you?"

"Boys on the beat don't hardly know me, Cecil."

"See?"

"See what I'm about to say, young man." Yep, Alex was going to turn this into another teachable moment. "Our job is to be largely unseen. That's the first rule of being a sleuth. You have to blend. And look at you, showing up to your detective work in a pink suit."

"It's salmon, I keep telling you."

***

By now, Liz Townie was just plain mad that this Gervais Garret asshat was trying to distract her, a female staff sergeant—these alpha pricks didn't know how hard it was—at work. He was on about how Wendy O. Williams wore electrical tape over her nipples as lead singer of The Plasmatics, but not on *MacGyver*, it being a family show with a Christian message, when Liz interrupted him, finally getting the plates. A wheelchair vanity job, M'HKN, as in *Last of the Mohicans*, she surmised.

"Mr. Garret," Liz said, "are you a wheelchair-bound person?"

Gervais paused, said, "Wot?"

"I said, are you in a wheelchair?"

"No."

"Then how come you have wheelchair plates?"

"I have an invisible illness," Gervais said. "Paperwork's in order. Beyond that, my caregiver says it's not right to ask."

His caregiver, right, Liz thought. His caregiver was probably some tweaked freak wearing a backwards Argos hat in the alley. This prick didn't get it. He was still being clever, lawyerly, sending all the wrong signals. So alright, okay, Liz was going to slow things down and get to the bottom of whatever he thought he was trying to pull here. She didn't ask any questions for a little while, saying shush when Gervais dared speak into the phone. She was punching the plates into the computer, hitting return, then seeing the bold notation at the top. CONTACT DET. A. JOHNSON AT X577 ALL MATTERS.

Yep. For sure, this Gervais was a fraud. That's why he was so lawyerly, already defending the guilty party, himself. "Priorities." Liz closed her eyes, digging knuckles into her sockets, rubbing. "If we fail to recover it, Mr. Garret, what do you say it's worth, the Nomad?"

Gervais told her it'd be tough to say. She knew how these things were. It was worth what some urban colonizer would pay. Less than she might think in spite of Chevy making fewer than seven thousand back in 1957.

Liz said nothing, waiting for a straight answer. Hello? Was she still there? "You're calling the insurance next," she finally said, "right?"

"D'you think?"

She still had her eyes closed, thumbs on the faceless man's windpipe in her mind. "What do you expect the insurance will say when you tell 'em no more Nomad?"

"Different matter entirely. It's insured as a collector's car, irreplaceable, by reason that they made fewer than seven thousand. I said that, right? How there were less than seven thousand."

"Yeah, you said. Now how much, insurance?"

"More or less?"

"Yes, Mr. Garret, more or frigging less, insurance."

"Roughly?"

"Say it."

"Two hundred thousand, roughly."

"Roughly? How about exactly?"

Gervais hesitated, said, "Two hundred thousand."

"Long frigging way home," Liz said. When Gervais didn't say anything else, she decided to speed him up, cause him to think on his feet, maybe make a forced error, telling him not to worry, that some determined detectives would be on his case in a matter of moments. And what number could Mr. Garret be reached at, all times? They were done when she read out the case report digits, 2001-867-5309. He'd need that for the insurance.

"Jenny," Gervais said. "Tommy Tutone."

"Who? What?"

"You'd know it if you heard it," Gervais said. "One-hit wonder." Bursting into song about how he's got her number, repeating 867-5309 over and over.

The way he was singing it, it appeared to Liz that Gervais was calling her a Jenny. Probably contemporary street talk for something derogatory about a dyke cop, so Liz wanted to say that she had Gervais' frigging number, too, then she thought better of it, that she'd let Alex Johnson do the legwork for her, that she'd help him bust this Gervais on whatever fraud he was up to.

SEVENTEEN

Hearing the electronic ring, Alex looked down, E. TOWNIE x119 on call display. Cecil watched, pointing his sneer at the phone as it rang again. "Just answer it."

Every time E. Townie appeared, Alex thought it was Jehovah himself telling him he deserved a break today on account of Theodore said make Cecil an effective detective. That was turning out to be more difficult than teaching a bird to speak, so Alex savored the sweet, knowing Liz had something for him, as always, making her wait, answering on the third or fourth jingle. "Elizabeth."

"Johnson."

"You know you can call me Alex."

"Says here to call you, Johnson."

"Well, you only need to say Alex. But really? It says that? Call me by my last name?"

"It just says to call you in particular about Gervais Garret. God, frigging computer says contact you on all matters, FYI. That's what I'm meaning."

"Right." Alex looked across the desk to Cecil. "Get me a pen." Watching as Cecil gave him that double-jointed smile, the kid reached for a desk caddy that looked like a paper bag, only it was ceramic, throwing a pencil like a knife. Alex stabbed it out of the air with his left hand, glaring. "How do you like that? Seven months later, I'm still grabbing David Carradine's pebble out of your slow white hand."

"Whoa," Liz said. "You guys need to stop making it a race thing. I mean, whoa Nelly."

"It's okay when I do it," Alex said.

"How so?"

Alex thought back to Sondra's words, figured they were worth repeating. "Racism is about power blacks don't have. Means blacks can't be racist."

Liz, laughing uncomfortably, said, "What's your source on that, Johnson?"

Alex, thinking Liz, flirty as she was, wouldn't appreciate him having a girl, said he read it in one of the alt-weeklies.

"Yeah well, whatever your hippy-skippy columnist wrote, it's theory. Regulations say no making it a race thing, all times. Way it's written, I'm pretty sure you don't get a gimme."

"Sorry." Alex glared at Cecil, blew a mean-spirited kiss. He could feel where the pencil lead had pierced the heel of his palm but didn't want to give Cecil the satisfaction, didn't want Cecil to see him bleed. "Got to keep grasshopper here on a short leash."

"I know," Liz said. "It's right here in last week's clippings, A1. Paper says, 'In a case of mistaken identity, fraud cop Cecil Bolan is accused of beating Ward 45 City Councilor Malcolm Tate repeatedly with his own cellphone.' Cause an international incident, why don't ya? Mind you, uniforms love it, someone getting to Tate. My sources tell me they have the articles taped above the urinals, morale purposes, cops all over town telling perps to kiss carpet, even when they're outside. They're treating this as a precedent. Best part is Tate facing that resist charge, and now I hear his wife's come forward alleging those panties weren't for her. Couldn't have asked for a better story arc. Did Cecil do it like that, like they say? In ladies' underwear?"

Alex said he couldn't quite see what was going on over in lingerie. Obstructed view on account of he was UC in the new western collection, Cowboy Couture, this year's line called How the West Was Worn. Cowboy and cowgirl mannequins wearing ten-gallon hats, rope everywhere, chaps. Looking across at Cecil, Alex added, "But yeah, it was close enough to that."

"I'm right here, you commenting." Cecil had another pencil ready and aimed. "Teddy said no commenting. No commenting means no commenting. Plus, you're lying. You weren't undercover in the western section when it happened. You were buying bedding to impress that bitch you bang. And thanks by the way for telling her that, fucking Serpico."

Alex shielded his face with both arms, telling Cecil don't call Chief Inspector Almano Teddy, Sondra bitch, or him, Alex, Serpico, then Alex spoke into the mouthpiece. "Now our man Gervais Garret, are you telling me he got picked up on something?"

"No, no. Gervais called us," Liz said. "He's reporting a stolen 1957 Nomad, *Last of the Mohicans*. At least I think that's what his vanity plates are trying to say."

"His MacGyver car," Alex said. "He mention episode 111?"

"Frigging told me all about it." Liz raised her freckled brow. "How the guy from *Barney Miller* was chasing some punk chick with electrical tape on her nipples."

"You mean Wendy O. Williams?"

"Her," Liz said.

"Well, I'm pretty sure she was covered in the MacGyver situation."

"That's what this Gervais Garret said. Point is, I could tell the prick was trying to distract me with all this trivial shit, wasting my time. Mostly, he pissed me off, so I did a little digging, and it would seem he should know better than to leave a classic car where he did overnight. Says here he also has a 1961 T-Bird."

"Bullet shaped," Alex said. "As seen on *Rockford*."

"And a 1969 Dodge Charger."

"Like the Duke boys drove."

"Sounds like he has a thing about cars from TV, that he's an experienced collector."

"Sounds like it because it is so."

"Yeah, well again, computer says to call you. This Gervais, I give him the report number, then he sings a song that incorporates the same number, his way of saying he has my number when he calls me a Jenny, implication being I'm a bull dyker, probably. He stinks of smug."

Alex said yeah, that's Gervais, another one of the lucky ones to fall through the cracks during that bust gone wrong out in Parkdale.

Operation Cooperation—the mayor named it himself, one of

this year's pet projects—was partly funded by an umbrella group for the insurance industry. It began with the arrest of the city's last three green hornets. They would routinely tag pre-1980 cars as abandoned, calling Jean-Max Renaldo, owner and operator of Renaldo's Auto Body. The shop was part of a ring that would then tow the cars to various remote locations, leaving them a few days to ensure they couldn't be picked up via an electronic tracking device. After that, they'd strip the car and market the parts individually, mostly through an assortment of sellers and online auction houses.

Alex broke the case, with a big assist from Cecil, through cell-phone records belonging to the last three green hornets—which connected them to Jean-Max—offering deals to two of them. Doyle Allenby and Doris Sabo gladly implicated another coworker and even sent Jean-Max after bait cars. It looked like both were going to testify in exchange for suspended sentences. That, and they would be shit-canned, put on probation.

"I forget all the names," Liz said. "Doyle and Doris the ones they lit up like Christmas trees at Mel Lastman Square?"

"Yeah, except we don't say they were lit up like Christmas trees at Mel Lastman Square on account of Cecil came up through school with that Doyle fellow, respect."

"Jeez, sorry. But how do you say it then, politically correct?"

"I don't know how you say it PC-like. Called Père Lebrun, traditional, Haitian slang for necklacing on account of Père was a car dealer who first got it like that. Idea is to humiliate the victim, usually a snitch, while they stand around mocking. In Doyle's case, residents heard someone call him whistle-blower, then say, hey, want some water? Mocking is key, make it ugly on account of they want to deter future snitching."

"Someone," Cecil added, "probably Doyle, also shouted Write in Dick Gregory for president. And fuck that big assist bullshit. I broke the case when I seized that biker's phone."

Liz said, "So why the frig don't we bring this Jean-Max Renaldo in, sweat him?"

"Can't, on account of he was at SkyDome, twenty-five thousand witnesses watching him on the jumbotron yelling at Billy Koch, air-tight shade. But Jean-Max still might be facing some minor fraud charges. Been pretty scarce since the last couple or few days or so. Sheff Dubois, I hear, is having a fit on account of Jean-Max gave H boys the shake, probably sleeping in their car."

"You saying the Frenchman is fleeing?"

"I don't think we can call it that yet, fleeing," Alex said. "His boat is still at the yacht club where his car is parked, last I heard, and he lives on the boat. Besides, without witnesses, it's not worth fleeing with what we have left on him, minor frauds, unlikely to do time unless H gets more than what we have to date. He's probably laying low somewhere until these murders blow over, my guess. Can't charge him for that, as much as everyone would like."

"You got anyone left to cop?"

Alex closed his eyes, the name Pam Jenkins, last of the green hornets, flashing in his head, wondering how witness protection was going to protect her. "Wouldn't be cool to say on account of you know why."

"Understood." Liz let out a breath. "Anyway, some interesting trivia you got there on the Brazilian necklacing."

"Haitian necklacing," Alex said. "Also popular in the former Yugoslavia."

Cecil piped in saying, "And don't forget it's, shall we say, dark-skinned people, Buddhists. Means Winnie Mandela, Nelson's wife, was a proponent."

Alex gave Cecil the shoo-shoo, saying Winnie was cleared on that and Nelson divorced her anyway, so it was wrong to blame Nelson for something his ex may or may not have done. Besides, that was just the way, people from all walks of life doing it, new-world order. But Alex didn't know where Cecil was getting that shit about Buddhists. They were pacifists, against it. Jehovah's Witnesses, too. And the Mandelas, they were both Methodist.

"That's all good and fine," Liz said. "But how can I, traffic, help you, fraud, with your asshole, Gervais?"

"You keen on him, huh?"

"It was his smug. 'Wot dat?' he says when I ask does he have a LoJack on his Nomad?"

"Oh, he's got one alright."

"But he said no, the lying bastard."

Actually, Alex explained, it wasn't like that. Gervais probably wasn't lying this one time on account of he didn't know, hopefully, that his ride had been tagged with a transmitter. See, Operation Cooperation had been expanded before the murders to focus on classic car people who sold their cars to Jean-Max cheap for parts, putting in bad insurance claims, as well as those who were believed to be buying stolen parts. In all, Alex and Cecil were ready to charge nine such people with phone, mail, and computer fraud before the necklacings.

Cecil said, "It's all kinds of fraud we would've charged 'em with."

True, Alex said but without witnesses, the case had largely and legally fallen apart.

As for Gervais Garret, while he hadn't made any recent insurance claims, his '68 Shelby Mustang, identical to McQueen's ride in *Bullitt*, went missing suspiciously in '98—a $130,000 settlement. But even when cops were able to trace a quarter panel on the Mustang back to another area vehicle, they couldn't prove Gervais knowingly did anything outside the law without witnesses.

"For the most part, I'd still made him more as a buyer of black-market parts," Alex said. "I just saw him as Richie Rich trying to save some money. Only here, the disconnect trends back to his behavior as per the '68 Stang in '98. Then, like now, I'm guessing he's made his car all it can be. Put that thing together bit by bit, enjoyed it. I'm thinking he's just done, maybe bored. Needs a new project, maybe even cash money for other interests, his duplexes. Maybe he wants to buy another car, another duplex, both."

So there was that, plus Gervais turned up in spy-cam shots with Jean-Max and his people—mostly this one guy everyone frustratingly knew only as the man who wears Adidas tracksuits—which encouraged a judge to sign off on paperwork allowing fraud to plant one transmitter on one of Gervais' vehicles. Funnily enough, Alex had picked the Nomad.

"You know it's still working," Liz said. "The LoJack."

"Oh, it's still working alright. Only the paperwork says we have to stop using that voodoo on Gervais at the end of April, yesterday. It being May 1st, Operation Cooperation is over for Cecil and I. Homicide's case."

"Doesn't mean we can't cooperate," Liz said.

Alex picked up her beat. "On account of that's how we operate."

"That's right." Liz felt herself really smile for the first time today. "Fraud must have other cases with LoJacks being deployed, active. I mean, if I were to sign you out a transponder on another investigation, but mistakenly set the device to track this Nomad, that'd just be cooperation."

"That's right," Alex said. "Cooperation."

EIGHTEEN

Upon reflection, Gervais did not care for the way his call to the cop shop went down. He knew that Liz woman, probably a vagitarian, didn't like him, his sense of humor, his cultural reference points, or even his vanity wheelchair plates. Mostly, he could tell she was suspicious, the way she said determined detectives would be on his case, so he decided to beat them to it by lighting a fire under Art's ass, get their business done.

First, Gervais thought about calling, then decided it was best to get himself over to Harwood's Select Auto Service and tell Art face-to-face. Gervais wanted the Nomad processed, dismantled now, the parts distributed, evidence gone. That way, there'd be nothing to find if and when some determined detectives came calling.

After phoning the insurance company and going through a similar drill, Gervais had a quick shower to get the alcohol stink off, towel-drying, pulling on a pair of Levi's, a long-sleeve white T-shirt. Over top, he decided on that oddball short-sleeve tee he'd bought on Carlton. Yeah, it was funny the first few times he wore it, but the joke was over, particularly to Gervais, who would find himself explaining Dick Gregory's legacy again today. Didn't matter. It was XXL, hard to source, and it was clean, so Gervais had to like it. Besides, he needed another layer, what with the slight chill, so he pulled it on, thinking at least it fit properly, felt good.

Since when did Gervais care what other people thought anyway? He'd studied *Death of a Salesman* in high school and the play's key message, at least so far as Gervais recalled, dealt with the false virtue of being well-liked, that the pursuit of the same was soul-sucking, that it would lead one to lose a sense of one's self. Of course, the playwright, Arthur Miller, went on to marry Marilyn Monroe who was universally adored, so maybe Gervais shouldn't have taken the key message to heart.

With that considered, he put on his glasses and looked at the keys to his Dodge Charger, remembering he'd already been drinking a little in order to work the courage up to report the Nomad stolen, that he actually told the lady cop he'd been drinking last night, which was why he left the Nomad parked on Parliament. That said, stupid, he decided to call City Taxi and arrive alive, or at least without running into some determined detectives looking to DWI him.

Out on Harbord Street, it seemed like every other kind of taxi but a City Taxi was passing and looking for fares, their available-for-hire lights on. At first, Gervais tried not to be a prick and waited on the company he called. Figuring he might end up on a City Taxi blacklist if he flaked, looking east and west impatiently, he really did do his best to hang in, until, eventually deciding he didn't care if City Taxi put him on their blacklist. If City couldn't answer his call, he'd never patronize them again anyway.

Incompetent pricks, he thought, flagging a Co-op cab. Talking nice, polite, addressing the colonizer driver—probably Dominican the way he talked—as sir, Gervais said please take him to Harwood's Select Auto Service on Eastern, closing his eyes, thinking about what was going to say, how he might put it, to light a fire under Art until he, Gervais, started fretting over walking into something else, or rather someone else, Jean-Max Renaldo wanted well-done.

The big problem here—what precipitated Gervais' involvement in all of this—was that he was increasingly in a deficit situation on his cars and his duplexes and his lifestyle. That's what got him in this deep in the first place. Showing off, banging broads, spending too much on cars and booze and clothes. But how did it get to the point where he was helping Art and Reggie necklace crown witnesses on behalf of Hells Angels? Perhaps Gervais was having a moment of clarity, despite being just the least bit tipsy, but was he still doing it, getting in deeper, just so he could bang more broads and ride around in more fancy cars for another day.

Opening his eyes long enough to see what had the cab

stuck—construction on the Carlton streetcar tracks—Gervais noticed the colonizer he bought the T-shirt from on the other side of Jarvis. Wondering if maybe the sighting was an omen, but not sure about what, Gervais closed his eyes again, thinking his life was too often stressful, what with the criminal things he had to do to make it all work. But watching the world go by from a cab stuck in gridlock was still better than having a job-job. He liked his life, his lifestyle, and he was going to do what he had to in order to maintain his level of comfort, whatever he was walking into at Harwood's Select Auto Service. And job-jobs? Job-jobs were for people born outside of the Greater Toronto Area, colonizers.

***

Cecil heard enough of Alex's half of the conversation to suss that he and Liz had been discussing that natural-walking man Cecil took to task outside The Beer Store. Seeing how it sounded like they might be running into him, Cecil waited for Alex to hang up, said, "This Gervais you were talking about, I had a thing with him, I think, last week."

"What kind of thing?" Alex blinked. "And you better not've been freelancing."

No, no. Cecil said it wasn't like that. It happened a week ago today. Right after Teddy sent them home from the mall, Cecil stopped by The Beer Store, picked up a case. Outside, he saw this bespectacled dumpling with wheelchair plates park in the cripple spot then get out like a natural-walking man. Cecil was already riled, so he was happy to find someone to take out his frustrations on. But seriously, all Cecil did was tell the guy, park in a natural-walking-man spot. That was it.

"Didn't he tell you he had an invisible illness?" Alex said.

"Yeah, and I told him, invisible illness my ass."

Alex didn't love the explanation, but Cecil's mild abuse of power rang true, so Alex avoided the temptation to turn it into a teachable moment and focused on the task at hand, a certain kind of file he told Cecil to locate. All he had to do was find an active case in which a LoJack was deployed. Just one. Couldn't be tough, and for Cecil to look under LoJack first.

"CBC coroner show from the sixties," Cecil said, opening a file cabinet. "Pretty good."

"No, no, no. You're thinking and hearing *Wojeck*. Man, you're not going to find a case involving a Wojeck. It's a LoJack you should look for. Check under *L*, I meant."

Seeing Alex snapping, Cecil swatted at something flying near his hip. Yeah, yeah, yeah. He knew. Take it easy. He was just having Alex on. Alex said Cecil was covering his dumbness, and did he even know what a LoJack was?

LoJack, Cecil said it was a tiny tracking device the size of a pacemaker sends an electronic signal. Invented to stymie auto theft, cops were now getting court orders to plant them on the cars of a range of suspect types. Of course Cecil knew. And hey, maybe he'd be able to find this faster if Alex shut the hell up. How could he just sit there anyway, yapping, while Cecil looked for some obscure piece of paper?

"You're right." Alex rose from his desk, throwing his flat-green TWA airline varsity jacket over a plain white tee. "Goin' down to Fran's, get my fancy four-dollar coffee, cinnamon sprinkles. Meet me there when you're done." Hiking his faded green Levi's, he walked toward the door, head down, squeaking the floor with blue-on-gold Pumas, turning back. "And hey there, Cecil, what's Freida got to do with that suit anyway? She lay your clothes out?"

Cecil looked down at himself. He reached into his coat, thinking about opening it to show off the secret pockets. Then he thought Alex would mock him for that, too, the prick.

"Don't leave me hanging," Alex said. "Why do you keep blaming that suit on Freida?"

Cecil pursed, saying, "Because she made it."

Alex brought a fist to his mouth, clearing his throat. Best thing he could say was that Cecil came off better than that guy who led the Soviets before Gorby. Allowing himself a full-on smile, Alex wiped it clean when he turned to the door. Theodore Almano was leaning on the frame, gangly arms crossed over a pale-blue polo with the police crest, the word FRAUD where a civilian might sport an alligator. "You know anything smells like Operation Cooperation gets turned over to homicide, Johnson."

Alex tried to look casual. "Was on my way to look for you, give you the FYI, Chief Inspector. Your call."

"Damn right it's my call." Theodore pointed at Cecil. "Just control young guns here. I have yet another message says call Chief Vogel regarding the poor city councilor trying to buy someone other than his estranged wife granny panties."

"Teddy," Cecil said. "Didn't we deal with this a week ago—last Tuesday? We talked about this before you gave me the week off as a reward. Vacation, you said."

Vacation? By vacation, Theodore told Cecil he'd been suspended, unofficially, except Theodore didn't want to do the paperwork and deal with Cecil's shop steward who was most likely an autoworker in another life—fucking Marxist would grieve his own conception—so Theodore was just calling it a vacay. Then Theodore remembered the pertinent parts of what he heard at the door, looking at Alex. "And why am I in the hall hearing you, fraud, talking about going after Gervais Garret, possible murder suspect?"

"Gervais might be into some mildly pagan things, slumlording, a little gentlemanly fraud," Alex said. "But I can't hardly make him for an assassin. No history of violence."

"Yeah, well everyone targeted in Operation Cooperation is now a potential suspect in the Doyle Allenby case, homicide." Theodore looked to Cecil. "All due respect."

Cecil rolled his hand. "The point, Teddy."

Theodore shot Alex a dirty look. Alex, as if he wasn't to be blamed, deflected, shooting Cecil a dirty look.

"It's also the Doris Sabo case." Theodore stroked his moustache. "These classic car people are in cahoots with people we hadn't planned on. People who kill for a near-mint '64-and-a-half Mustang ashtray, a pristine '59 Coupé de ville bumper. This's all turned into a real hornet's nest, no pun intended. Now I understand Cecil knew this Doyle from school. As I've said, I empathize. I do. But like I keep trying to tell you, we're fraud, and fraud does fraud and nothing but."

Alex nodded, thinking how many times am I going to hear this? Playing along anyway. "Kind of like the colonel when he just did chicken."

"And he used to do it right," Theodore said. "Until he started doing the super crunchy recipe, followed by crispy, extra crispy, which of course opened the door to the fucking nuggets, brownies, colonel piggy banks, and all the other shit. Now the colonel's got free watches that talk like him when kids press a button. What it was is, the colonel lost his focus."

"Focus," Alex said. "Very important. We have got to focus on the task at hand, fraud. Yet here we have a murder suspect, you say, who I say is a fraudster. His Chevy Nomad, the one we have an expired tracer on, goes stolen last night on the ghetto's edge, St. James Town or Cabbagetown, depending on your urban studies geek. Makes me say, hmm, fraud, us. Now, are we going to let the trail get chilly while it gets all bureaucratic-like? Or, are we gonna bust fraudsters? Asides, homicide has a hogtied floater to deal with, discovered by pleasure boaters, I heard on the radio coming in, must be a little, hmm, resource challenged."

Theodore nodded, saying he'd just returned from a budget meeting with Sheff Dubois. "Grisly, little amateur job, terrible. Thought they were smart, putting the deceased in a metal cooler, shooting him through it. It made sense to them, seeing the holes fill, the cooler sinking."

Cecil, dissatisfied with the explanation, said, "So school me, Teddy. I don't see the mistake. Floater's been dead a few days or so, hasn't he, Teddy? And the killers are probably long gone, the trail cold. What'd they miss, Teddy? Educate me."

Oh, that is a whole lot of Teddys already, Theodore thought, getting madder. "Listen, Cecil, I know you're chippy about being taken off the identity-theft case, which strikes me as dumb cause

I don't think you wanted it in the first place. Either way, too bad, your cover is blown and they don't want you back at ladies' un-mentionables. As for the floater, they killed him alright, but they didn't weigh the cooler down to keep it sunk. So, what happened is, the body bloated enough to bring the cooler to the surface. Now, if you didn't need so much seasoning, you'd know that means Sheff Dubois' boys are going to find out who's dead, con-sider motive, and that's going to flush out evidence necessary to convict an amateur killer making emotional decisions."

"Sounds like H ought to be hopping," Alex said. "Too busy to deal with Gervais. I don't want to press, but whatever his list of crimes, mayhaps we should solve this Nomad caper before they strip it and ship it, then pass anything we find pertaining to urban death squads on to H."

While Theodore weighed his options, Cecil was thinking aloud and closing the deal. "Hey Teddy, didn't I cut you slack when you popped me a cheap shot? I didn't bitch to the union. I'm so solid I lied to Freida about how I hurt my lip, and you know it, because she'd march down here and whip you with your own belt, emasculate you. So how about it? How about you do us a solid like I did you?"

Theodore figured Cecil had him here. Theodore could be as disgusted as he wanted, but it wasn't his place to pop cops, es-pecially now that most everyone attached to the force was cele-brating what Cecil did to the city councilor. Also, he was afraid of Cecil's wife, so he said alright just to get rid of them, never daring a mild dig at that pink suit she'd apparently made.

"But." Theodore held an index to Cecil. "Anything else goes wrong, you'll be busting able-bodied persons using wheelchair plates to park in cripple spaces full time. That, and I'll have you in the sensi-tivity training over how you talked to the sales lady in lingerie."

Alex looked pleased, crossing his arms, a united stand. "The two-hundred-pound rockabilly girl telling Cecil don't ornamen-talize her."

"Yeah," Theodore said, "only you don't call her that anymore."

Alex looked confused. "Why not?"

"Because she got wind of it, what you all were saying."

Cecil pointed. "You said it, too, Teddy."

"Not anymore." Theodore looked away. "What I heard is the fastest way to get yourself an appointment with the two-hundred-pound rockabilly girl says don't ornamentalize her is to call her that. Apparently, there's amnesty for anyone who said it in the past, a fresh start, but it will result in disciplinary action going forward." Re-establishing contact with Cecil, then Alex. "And don't forget. She's part *polizia*, has an investigative budget, her own techniques."

"Fine," Cecil said. "So what do we call this bitch?"

"Call her Angelique." Theodore blinked, holding it. "Angelique Royale."

"Sounds hot," Alex said. "Angelique Royale."

Cecil, laughing so hard his shoulders shook, mimicked Alex. "I likes 'em big."

"Seriously." Alex looked at Theodore. "That's not her name."

"Afraid it is, or at least how we've been told to address her, Angelique Royale."

"I bet she gives great head," Cecil said.

"Okay, enough." Theodore clapped once, saying Alex and Cecil had a day to chase Gervais, one. But Theodore didn't officially know anything about an expired tracer. "And." He wiggled his thumbs back and forth. "If I find out this is a homicide investigation, that you're holding out, gatekeeping so you can freelance behind my back, you will be chasing able-bodied people using wheelchair plates—that's fraud—until Labor Day."

Cecil counted on his fingers. "Four months. Little extreme, isn't it, Teddy?"

"One other thing." Theodore looked at Alex, pointing to Cecil. "I'm telling you for the last time. You, Alex, are responsible for him, Cecil."

Hands on his hips, Alex looked down, calling the chief inspector Teddy in his head.

***

Art Harwood looked at Miss April from this year's Harwood's Select Auto Service calendar. Some skinny white girl with bad skin wearing a lime bathing suit a size too big, buffing an apple-green MGB, the colors wrong together. Jeez, where did the desktop designer/photographer/print consultant get them? Then it dawned on Art that April was mercifully over.

He stood at his desk and removed a white thumb tack, turning the page to Miss May. Her canary-yellow bikini with jade details was too small, didn't match the piss-yellow Vette she was hosing down, either. God, she was as spooky as April with her penciled-in brows. Poor thing, probably a Gemini, couldn't stop plucking, and now she looked like a mutant in a blonde wig.

Sitting, shaking his head, Art was already thinking it was going to be another long month when his private line rang. He saw that the call was from a Bell Canada payphone, which wasn't unusual, but why would anybody be calling from the 705? Figuring yeah, some overachiever took his streeter up north to show off at the cottage, got in an accident, and needed help getting it home for repairs, Art had to answer, business. He picked up, saying, "Harwood's Select Auto Service. How may I help you with your vintage vehicle?"

"Hello, Art. I have another message from J-M."

"Antoine." Art tried to smile. "Where are you calling from?"

"Art, yeah, I'm good. I—"

"Didn't ask that. I asked where are you calling from? Are you in Barrie? Sudbury? I see the 705 area code on call display, can hear the highway."

Sighing into the phone, Art already being a problem, Antoine looked up at the sign, WAUBAUSHENE TRUCK STOP, and ignored the question, asking when was that outstanding work J-M paid Art, Gervais, and Reggie half in advance going to be done?

When? Well, Gervais said the timing of the job was in limbo for three reasons: One, that last hornet still had a lookout on her. Two, J-M hadn't paid anything yet on that market mayhem.

And three, nobody had seen or heard from J-M since last week. Where the hell was he anyway?

"Busy," Antoine said.

Fine, but then Art wanted to know, had Antoine seen J-M since he was yelling at Billy Koch? For all Art knew, J-M was MIA, so Art didn't know whether to go ahead with the job or not. Was Art even going to get what he was owed?

"You know J-M always pays," Antoine said. "And at all times, you have access to his lawyer, a good one, so just get it done, soon. He returns and the job's not finished, I'm going to hear it first, you second. And you will not like the message. Hear?"

"Fine," Art said. "We're ready, have the tire soaking. But when did you last hear from him, J-M?"

"Yes, I've heard from him."

"When, I said, not have you? When did you hear from him?"

Antoine cleared his throat, said, "It doesn't matter when, just that I have. And the last time, like the time before, it was J-M saying, Antoine, why haven't Gervais, Art, and Reggie finished the work I commissioned them to do? He is trying to be understanding, reasonable. In fact, he told me to wait until today, Tuesday, to deliver this reminder. He wanted you to have a break, a reward. In addition, he wanted you to know he was pleased with your use of 'Playing with Fire' by The Rolling Stones to satisfy the avec mocking part last time. So pleased, in fact, that he has a request for this last hornet. This time, he wants you to sing 'We Didn't Start the Fire' by Billy Joel, the three of you a cappella again."

"Are you kidding?" Art said. "It's a dissertation of a song documenting forty years of history up to the end of the Cold War. We're never going to learn all the lyrics."

"Perhaps just the chorus will suffice," Antoine said. "It would please J-M to learn that the chorus was sung to satisfy the mocking part. Otherwise, J-M said he loves and respects you all, but if he returns and the job's still not finished . . . "

"Alright," Art said. "Alright. But you can see why—"

"Look, I am just the messenger. I don't care so much anymore what the answer is. Just tell me so I can tell him next he calls, will the work be done?"

"Yes," Art said. "Just needed to hear from someone. I guess from you is good enough."

"Well you've heard now, and make sure Reggie and Gervais get the message. Especially about how J-M loves them and respects them. He wanted them to hear that, too. And no more phone calls, as I've been saying, from any of you."

"I will pass it on. Reggie has the apparatus prepared, like I said. It's just, also like I said, we were waiting to hear something before going ahead and installing the part, so to speak. And hey, where are you calling from again?" Hearing a click, Art waited a beat. "Hello?" Then another. "Antoine?"

NINETEEN

With paperwork concerning a Mercedes SUV belonging to one Bonaventure Healy—suspected star counterfeiter in a concert-ticket caper—in hand, Cecil fetched Alex from Fran's diner. Cecil wanted a black coffee to go, but Alex put the ixnay on that, saying Cecil needed to cut his caffeine intake, leading him outside. Cecil said he watched a documentary while they were off and he didn't think Jehovah's were allowed to have caffeine, period, so how did Alex square his shit up? Alex said there was a lot shit that didn't square. And what religion was Cecil again? Anglican, Cecil said, but he wasn't practicing. Organized religion was on his fighting side.

The diner was attached to the same building as headquarters where they reported to traffic on the ground floor. Liz Townie tried to toss her red hair, only it wasn't long enough to really whip it. Playing with the snap buttons on Alex's TWA jacket next, she turned to Cecil, nodding to his outfit. "Your wife make that?"

Cecil gave her a tentative nod, shot Alex a look.

Liz snatched the paperwork from Cecil, studying it. "Alright, everything's in order, sort of." Pointing at a small black briefcase on the counter. "This is all set to track Gervais Garret's Nomad. You luddites know how to use this?"

Alex said yes on account of a seminar at the annual retreat. You just plug it into the cigarette lighter, follow the signal as it gets louder. And sorry, but they had to go.

"K," Liz said. "Get that prick, singing he has my number, calling me a Jenny. Get him."

Alex promised to do his best, leading Cecil out. Alex carried the briefcase in one hand, latte in the other, placing both on the Cougar's roof as Cecil let himself in on the driver's side.

"Pop the trunk," Alex said.

When Cecil complied, Alex unhitched his cuffs, saying they were digging into his love handles and threw them in along with his cell, shutting the trunk. Gathering his things from the roof, he climbed into the Cougar's back seat, opening the case and handing Cecil a wire to plug into the cigarette lighter. That done, he said don't hit anyone as Cecil turned the car around.

"What time you got?" Alex said, opening the case.

Cecil looked at his watch, shaking it, banging the steering wheel. "Fuck, fuck, fuck."

"The time, Cecil." Alex didn't understand what could be controversial. "Can't be that late. Just tell me the time."

"I don't know the time. Just had Freida fix my watch and it's stuck on seconds."

"Again?"

"Yes, again. And since your dash clock is also buggered, says it's afternoon, leave me alone about my watch." Cecil looked over his shoulder. "Besides, you mean that thing in the briefcase doesn't tell time?"

"It's a transponder, Cecil, not a clock."

"Clocks on everything now, is what I'm saying. Check your cellphone."

"Check yours. I left mine in the trunk."

"Yeah, well, mine's at the office so as I don't have to take calls from Teddy."

East on College, Cecil noticed the digital Scotia Bank billboard at Yonge. Tilting his head, he said it's 10:48 a.m., stopping for the light. The cuffs on his belt were digging, too. If Alex didn't have to wear cuffs, Cecil didn't either. Besides, if push came to shove, Cecil had his spare set in a secret pocket, so he unhitched his service cuffs, sliding them under his seat. Hitting the gas before the light turned, nearly clipping a pedestrian he deemed to be lollygagging.

Another red stopped him after College turned into Carlton. Seeing they'd be held up because of construction ahead, Cecil said, "C'mon, c'mon, c'mon . . ." until Alex told him to zip it. On the upshot, the lights at Church Street were working. Cecil was waiting on the red when he shook an Export 'A' out of his pack, lighting up with a book of matches tucked into the cellophane. Leaning out the window when he saw something.

"Hey lady, lady."

Alex looked up to see what Cecil was on about, a tall auburn-blonde. She wore a peach babydoll with fluffy frills at the bust, walking the intersection in black spikes. Making the corner, facing them, waving. "Hey back."

"Cecil, you're coming onto a man," Alex said. "You know that, right?"

Cecil fanned the cigarette behind his head. "Yeah, yeah, yeah."

"Her shoes, Cecil, elevens from where I sit. Same size as me. About the same height as me, too, a pinch over six feet, and that's before you account for heels."

"Just a wholesome girl," Cecil said. "Substantial, something to grab on to."

"Oh, she got something to grab, alright. Get her to talk."

Cecil leaned out the window again, raising his voice. "Down with the economy, up with hemlines, huh?"

She cupped a hand over her organdy-painted mouth. "That's what they say, sweetie."

Convincing, but too campy for a natural woman, Alex turned his mouth down. "Now ask who's got the candy? Settle it."

Cecil made a megaphone out of his left hand. "Who's got the candy?"

Half-sitting on a green *NOW Magazine* box, she said, "Mama's got the candy." Giving Cecil the thumbs up. "And nice jacket, by the way. Salmon is the new black."

Cecil spoke over his shoulder, saying, "See?" as the light turned, advancing east. Alex said shut up. That mama's got the candy means it's a man, code. And shut up again. Alex was operating the transponder, complicated enough without Cecil hitting on traps. What would Freida think, because it was starting to look like Cecil was extracting favors, same as the drug squad. Cecil said Alex knew better. Also, girls like that didn't appreciate being called traps. And Freida wouldn't say fuck all, because that girl was on the Neighborhood Watch Committee, same as Cecil and Freida. Her name was Kendra—Kendra Mann from the Hugh Garner Co-op—and Kendra says our cops are tops. No doubt, Alex said, only Kendra meant it different than Cecil. Ha, very funny, but Cecil's point was that letters nation people who don't do meth made good neighbors, that they scaped their land like chest hair, improved property values.

"Really?" Alex said. "What do they say about you never cutting your grass?"

"I cut my lawn already, I told you on the phone yesterday, so drop it."

Alex couldn't decide what he was more surprised by, Cecil looking at Kendra Mann as an actual girl or mowing his lawn. Whatever, so long as Cecil wasn't extracting favors—and the funky he-bitch didn't appear hostile—what did Alex care? He was a busy bee, turning gray knobs inside the briefcase, flinching at feedback then switching it back, leaving well enough alone when Cecil sniffed out something else, pulling over.

"What now?" Alex said.

"There's a guy selling T-shirts across the street."

"What? You see one you like?"

"Wait here." Cecil opened the door, stepped out, jogging to the T-shirt vendor, pointing. "That write in Dick Gregory for president shirt. Let me see." The guy reached, handed it over, Cecil studying the design. "How many of these you sell?"

"You a tax cop?"

Cecil was impatient. "I'm not from Revenue Canada, no, or even city licensing. But if you wanna be a hard case, I can have 'em both up your arse for the DP. Instead, I urge you to cooperate. Now, I'm looking for someone bought a shirt like this, so how many you sell?"

The guy put his hands up, said thirty, maybe forty, not that he was the only one hustling them. They were all over the streets, in the head shops, twelve to fourteen bucks. Cecil thought about grilling further but couldn't see as how the guy was going to know anything worthy, so Cecil did an about-face, hightailing it to the car, shirt in hand.

"You gonna pay?" the vendor shouted.

"I'm confiscating it, evidence," Cecil shouted, stepping back into the Cougar.

Alex had seen the whole thing. "Did you just steal a T-shirt?"

"I'm telling you the same thing I told the guy. I'm confiscating it, evidence."

"Evidence of what?"

"Evidence of Doyle's last words were 'Write in Dick Gregory for president.'" Cecil threw the shirt at Alex. "Whoever killed him was wearing that shirt—twelve to fourteen bucks, depending on your vendor or head shop."

Alex said Cecil was misusing the word evidence, that the tee was merely a sample of what real evidence might look like, an example. In other words, he was saying, the tee was something to be curious about, a clue at best. Then he heard the familiar sound of a squad-car horn, double-beep, looking through the back. "Uh-oh."

"Uh-oh, what?" Cecil said.

"Looks like we're getting pulled over."

"The fuck?" Cecil glanced in the rearview, hitting the indicator, looking back at Alex. He was shaken, eyes forward, and Cecil couldn't understand. "Why are you a scared of a uniform?"

Alex took a breath, closed his eyes. "On account of it might be about I had to liberate this here car from Svetlana this morning."

***

It was often said there were two seasons in Toronto, winter and construction, so why did Gervais own any cars? Unless it was night, late, it wasn't fun to drive here, nowhere to run. Like, Gervais wasn't sure how long it was taking to get across town. He wasn't timing it, but fuck him, it would've been faster to walk. Well, maybe not walk, but he was thinking he would've arrived sooner on bike when, at long last, the Co-op cab jerked to a stop on Eastern. Gervais thanked the colonizer driver, telling him to keep the change on the twenty and the five—a ridiculous $21.20 fare for the privilege of advancing seven kilometers through construction, detours, and morning gridlock—hoping the driver wouldn't think of Gervais after this. Just a polite, quiet, respectful passenger who minded his own business and tipped well, but not too well. Faceless.

Out on the avenue, Gervais turned the metal wheel on his Chevy Zippo, scratching the flint and lighting up in front of Harwood's Select Auto Service. Dragging his cigarette, he thought about going around and in through the back, then remembered that stupid dog-barking alarm system Reggie installed. Well, it was effective enough to scare the bejesus out of anyone, so maybe it wasn't stupid, these times. What with a little chaos in his head over his life and the man he'd become, in addition to the hangover, Gervais didn't want to hear it anyway, crazy dogs, so he finished his cigarette, casual, walking in through the front door like any other patron.

Seeing Reggie first, Gervais was miffed at the optics of his '61 T-Bird on the lift when Reggie should've been stripping the Nomad. Nonetheless, complaining to Reggie wasn't going to solve anything—Art was the man with the plan here—so Gervais casually walked over and asked how the bird looked underneath.

"At this point everything appears tip-top," Reggie said. "If it doesn't need more than an oil change, Art'll probably let you drive it home once you have a couple of his tiny little coffees, sober up."

Gervais wanted to ask Reggie how he knew he'd been drinking—he'd only had a few splashes of Smirnoff—but figured any question would set up another smart-ass answer, so Gervais cut to the chase. "I need to see Art. Have to have speaks."

Reggie grabbed a rag, wiping his hands. "I'll tell him you're here."

Walking across the shop to Art's office, Reggie knocked, waiting a beat before opening the door. There was a brief exchange, but Gervais couldn't hear what they were saying over the Nina

Simone song on the radio, "Trouble in Mind," how appropriate. Moments later Reggie rejoined Gervais, pointing past the row of blue plastic chairs. "Art will see you now."

Gervais thanked Reggie and proceeded to Art's office, walking through the now open door, plopping his ass down on a nicer chair, leather, on the other side of Art's desk. "What? Reggie's your secretary now?"

"I'm sorry about that." Art held a pen out. "No offence, but I have him running interference on everyone who comes through, just in case. You have to know how it is, a bit warm already, heating up."

Yeah, well that's why Gervais was here. It was hot, which was why he wanted to see Reggie chopping up the Nomad and getting it gone, not doing an oil change on the T-Bird.

"Why not? If all it needs is an oil change, Reggie says you can drive it home today." Art thumb-pointed to the De'Longhi machine behind him. "And hey, can I get you an expresso?"

No, Gervais didn't want a pretentious little goombah coffee, nor did he have a fuck to give about driving the T-Bird home today. He wanted the Nomad stripped, the parts shipped before some determined detectives came looking for it.

Art looked at Gervais longer than appropriate then pointed at the door. "Will you shut it please?" When Gervais said sure, doing as requested, Art said, "Look, I'm glad you're here. There's a reason, a bunch, actually, Reggie's not started on the Nomad. This situation is fluid, and we have to talk about that, take the necessary steps to protect ourselves, and chopping up your car might not be one of those steps after I get through telling you what I have to tell you."

* * *

"You mean to say." Cecil paused, looking over his shoulder. "I'm behind the wheel of a stolen detective car as we, two detectives, search for another stolen car?" First, he was mad at Alex, thinking how he might use the word ironic in a sentence. Then Cecil thought maybe this would give him something to work with, leverage to hold over the old man. "Don't worry, pards. I got your back."

Hands high, badge in his right, Cecil stepped out of the Cougar, saying, "And a good morning to you, Officer."

The driver of the squad car did a double take at Cecil's face and badge. "Are you Detective Bolan, sir?"

"Why yes, Officer." Cecil hitched his pants. "One in the same."

"Well." The cop moved forward with an open right. "I just want to shake your hand for putting that anti-cop city councilor in a hole. The bad-mouther, telling media our guys are dropping dirty guns while he's purchasing panties for someone other than his spouse, likely a loose-liver herself. With respect, sir, fuck him."

Cecil shook the uniform's hand while he went on about how all the coppers appreciated it. Saying cheers, removing his hand, Cecil asked, "You pulled me over to say thanks?"

"No, sir." The cop looked at his boots, sheepish. "It's just the car you're driving's been reported stolen. Not just that. It's said to be a two-person job, possible hate crime. A female black in tiger stripes driving another vehicle, teal Nissan—we're also looking for her—apparently ran down the owner of the home where the car was stolen from, made slurs, comments about gender, skin color. Anti-eastern European sentiment was expressed."

Cecil chuckled quietly, asking the uniform if he ever had marriage problems? No, the uniform said he wasn't married. Cecil rolled a hand, saying yeah, but the cop had to know a lot of fellow officers had marriage problems, right? The uniform thought on it, said sure, he knew lots of fellow officers had marriage problems. Why?

Putting his hand on the uniform's shoulder, Cecil led the officer back to his cruiser. "Well, this is a false report because of my partner's marriage problems. And if you value me putting that bad-mouthing, loose-living city councilor in a hole, I'd value you putting this down as a false report by reason of marriage problems, close the book. Can you do that for me?"

The uniform thought some more, said yeah. He could do that

so long as Cecil's partner returned the vehicle by midnight, and not a second later. Cecil promised Alex would, thank you, asked for the officer's name, Piper, said he'd look out for him.

Back in the Cougar, Cecil told Alex not to worry, just to have the car back tonight and it would go down as a false report due to marriage problems. Yes, Alex heard everything, most of it anyway, and thanked Cecil for bailing him out. Still, Alex couldn't help but think how this meant he wouldn't be able to attend church, again, on account of there was no way he could do that, plus return the car, and make it back to Sondra's condo in time to talk about their relationship.

Putting the car into drive, Cecil said, "You owe me."

Alex figured it was more like he was finally getting paid back for all the times Cecil owed him, but just said yeah, he owed Cecil. Besides, Alex didn't deem the timing right for a teachable moment, telling himself a new opportunity would soon present itself.

South on Parliament, the transponder's signal grew stronger as Cecil picked up speed. Passing through the Regent Park projects, Cecil remarked on black kids playing Hackensack near the streetcar stop, that they should be in school.

"It's hacky sack," Alex said, already finding, yep, he guessed it, a new opportunity for yet another teachable moment. "Hackensack's a place in New Jersey."

The signal grew weaker as they approached the Gardiner Expressway.

"Turn around, north," Alex said. "Try King or Queen, east on one of them. Seems strongest around there."

Cecil made a sloppy U-turn, establishing eye contact with a southbound man skidding to a stop, leaning on the horn of his gunmetal-gray Honda. Cecil flashed his shield. Asked if the guy knew what happened to Arabs who fight cops? The man shouted he was a Turk, that Turkey was allies this time. Then why, Cecil wanted to know, was City TV telling people don't go to Turkey unless they really, really had to? Huh? Why were they saying that if Turkey was allies? If Turkey was allies, City TV would be saying go, have a delight. Not stay the hell away.

Alex had punched the rest behind Cecil's head three times by then. "North. Just hit the gas, north. Yelling at some Turk he's an Arab—probably goes to the same church as me."

"In the documentary," Cecil said, "they mentioned Jehovah's go to Monarchy Mansions."

"It's Kingdom Hall, Cecil, and church is close enough for you. Now north, man. You've got to be kidding—spouting foreign policy during road rage. Yeah, we on the case." Wiping at the fresh coffee splotch on his white shirt, he hit Cecil's headrest again. "You made me get latte on my brand-new Gildan Ultra Cotton. Young motherfucker, I wore it one morning, one. Now look. I'm telling Theodore a session with the two-hundred-pound rockabilly girl says don't ornamentalize her is right for you."

"Angelique Royale, huh?" Cecil looked in the rearview, gunning it to seventy in seconds. "I just talked that uni out of arresting you, a fellow cop, impounding your car, and that's what you want for me? The thanks I get?"

"Please go slow," Alex said. "I was just kidding about the sensitivity training. Honest."

"The fuck?" Cecil eased up, bringing the Cougar down to twenty-five. "This's like trying to find an earring with a bullshit detector on a beach."

Alex played with the buttons, more feedback, jerking away. "Pretty close, Cecil, pretty close. Except this here earring, transmitter on the Nomad, sends out a siren call all its own. Means our briefcase will find the transmitter. Just hope it's still attached to the Nomad, that they haven't stripped it and shipped it yet, like I told Theodore."

"Where'd the techies put it, the transmitter?"

"Inside the hole where the hood ornament goes. After that, they reinstalled the hood ornament—looks like a rocket—on top. Now, I'm willing to bet the hood ornament is most valuable when still attached to the hood. Only a hundred sixty-five American on its own."

"How do you know that?" Cecil said. "What it's worth."

"Because that's how much Gervais paid on eBay, got his emails. You want to find out what something's worth, go to eBay—see what someone will pay in the global marketplace—and the highest bid was a hundred sixty-five American, plus shipping, Gervais."

Signal growing stronger as the Cougar made King and Parliament, Alex said turn right at Queen. Cecil did as he was told, the signal stronger still.

"That sound," Cecil said. "You make that to be a tick-tick or a beep-beep?"

"Something in between," Alex said. "Like Pac-Man gaining on Chernobyl." It faded again when they passed Eastern Avenue. "Okay. Turn it around again, west."

Cecil pulled another U-ie, cursing when he turned too wide, bouncing off the curb.

"Mind the Goodyears." Alex pointed at the intersection. "Go right on Eastern, pull over."

Cecil took the right, looking around. "Pull over where?"

"To the side of the road, Cecil—where?"

"You gotta pee?"

"Just you pull over here." Alex lurched forward between the seats, pulling the wire out of the cigarette lighter. Gathering it, he forced the briefcase shut over the lump, snapping hinges. "Not supposed to be using this voodoo on Gervais as of yesterday."

"You speak of him like an acquaintance."

"A client, Cecil. Just a little gentlemanly fraud, good for business, our business. That's all I see so far. Now pop the back." Alex stepped out with the briefcase, dropping it into the trunk, slamming it, walking to the driver's side. "You know where we're going?"

"No."

"Then slide over."

Cecil thought Alex had a lot of control issues, a guy his age, sliding to the passenger side anyway. Alex sat in the driver's chair, punched the car into gear. A half block later, he pointed to a sign, HARWOOD'S SELECT AUTO SERVICE, remarking on Cecil's untrained eye, pulling onto the gravel. Oh yeah? Untrained eye, huh? Cecil wanted to know if this was going to be a teachable moment about, wait for it, grand theft fucking auto.

ervais put his hand on Art's desk, pastel sticky notes everywhere. "I don't know where Jean-Max is. I mean, he's not answering the burner he told me to call in case of emergency. Or, someone else is answering hello, not bonjour. I don't know, but I don't like it."

"You don't like it?" Art said. "What about me? I told you, don't phone Jean-Max. You know why?" Pointing at his landline. "Because Jean-Max doesn't want us phoning."

"Yeah, well Jean-Max owes me money. And, at least in part, that's the reason why I've got to lose the Nomad now, cash flow."

"That's exactly why I'm having second thoughts about stripping your car at this point." Art gripped his leather armrests. "That's what scares me, one of the things anyway, money."

"Little late to get scared." Gervais looked at the Harwood's Select Auto Service calendar above Art's head, some poor girl with penciled-in eyebrows wearing a bikini that didn't fit hosing down a '71 Stingray. "I've already reported it stolen, Art. Called the cops, the insurance."

"Then maybe you need to un-report it." Art leaned back in his chair. "Maybe we have Reggie ditch it somewhere, let them find it, forget the whole thing, okay?"

Gervais shook his head. It was not okay. Reggie wasn't driving the car anywhere. Gervais needed the money, and he couldn't exactly allow the car to be found then pull the same stunt a month later once Art grew a pair. Aside from that, if Art was screwing Gervais today, why should Art be trusted tomorrow? Same as when someone lies. If they lie once, how do you know when they're telling the truth? Didn't the urban colonizer see what Gervais was saying? Art's word was on the line here.

"My word?" Art leaned forward, elbows on his blotter. "It's just I've been thinking."

"Oh good. You, having revelations, deep thoughts."

186

Art pointed a pinky. "And you, having a previous theft of a big-ticket vehicle, the subject could get raised if that Oreo duo all over Renaldo's Auto Body comes scumbagging around here. I mean, I don't mind doing this. It's good business for me. But so far as the authorities are concerned, money is always the handiest motive for getting at anything. This case, peepers are watching Jean-Max, means maybe peepers are watching you. Which, in turn, means they might be watching me, because you came here. Were you tailed?"

"That's why I took a cab," Gervais said.

"Because you didn't want to risk a DWI?"

"No, because I didn't want to be tailed, you fuck."

"Well, they can follow you in a cab just as easy if you're too drunk to look. You don't know, is the point. You're too busy chasing money to look over your shoulder. I'm telling you, maybe this is not the time to be pulling one over so far as money is concerned. Just giving you words for the wise."

"Thanks." Gervais shook his head in fast jerks, smiling. Art giving him guidance. Man, Gervais thought, Art was in no position to judge anyone. The fact that he did anyway was what made Art, Art, another flawed humanoid. "But no thanks, all the same." Tapping a cigarette out of his pack and onto the desk. "Just go ahead, strip the Nomad, and I'll really thank you, properly, have one of my honeys bounce on your lap. So, unless there's anything else..."

Watching Gervais place the cigarette in his mouth, Art slid an ashtray made out of a mini-Goodyear tire, 1873, across the desk, saying yes, there were still some items on the agenda.

First, Gervais had to understand how this might look, him in a hurry, like he knew something Art didn't. Maybe Gervais might need money to pay a lawyer, unexpected expenses, leaving Art and Reggie twisting in the wind.

Second, wasn't Gervais making enough from his duplexes? Not to mention the money Jean-Max owed all three of them. And Jean-Max always paid.

"Third," Art said. "It's bad enough we still have to get the other one now, the last of the green hornets, Pam Jenkins. Jean-Max originally told us to do that, what, almost two weeks ago? So maybe it's not such a good time to be screwing over your insurance company."

***

No one was at the cash. Alex said c'mon, leading Cecil to the shop floor, a gray-haired guy wearing dirty overalls green as Lake Ontario on a no-swimming day. Looks tired, Alex thought, face shiny, hair all over the place. Reading the name crest, REGGIE, Alex introduced himself, Cecil, then said, "So listen, Reggie. You are an employee, right?"

"Yes, sir, Detective Johnson. An employee."

Alex held his hands like he was cradling something valuable. "So, I don't see how this involves you, personally, you know? But we have reason to believe a 1957 Chevy Nomad, parts of one anyway, are on this premise or somewhere thereabouts. Same car as MacGyver drove."

"Haven't seen none." Reggie pointed to the lift. "Oldest thing we have is a '61 T-Bird."

"Also Gervais' car," Cecil said.

Alex looked impressed, Cecil paying attention. Reggie just said yeah, it was in for an oil change and an estimate on security options. Removing a cigarette pack from his coveralls, Player's, lighting up. "And MacGyver drove jeeps, Cherokees and Wranglers, if memory serves."

"Your memory does serve, most of the time," Alex said. "But sometimes MacGyver drove the Nomad his granddaddy willed him. Like that time Abe Vigoda got out of prison and double-crossed MacGyver, Abe thinking there's a priceless diamond pendant hidden inside."

Cecil, watching Reggie stroke a thin yellowed moustache, spoke to Alex. "So now there's a diamond in this ancient heap we're looking for?"

Alex said no, but would Reggie mind if they went out back to take a look?

"You have to talk to Art Harwood himself, you want to do that." Reggie took a drag, held it. "Art's the one to bring you back there. It's not for me to do that." Exhaling, pointing his cigarette at Alex's chest. "And you know you have coffee on your shirt?"

Alex took a step, leaned in closer. "You going to stop us?"

"No sir, Detective Johnson. I just tell you this is private property and to talk to Art. You don't listen, you are at your own risks. Two Doberman, a pit bull—answer to names of Gibson, Rusty, and Ed Van Impe Junior, respectively. Art named Ed after a hockey player, the guy flattened the Russian in the seventies."

"Soviets wouldn't play for twenty minutes after that, the Flyers were so violent, Ed Van Impe in particular," Cecil said. "So if this Ed Van Impe Junior pit bull is gonna bite us, cops, maim us, how about I shoot him, put him down? You, keeping a dog so violent you call him Ed Van Impe Junior, obviously bred to be a toughie."

"You can't shoot 'em because we got security tapes pick up everything, including signs that say Do Not Trespass, Beware of Dogs, all that. Everything is recorded." Reggie, looking at Alex, pointed his cigarette to Cecil. "He starts shooting dogs they'll lock you up, too. Him just saying he's shooting dogs, he can't say that. And you—you have to express immediate disapproval in a situation such as this. Besides, I haven't seen a warrant. That's what Art would want me to say. You have one?"

Alex put his hands on his hips. "I'm not sure I ever heard so much law talk from a man doesn't have to have something to do with it, an employee." When Reggie took another drag, Alex looked at Cecil. "How about you?"

Cecil smiled tightly. "How about me what?"

"It's like he's not a lawyer, but he did stay at a Holiday Inn last night."

"So what are you asking?"

"What I'm asking is, did you ever hear so much law talk from a man doesn't have anything to do with it?"

Cecil rubbed his index and thumb together, money. "That city councilor I made kiss the carpet, Tate, he also talks a lot of law for a guy had nothing to do with it."

Reggie pointed at the radio. "That was you?"

"Me." Cecil thumbed his chest. "Tougher than a dozen nights in jail, *All News, All the Time* says, so don't think this Ed Van Impe Junior intimidates me. If he attacks, I know a pit bull's weak spot, its front legs." Holding his hands together in fists, spreading his arms abruptly. "You just grab 'em and split 'em like a wishbone. Good doggie."

"Other than the city councilor." Alex clapped in Cecil's face, focus. "Did you ever see a man talk so much law got nothing to do with it, anyone like this Reggie?"

Cecil shook his head. No, he'd never seen a guy had nothing to do with it talk so much law as this Reggie. Other than, like Cecil said, the city councilor, Tate.

"Look, you guys are on camera talking about shooting dogs and Art's in a meeting." Reggie looked at a closed door. "You have to wait."

"This is a police matter," Cecil said. "Tell him, Art."

Reggie pointed again. "See that sign?"

"No Smoking?"

Reggie took another drag. "Art doesn't recognize that, just an ordinance requiring him to post it, so smoke 'em if you got 'em." Exhaling. "The sign hanging on the doorknob. What does it say?"

Cecil squinted, reading it aloud. "Pompano Beach Days Inn?"

"Right sign, but the message beneath that."

"Do Not Disturb?"

Reggie said that was the one. And, other than No Smoking, Art Harwood meant what he said when he hung a sign. Pointing at the row of blue plastic chairs near the cash, Reggie said take a load off, wait. Cecil walked to the back door instead, opening it, setting off three dogs barking. He didn't know which one was Ed Van Impe Junior, but even if Cecil couldn't see the dogs, one sounded particularly pissed off, vicious, so Cecil put a hand on his piece.

"Let's just wait the man out, Cecil." Alex eyeballed one of the cameras. "Step light."

***

Art wondered what the fake dogs were on about. For a moment, he considered directing Reggie to shut the system down, dismantle it, complaining that it was sending a little jolt up Art's arse every time. But that wasn't it. Reggie had assembled a fine DIY security system. Nobody wanted to mess with dogs sounding off like that. Besides, first it was Antoine on the phone and now Gervais in person really pissing Art off, not Reggie's fake dogs.

From across the desk, Gervais held his unlit cigarette in front of Art's face. "Like I said, Jean-Max still owes me, and he's MIA. So, until we hear something from the Quebec colonizer, I say we put this nasty little job of his off, on hold, deal with my car first."

"Can't put the Pam Jenkins thing off, on hold. Wherever Jean-Max is, his right hand says he loves and respect us, but this has to happen." Pointing at his landline, Art thought about saying Antoine phoned from the highway, but decided not to mention that part, that it wouldn't help. "I was just talking to Antoine, so the message is field-to-table fresh. And please, don't give me any more shit about Jean-Max paying. I told you, he always pays, and, if things ever get hairy, he always has a lawyer at the ready, a good one."

"Antoine, he's the houseboy, right?"

Art said, "The messenger, Jean-Max's personal go-between, his delegate, and that's another thing. You can't disparage these people, calling Antoine houseboy, Jean-Max a colonizer. You have to remember that, in their minds, we are not like them, and cannot be seen or heard disrespecting them."

"Not like them, how?" Gervais said "We're white. We've done everything they've asked, some of which was well above and beyond, so how are we not brothers in arms working hard, living hard, and playing hard? You mean to tell me we can't horse around?"

"We are not bikers and we are not French. They take care of

their own first, the bikers and the French."

"Well, at least I have a French name, close enough. Also." Gervais flashed his cigarette pack. "I smoke Gitanes."

"You are from Burlington and you don't speak a word, so it's not close enough. Jean-Max isn't going to let us shirk this off because your name sounds French and you smoke Gitanes. We're in no position to walk away from a job we're already half paid for by a Hells Angels president, so let's concentrate on that, get it done, and try not to do anything else—like chop your car—that might create the illusion of us having criminal connections to Jean-Max whilst we are doing more serious criminal bidding on his behalf."

"Don't worry about your guy's bubble touching mine." Gervais shook his cigarette at Art. "They've got nothing between Jean-Max and I, other than I had his shop do some work, nothing between you and him and I in terms of being parts of a ring. For all they know, you're a competitor." Pushing his glasses up to the bridge of his nose. "Me, I'm just a keen customer looking for value, A-1 service at an A-1 rate."

"But I am worried," Art said. "For starters, you didn't follow protocol and leave the Nomad somewhere for a few days to ensure it doesn't have a tracking gizmo."

Gervais said he knew his car didn't have a gizmo because it was, well, his car. Not something they were stealing from a stranger.

Art pressed the point anyway. "Ever think maybe the cops planted something?"

"There'd be no basis for that," Gervais said, "legally."

Art rubbed both eyes with one hand. "Goddamn this whole thing. I mean, why can't we just take care of Jean-Max, do what he's contracted, get him off our books, lay low, and forget everything else?" Looking at the unlit cigarette in Gervais' hand. "You gonna light that?"

Gervais put the cigarette in his mouth. "You see me on *America's Dumbest Criminals?*"

Art looked at him, what?

"I said, did you see me on *America's Dumbest Criminals?*"

"No."

"And you're not going to." Gervais reached into his hip pocket, finding his lighter. "You know why?"

"Because this is not America?"

"Because I think things through." Gervais opened his Chevy Zippo with a swish, turning the metal wheel and scratching the flint. "Like MacGyver."

TWENTY-ONE

With Cecil sitting next to him on the row of blue chairs, Alex wiped in vain at the coffee stain on his shirt. Fidgeting, noting the pattern, he realized DJ Dwayne was now playing divas every song. Singing softly with Dianne Reeves, "Old Souls," on the paint-spattered ghetto blaster, Alex figured it must've been some kind of special fundraiser aimed at lady listeners.

After Dianne, there was a sports break with a new girl talking about Billy Koch managing to earn his seventh save last night, despite posting an earned run average of 4.15 for the month of April, preserving a 2-0 shutout against Anaheim.

"The drama," Alex said. "A closer with an ERA above four."

"Can't believe Buck Martinez stays with him," Cecil added. "Lots of good young arms in the bullpen, guys who can find the plate, hit the corners."

After a soundbite from Buck saying that Billy was his guy, the board op played a spot for a free jazz picnic at Cherry Beach before throwing to poor old Ryan Flanaghan. He was in a cab, reporting from a cellphone, en route to police headquarters for a noon press conference where it was expected that top homicide cop Sheff Dubois would ID the hogtied floater tourists happened upon yesterday on Lake Ontario. Then it sounded like the cab hit something, boom, dead air.

Casual, Cecil said, "I just want to note this Reggie's wearing coveralls."

Alex knew where Cecil was going and tried to put an end to it, saying Reggie was a mechanic, that mechanics wear coveralls.

"Okay, what about this '57 Nomad?" Cecil said. "Everyone keeps saying it's the same kind of car a guy named MacGyver drove."

"That's right."

"Everyone, except for me, seems to know of him. He's a real guy, this MacGyver?"

Finally, DJ Dwayne put on a record, Irma Thomas, "Time is on My Side." Thinking, yeah, nothing but divas, Alex decided maybe Leamington didn't get ABC and that it'd be fun to pull Cecil's chain while they waited.

"Angus MacGyver," Alex said. "Agent for the Phoenix Foundation in the late '80s and early '90s, kept the world a safe place. This one time, Cold War situation, MacGyver saved us all by disarming a nuclear warhead with a paper clip."

"And how'd he do that?"

"Just did, education and training. That Leamington school, they teach history?"

Alex looked straight ahead, fighting his smile while Cecil insisted history was in fact core curriculum at Leamington Secondary, and so what if he never heard of the Phoenix Foundation? Maybe Cecil was feverish that day, pissing out shits. What? He was supposed to know all the foundations? There was going to be a foundations test?

Serious now, Alex put his hand on Cecil's thigh. "Again, I am sorry about Doyle. Guess none of us knew what we were getting into. Bad business, this Operation Cooperation."

Cecil pushed Alex away. "You know Jean-Max did this."

"And you know he was at the ballgame hating on Billy Koch." Alex stopped himself from turning this into a teachable moment, pulling back. "Again, I'm sorry. Just so sorry."

Cecil shook his head, saying Doyle did it to himself, really, and the drinking didn't help. Thinking back, school days. "A mischief-maker was what he was, always pouring something on something back when we were kids."

"Pouring?"

"Pouring, that's right."

"For instance?"

"Okay, this one time, he came into class early, poured Tabasco on the science teacher's chair. Rest of the day, Mr. Higginson's scratching his arse, wondering why it burns. That was Doyle's thing, pouring, running away, and watching the results from afar."

Cecil laughed sadly, gently. It hadn't been much more than a dozen years, but he could barely remember the little snippets anymore, memories fading. "Used to be, Doyle worked with the animals just outside of town. Junior warden-something-something. That's why we got rings for the championship, not leather jackets. Doyle wouldn't stand for it, us wearing leather. That's also why he was wearing a pleather jacket the night he got it. It was because of the animals."

"Leather would have never taken the flame like so," Alex said. "Guess you could say it was on account of the animals he died."

"How could you say that?" Cecil looked sideways. "That the animals had something to do with it?"

"Just that he loved them so much he wouldn't wear them. And, in turn, he died—at least in part—on account of pleather being such a quick combustive."

Cecil said yeah, but then Doyle would break down and eat the animals every once in a while, so he couldn't have loved them that much.

For the first time—no, it happened twice before—Alex felt something for his young partner. And oh, he didn't want to feel something. Didn't want to have to say something, but there they were, stuck with each other; Alex near the end of the line, Cecil still learning on the job when he really should've been back in uniform, at best.

"Everything else aside," Alex said, "I was impressed you didn't say let Doyle slide on account of you knew him. You, becoming an effective detective after all."

"Thought I was favoring him enough by seeing to it they offered him a deal first. He was only helping rich people steal from other rich people. It's not right, but he wasn't hurting those in need, just lazy at some things. That's what they said. After high school, he briefly played for the University of Windsor team, the Lancers. Cut for being so lazy, some said." Cecil held his forehead, balancing an elbow on the arm of the chair. "Means I got him killed for being lazy."

Alex let out a laugh. "That empathy you displaying?"

Cecil, straightening his back, said, "Of course, some said he just needed more seasoning. With the Lancers, some said his work ethic was fine, but he needed more seasoning." Alex wanted to ignore that, let it slide, too, but Cecil looked him in the eye, going on. "Bad enough it's your words I hear coming out of Teddy's mouth, seasoning, then today that old traffic tootsie you flirt with, Liz, asks, did my wife make my suit? That's insider information."

Alex looked Cecil up and down. "Elizabeth said that on her own."

"Right."

"I shouldn't have said anything to Theodore about seasoning. Give you that, but I didn't tell Liz about the suit. It actually does look like your wife made it. And it's pink, Cecil."

"I don't know how many times I have to say, it's salmon."

***

Art watched Gervais drag on his cigarette, saying fine, Gervais, you're a very intelligent man, smarter than MacGyver. That Gervais probably read books with no pictures, too. But as smart as Gervais may or may not have been, Millhaven was home to hundreds of guys who also thought they were smart. Guys who thought they were smarter than their computers, smarter than guys on TV.

That was the key point Art was trying to make. Nobody ever figured on getting caught. And risks considered, there wasn't all that much money in what Gervais was doing with his Nomad, so why was he even thinking about it? Art thought Gervais loved that car.

"I do love the Nomad." Gervais flicked an ash into the tray. "But this is all about business. Business is all about money." Tapping his chest. "And me, I'm all about business."

That's exactly where Art was going, sure, looking at it as a business-type circumstance. What Art meant to say was, was it even worth Gervais' while when he considered Art would discount the merch deeply now that they had to move it briskly? Art didn't know how Renaldo's Auto Body worked it, but here, Art was going to have to pay Reggie to break up the parts. Did Gervais understand that? See, everyone shared the yield, reciprocity. Multiple people were involved. Aside from Reggie, Art had to pay the desktop designer/photographer/printer consultant to covertly advertise the stuff online through various sellers, who would also take a cut, and did Gervais think about that while doing the math?

"I've done this before," Gervais said. "Remember? The insurance is what I'm really after. Anything you get on the open black market—so long as it's fair—is beer money. You know?"

"Yeah, I know." Art looked up to Miss May again. Oh God, how was he going to talk his way out of this? "But you've got to know guys aren't going to stay shut up if they get caught. Once they're told murder is part of the sitch, they're going to sing like stars."

Sitch? Gervais had heard enough. This was why people didn't like him, because he stood up for himself, and there was no way he was going to let Art bullshit his way out of this fucking *sitch*, not this late. "Look, the thing you have to remember is that none of these guys are likely to put money aside for rainy days." Gervais hit his smoke. "They spend lavishly on booze, broads, good times, like us." Exhaling. "They show off, also like us. That's why we're all in this business. That's also why none of us have families bogging us down. We like our cars like we like our dicks, big. And the only way to keep those cars going—figuring in gas, insurance, improvements, and upkeep—is money, lots of money. That's how I know these guys won't sing like stars. They want to stay on the money train."

"Money," Art said. "I keep telling you, that's what worries me. It all comes back to money, something to follow."

"How?"

"You, a guy owns a half a dozen duplexes wanting so much money so fast. This car is your pride and joy, then you want to get rid of it all of a sudden? The more I think, the way you're pressing, maybe you really are prepping in case you're hit with lawyer's fees, big time, because the lawyer's going to know you're guilty of something. Like maybe you know something's coming or are scared of something you're not telling Reggie and I about."

"C'mon." Gervais took another drag, speaking as he exhaled. "If I was really afraid of... If I thought something like that could happen, we wouldn't be having this conversation. In fact, the only thing I am afraid of is getting caught on the Nomad thing because we didn't dismantle the car and get the parts out of here fast enough. Our window is now."

"What I'm saying is." Art loosened his Chianti-on-navy striped tie, undoing the top button of his checked shirt, same colors, wondering if he was getting away with mixing patterns. "The more I think, you've got a motive for why you'd get into the insurance scam, at least so far as cops are concerned. And me, you could see how I'm thinking maybe your lawyer, knowing you're guilty of something, is demanding a bigger deposit with the kills in the papers."

"You're going in circles on this lawyer thing." Gervais scratched his cheek. "I mean, you just got through telling me, again, that Jean-Max would have a lawyer at the ready, if we ever need, so why would I be fundraising for Johnnie Cochran?"

"Because you're part of the self-preservation collective of one."

Gervais said fuck that, and fuck you, too. What was Art, paranoid? He knew they hadn't looked at Gervais for anything violent. It wasn't in his historical nature, and he couldn't see how he was drawing any attention, as per the necklacings, so why couldn't Art just tell Reggie to chop the Nomad and get it out of here before some determined detectives came dicking around?

Art tilted his head, closing his eyes.

"Now." Gervais took another hit then butted his smoke in the tire ashtray. "Are we going to do this or not?"

Art opened his eyes, thinking maybe he was overreacting, paranoid like Gervais said. And well, Art had already agreed to do it, told Antoine sure, he'd deal with Gervais' car, which was the same as making a pledge to Jean-Max personally. If Art had reservations, it really was kind of late. So okay, fine, to keep the peace, Art would tell Reggie to dismantle the Nomad this aft. But there was no wiggle room on this Pam Jenkins thing. They still had to take care of the last of the green hornets, and relatively fast. Did Gervais understand that they no longer had a choice in that matter? Gervais hesitated, saying yes, he understood.

"Good," Art told him, "because it gets better. It appears Jean-Max was impressed by your selection of 'Playing with Fire' by The Rolling Stones as fulfilling the mocking part of the assignment. Very impressed."

"He liked that?" Gervais said, pleased Jean-Max was pleased.

"He did. In fact, he liked it so much, he has a request, wants us to sing 'We Didn't Start the Fire' by Billy Joel this time, also a cappella."

"Come on." Gervais wasn't smiling anymore. "Even Billy Joel doesn't like 'We Didn't Start the Fire.' I saw an interview where he said it was the worst melody he ever wrote, that it sounds like a dentist's drill."

Art wanted to scoff, thinking there was no way Billy Joel didn't like his own song. Instead, he just said, "Well, that's what Jean-Max wants."

"Fuck me." Gervais held his head in one hand. "It's a long list of names, places, international incidents, scandals, books, and movies. I don't know the words."

Art said it was okay, that the chorus would suffice, that they could just learn the chorus.

TWENTY-TWO

Cecil was on about the time Doyle started a riot at an exhibition football game, pouring grape juice on the Assumption Purple Raiders' cloth signage, staining it. The way Cecil told it, the Purple Raiders' half of Windsor Stadium emptied, spilling onto the field.

"But Doyle." Cecil let out a weak smile. "He'd left the stadium. By the time people were actually out there, fighting, they say Doyle was in the parking lot sitting in his Ford Elite, having a beer, watching the whole thing. It was his first and only car." Motioning to the shop floor. "He took care of it, oil change every three months or five thousand kilometers whether it needed one or not."

Alex raised a brow. "But all cars need a lube and filter every three months or five thousand kilometers, Cecil."

"So?"

"So, you said he changed the oil whether he needed to or not. Just saying it sounds more like he changed the oil as needed."

Cecil thanked Alex for splitting that hair, prick, saying the point was Doyle had been babying and rebuilding and upgrading the car since before he even got his license, that it was willed to him by old man Allenby—who made ketchup and other Heinz products by day and volunteered for the fire department at night.

"Your parents," Alex said. "They still in Leamington?"

"Yep." Cecil was tempted to spark up another butt but resisted. "Only we're not talking. And before you ask, it's because they give too much money to St. John the Evangelist."

"And that's why organized religion is on your fighting side, huh?"

"It's in the mix." Cecil nodded. "But I don't think any of the religions would approve of me, so I don't approve of them." Thumb-pointing at himself. "I have my own moral compass."

"No doubt," Alex said, sitting there with his hands folded in his lap. "No doubt... Your other teammate from buttfuck, the young brother, Milky Way Jones?"

That caught Cecil's attention. Why was Alex asking about Milky? Cecil looked up for a sign pointing to where Alex was going with this. No expression in face, but there was a hint of a smile in his old-people eyes, freckles disappearing as the skin around his face creased. Feeling himself gulp, Cecil said, "Yeah?" and held his breath.

"What's his real name?"

"Jimmy." Cecil smiled, looking down at his white shoes. "Jimmy Jones."

"Jim Jones." Alex nodded in satisfaction. Yeah, he knew it was going to be something like that. "No wonder a man pushing thirty goes by his high school handle. I get it. He's probably just tired of Kool-Aid jokes."

"You know it."

The two men were sharing a laugh when Alex said, "What with you so attuned to the black arts of African brown ball, a champion yourself, how come I never hear you say anything about the Raptors. Not a word."

Elbows on his knees, hands held together, fingers intertwined, Cecil pondered the question before answering. "They have some nice players, talented individuals—Vince Carter, Keon Clark, Charles Oakley—but not much of a team. I mean, yeah, Carter's a human highlight reel, but he's way cocky for a guy hasn't won more than the Slam Dunk Contest. If they ever get together as a team, I will follow." Snapping his fingers as something occurred. "And hey, you must've talked to Hermosa by now about Doyle's expensive white-girl lawyer, right? Told him to find out who's paying?" Cecil waited a beat, another. When Alex didn't answer, Cecil pointed in stabs, saying, "I wish I could take a pill to forget every one of your teachable moments, you gatekeeping motherfucker. I ask you to pass along one thing, pertinent, twelve days ago. I follow up I don't know how many times, and you still don't do it?"

Alex was talking fast, saying he called Hermosa about this specifically on Thursday, but Hermosa told Alex to butt out, called him *mayate*, so Alex figured maybe Cecil was right for saying Hermosa was an uppity spic being racist, although Alex would clean that up a little and say maybe Hermosa had problematic tendencies towards all peoples. Now that Alex thought of it, maybe Hermosa wasn't a racist at all. He did, after all, seem to treat blacks and whites with equal scorn, so maybe Hermosa was just another asshole.

Cecil turned away, muttering "empty words, empty words" as the office door opened. Art Harwood walked out doing up the inside button to his blue-black double-breasted suit, Chianti pinstripes matching his shirt and tie, narrow lapels. Seeing Alex and Cecil, he stopped as if he'd stepped on something, taking a split-legged stance.

"You got a gun?" Alex said.

"No, sir." Art raised his hands halfway. "No gun."

"Then why are you reacting like that, standing all Curtis Sliwa like? You a Guardian Angel, a vigilante, standing like that?"

When Art didn't answer Alex, Cecil stepped forward, more or less repeating the question. "Are you Curtis Sliwa, my partner said?"

"No, no." Art took a half step back. "Just surprised, is all."

"Also used to holding a gun, training it on someone," Alex said. "That's how you reacted to seeing a cop, the position you assumed."

Stepping aside, dropping his hands, Art cleared the door. Gervais Garret came out from behind, wearing utilitarian dark-framed glasses, a long-sleeved white T-shirt beneath a short-sleeved black tee with a message printed across it.

"And looky-loo." Cecil took a couple steps forward, glancing back at Alex. "This is the bespectacled dumpling I was telling you about, the man with the invisible illness."

Alex put a hand up, said it was legit.

Gervais smiled wide, whitening strips giving him the confidence to answer in the affirmative. His paperwork was in order. Also, as per his caregiver, he said it would be inappropriate to ask further questions about his invisible illness, lest the detectives wanted to violate doctor-patient confidentiality.

Alex held an open hand to Cecil, said, "See?"

"See what?"

"It's shit like this, mocking an invisible-illness survivor of size, going to put you in front of the two-hundred-pound rockabilly girl says don't ornamentalize her."

Cecil glared at Gervais, speaking to Alex. "Her name is Angelique Royale."

"That can't be her given name," Alex said. "And before you ask, no, I don't know why Theodore said call her that. He's probably pulling our legs in such a way as we get in even more trouble for calling her Angelique Royale, code for something terrible dirty, pagan."

"Well, it's what Teddy told us to say, officially, so I'm not calling Angelique the two-hundred-pound rockabilly girl in front of suspects."

Gervais didn't know what this was about, but figured Alex was playing with him, reverse psychology, playing the good cop whilst sneaking in two fat jokes—one against this rockabilly girl and one against Gervais himself—when Gervais noticed that Alex had a coffee stain on his shirt, mentioning it, helpful. Then he said, "Detective Johnson, sir." Looking at Cecil. "And it's Detective Bolan, right?" Cecil nodded, Gervais opening a hand. "Coupla good crusaders—meet Art Harwood."

They all nodded at each other, after which Cecil turned and glared at Alex, chin-pointing as if a clue was on the other side of the shop. "I need to borrow you a sec, pards."

Alex made a face, but said okay, telling Gervais and Art not to go anywhere without permission, following Cecil. Satisfied they were out of earshot, Alex spoke in a low voice. "I'm just about to sweat Art and Gervais on the Nomad, Cecil—what?"

"Check out Gervais' T-shirt."

Alex didn't bother, holding eye contact. "Says write in Dick Gregory for president."

"Yeah, well we have three guys matching the descriptions: a guy in coveralls, another in a suit. Even more specifically, somebody in one of those buildings said he heard someone, probably Doyle, scream 'write in Dick Gregory for president.' Now we're here, and it says write in Dick Gregory for president on Gervais' T-shirt."

"Indeed." Alex nodded. "Same time, approximately. Only so far, I'm calling this, hmm, a coinkidink on account of I already told you mechanics wear coveralls, so that part doesn't mean anything. And a guy in a suit? C'mon Cecil, there are hundreds of thousands of men, some women, wearing a suit in Toronto on this very day, and there's no way I can treat 'em all as murder suspects. Also, when Hermosa was still talking to me, he said the man who heard 'write in Dick Gregory for president' is a confirmed member of the American Peace and Freedom Party—'68 freak ticket that I schooled you on, split the vote, sent Richard Nixon up the middle, made him president. Worse, the witness is a winehead, as we already knew. And we now know he's wanted in Inkster, Michigan in connection with a rash of exploding mailboxes. So there's that, plus a lot of shiny, happy, lefty, white kids are wearing the same shirt this season, like that vendor told you, twelve to fourteen bucks depending where you buy."

"Okay," Cecil said. "Fine. I hear you on the coveralls and suit, but I can't ignore them together with the T-shirt when we also have witnesses say a guy was wearing a shirt, size lardass, that looked like a Rage Against the Machine shirt."

"Right, and Gervais is not wearing one says Rage. You just said so. You said, Alex, it says write in Dick Gregory for president, Gervais' T-shirt."

Cecil was getting madder, the gatekeeping old prick mocking the way Cecil talked, as if. "Look at the metrosexual design, is what I'm telling you. Same coloring—yellow, white, and red on black material. It looks like they put a picture of Dick Gregory the same way those Rage T-shirts have the uppity Commie spic they named Che Stadium after. Supposing somebody only thought it was Rage Against the Machine, from a distance, because of the metrosexual design."

Alex supposed briefly, saying it was a stretch. Beyond that, Alex said Cecil had the wrong Che. It was Shea Stadium, not Che, that Cecil was propagating an urban myth borne out of a mockumentary on a fictional rock band known as The Rutles, and it was mistakes like that, along with racist tendencies, that cost a cop cred during critical arguments. There. Another teachable moment.

Crossing the floor again, telling Cecil to watch and learn, Alex led this time, strutting toward the two men. Alex said it didn't look good, what with Gervais at a chop shop the morning his ride leaves without him.

"That's not nice." Art creased his eyes. "Chop shop?"

Gervais put his arm in front, protecting Art. "I'm here checking on my T-Bird, Detective Johnson. Art's man Reggie here is one of my mechanics."

"Because Renaldo's Auto Body is too hot," Cecil said.

"Listen to me." Gervais pointed at himself. "At Renaldo's, I've always dealt with Jean-Max, personally. None of his serfs, just Jean-Max himself. But Jean-Max, I haven't seen, so I'm going with Art today. Just here getting an oil change, Reggie's professional opinion on the state of my undercarriage and trying to figure out security matters on my little fleet. That's the other reason I'm here, to consult Art and Reggie on security because I've just had a car stolen. You see a crime in that, taking preventative actions?"

"No," Alex said. "Not so long as there aren't parts here belonging to a 1957 Nomad out back. If there was, could be a false report, wire fraud, insurance fraud, conspiracy—"

"It's all kinds of fraud we're here about." Cecil hitched his pants. "See, it's the fraud interests us."

Gervais shook his head, giggling, saying he didn't think Art was that kind of man.

"What do you mean," Cecil said, "that kind of man?"

"I just don't think so, as in I don't think Art Harwood is that kind of man." Gervais opened his arms. "From the few dealings we've had to date, it's just a feeling that I have." Looking at Art. "He's always been honorable with me."

Alex pointed behind his own shoulder with a thumb. "Reggie here says." He stopped, seeing Art looking past him, confused.

"Here, where?" Art looked everywhere and nowhere. "I don't see a Reggie."

Reggie gone, Alex faced Art again. "The mechanic that was just here said you and only you could call off the dogs, let us out back."

Art sucked his lips in, waiting, bracing himself when he heard the great family sedan roar. Alex pulled his Glock, running to the back exit, outside into a cloud of dust. Too distracted by the barking to get a good look at the car pulling away, aiming his gun all about in case he had to shoot a dog coming at him.

Cecil ran out in tow, catching a glimpse of the sea-blue-and-ivory Nomad, firing at the backside of the car pulling through an open gate, clipping a taillight, putting marks in the wall.

"The hell're you shooting at?" Art said.

"This is not a gun situation." Gervais ran past Art near the doorway. "That much about Canadian policing I do know."

"Dogs?" Alex looked all about. He could hear the animals, but he didn't see any. "Three dogs barking?"

"Ed Van Impe Junior," Cecil said. "Where is he? I'll shoot him, barking at cops."

Art fanned dust away, laughing. "No dogs. Reggie just says that—protecting me, protecting the shop. He's the one put up signs say No Trespassing, Beware of Dogs. It works as an alarm, keeps out vandals, intruders." Art shut the door, taking three steps into the yard, pointing to a white speaker mounted over the door until the noise of savage dogs stopped. "You could say he kind of MacGyvered it to activate a tape deck inside when the door opens. He's only making it seem like three dogs—Ed Van

Impe Junior being one. It's an inside joke."

"Gas." Cecil sniffed once, twice. "I smell gas."

It's a garage, Alex said, lots of nasty business. Gasoline, oil, acids, additives, ammonia, wax, Turtle Wax, chemical soup. Scanning the yard, he saw scores of tires, hoods, quarter panels, bumpers—a wasteland the size of those miniature golf courses on the highway—but nothing that looked like it came from a 1957 Chevy Nomad. Like Alex would know anyway.

"How come there wasn't any barking when Reggie snuck out?" Cecil said.

Art extended his right hand as if he was holding something. "He's got the doohickey to control it, a remote. Probably has it with him. Probably turned it off to leave, then on again when he cleared the door."

"You two are still double busted," Alex said.

"How do you figure?" Gervais stepped forward, smug. "I mean, whattaya got?"

Alex pointed at cameras sprinkled throughout the yard. "Art here taped it, got the whole thing on his security system. Tapes will pick up the make, Reggie scrambling out of here, driving away, probably even the wheelchair plates, at least partial, and how many Nomads in Toronto have wheelchair plates and a shot-out taillight when you know there were only seven thousand made?"

Cecil said yeah, thinking that ought to stop Gervais, but he was still snickering. Art had lightened up, too, crossing his arms, cracking a smile. "Those cameras are decoys, like the Beware of Dogs sign, Detective. Kind of like the Trojan horse, only opposite." Warm out in the sun, Art fought out of his suit jacket, throwing it over his shoulder, looking to the end of his yard, Cecil's bullets marking graffiti in the alley, Virgin Territory. "Reggie figured it would be enough to make people think they were on tape. Guess you could say he MacGyvered that, too."

Alex watched them laugh. And indeed, it was getting warm, pollen in the air, so he took off his TWA jacket, tying the arms around his hips. Laughing along with them. "Now Gervais, what time did you report the Nomad stolen?"

"Just after nine this morning."

Alex kept his eyes on them, speaking to Cecil. "What time you got, junior?"

Cecil looked at his Accu.2, hitting it with a backhand slap. "My watch is stuck on seconds, I already told you, so stop asking. Only Freida can fix it."

"It's just past eleven thirty." Gervais held up his Timex, smiling. "Anything else I can help with, I am here for you, Detective. Now that I am, how is the time even germane?"

Alex kept looking at Gervais, deadpan. "Time is germane because we found your car well inside three hours the first instance, right?"

"You haven't found anything." Gervais looked to Art. "You see my Nomad?"

"No." Art shoved his free hand deep into his pocket. "No Nomad."

"Put it this way," Alex said. "If we found it well inside three hours the first time, how long you think it's going to take us to find it again?"

"This some sort of math problem?" Gervais said.

Alex tapped the side of his head with his Glock. "Figuratively, it's kind of like that episode where MacGyver hid the evidence in a lamp post so it would be there for later."

"Episode?" Cecil was beside Alex now, reaching, grabbing his arm. "He was a real guy, you told me, this MacGyver."

TWENTY-THREE

Gordon Sung looked around the Coffee Cup. Nobody was paying attention, so he dropped half a Perc and washed it down with coffee. He was anticipating the velvety kick, reading a piece in *Eye* about the neutering of gay film characters when his work phone went off, the deputy news editor calling. Apparently, the deputy was in tight over a columnist chronicling his recent fling with heroin, and it was turning into a bit of a lark. See, the deputy wrote a headline saying the columnist had shot heroin, when, in fact, the pussy only smoked it, and now the columnist was firing off emails to brass, demanding clarification. The deputy couldn't see as how he was in any real trouble over this, and in fact, was more relieved that nobody seemed to be complaining about *Eye* glorifying junk. Anyway, the reason the deputy was calling was that police had scheduled a noon presser where it appeared they were going to reveal something about the discovery of that hogtied body on Lake Ontario, and could Gordon attend? Knowing the deputy would understand, Gordon said no, he had an appointment, and could the deputy send Schmidt? Yeah, no problem, but what was Gordon working on and when could the deputy expect copy?

"I'm just confirming some facts," Gordon said. "Nothing I want to get too, too excited about yet. Give me a few hours and I'll get back to you with deets."

"Okay," the deputy said over someone yelling in the background. "A few hours."

Gordon crinkled his eyes, smiling. "Is everything okay?"

The deputy said the damn columnist just walked in, and he was pissed because now his mother thought he shot heroin when, in fact, he only smoked it. More later. The deputy had to go.

Checking the clock as the deputy hung up, 11:33, Gordon was waiting on Helen Tyndall. She was the reason he wasn't attending that presser. She'd be calling soon, as agreed during their preliminary talk last week.

Deciding to make use of the time in between, Gordon collected all four dailies one by one as other patrons left them behind, and looked for the story within the story, just a piece, a slice of pie that he could cut off for himself to localize and turn into something bigger. Maybe something with a social justice angle. The deputy news editor always liked that. Or maybe something was going on at the raves, the way cops were still getting paid $50 an hour by promoters to over-police themselves. Nice work if you could get it, and what a scam, especially in light of all the important work Gordon had done on the subject in terms of exposing misinformation, abuses of power, conflicts of interest, and bald corruption. But alas, he hadn't a clue as to what he was going to write about this week, nothing new.

He was thinking maybe something would come up. It always did. Then he repeated his thought. Something would come up, eh? Well, something already had come up when he saw Cecil Bolan walking out of Venus de Milo's place one week ago today. A freshly showered fraud operative walking out of a hooker's den with the hooker early in the morning? That was the story. Who, what, where, when, and why. Gordon could've had it all. Or, at least most of it. But of course, once Gordon called Jean-Max and told him about it, drawing attention to Venus' man in the boat comment, it was obviously best that Gordon duck and otherwise pretend he didn't know any of the 5Ws on that one. Talk about conflicts of interest. There was no way Gordon could tell that story, and he wasn't a good enough reporter to look the other way when something like this did fall into his lap.

Mind you, it wasn't just Gordon who was slipping. It was *Eye* itself, compromising its people, talking one of the scribes into posing with a bottle of Steam Whistle on the cover, product placement. Soon, editors were being told to take story ideas from the marketing department, more product placement and more advertorials all around, which meant they were unofficially packaging stories and selling them along with ads, so pretty much everything Gordon had learned was out of the window. Worse was the trend toward me-journalism, whereby, increasingly, columnists were hired on the cheap, instead of reporters, to merely read the news and state their opinions without having to do any of the dirty work, the digging. And what was the result? A lot of bold, declarative statements from hyper partisans.

Gordon didn't see himself as a me-journalism kind of guy, nor did it respect his training, so it was hard to look to the future and think there was going to be a place for him, say, five or ten years from now. Who cared about his thoughts, his opinions? No one. And why should they? Gordon was trained to withhold his opinions, to just dig up facts, report them, let people form their own views. And that didn't seem to be on the correct side of what was becoming the course of recorded history, where more and more, establishing truths—or just repeating established truths—could get you hated, hunted, and yes, killed.

As standards slipped all around, even at the mothership, Gordon didn't see how doing shitty journalism was going to pay better than the real thing, so of course, why shouldn't he have at least tried to make it work like most everyone else? The guys in the music department had boss LP, CD, cassette, and T-shirt collections without buying much of anything. Book critics stocked up, even on works they didn't review, holiday shopping done, and a fair number of the rest seldom paid their way into anything, often finding a way onto the list. Even the people who wrote about sex were getting goodies in the mail—beads, plugs, probes, ticklers, aromas, flavored condoms, lube samples, plus an assortment of things that vibrated. And what was Gordon's payola? The odd CD no one wanted and enough free beer to blow over the legal limit.

Fuck, Gordon couldn't even sell out properly.

Whatever the rest of them had been up to, Gordon used to take pride in the fact that he was one of *Eye's* last real reporters, somebody to go out and find the story, cutting through the mendacity of headquarters. At least he had tried to practice the lost art of reportage, for a while anyway. The here and now, however, was another news item entirely, because, clearly, Gordon ended up crossing more ethical boundaries than anyone.

He was now fully compromised, in bed with lowlifes he used to chase with his camera and notebook, and pretty much dead professionally. But now that enough time had passed for the Perc to do its thing, literally depressing Gordon, he was beginning to understand the depths of what he'd done to Venus.

Like thieves, wasn't there supposed to be a little honor among drug buddies? Of course. Drug buddies were supposed to look out for each other, keep each other posted on narc behavior in the vicinity, help each other hook up, score, even front each other in times of need. So what did Venus do? She played a dangerous game, trying to pry information out of Gordon so she could deliver it somewhere else, to someone else—Cecil Bolan, most likely—and that wasn't going to be exactly good for Gordon. If he'd allowed her to do that, became her snitch bitch, maybe it would have been Gordon getting mocked and necklaced instead of Venus, so what choice did Gordon really have?

He was staring his second DWI in the face, maybe looking at a little jail time, more probation, the loss of his license, again, random piss tests, and they were going to fire him at *Eye* if he was found guilty a second time, meaning he'd end up on the street or in his mother's basement. Gordon didn't have money for a decent lawyer, not on what he made, so what was he supposed to do but accept the help when Jean-Max reached out?

Closing his right eye, itching his forehead, reminding himself this was about survival, Gordon tried to pep-talk internally about digging deep and clawing and scratching his way out of this. Just hang in there, he told himself.

Refocused, he looked out onto Kensington Avenue. You're Not the Boss of Me was hollering at someone in front of his fruit stand. The subject of today's rage was an old man, and he was yelling right back, picking up his walker and pointing it. About then, Steve Goof walked into the scene and had something to say, too. Gordon turned away, sick of the sight of them, the usual suspects with the usual routines, and all Gordon could think was, how did I get here?

Now that he was coming to terms with his cerebral geography, Gordon could no longer avoid the common reference point of his every success and failure.

Fear had always motivated him. Fear of disappointing his mother and failing to graduate. Then the fear of being unable to secure a decent journalism job followed by the fear of being good enough and smart enough and tough enough to stay, let alone advance. Sometimes, there was even a fear of dying, ill health, disease.

Fear—that's why he found himself working in feverish fits and starts, lots of off days in between. The upside was that fear inspired him to get incredible amounts of work done in shockingly little time, like that exposé on 51 Division officers essentially kidnapping a homeless man, Thomas Kerr, bringing him to Cherry Beach for a beating, then tampering with evidence, landing Gordon an honorable mention at the Babstock Awards. Fear shocked his adrenaline glands into gear and Gordon simply rode the rush to outwork them all on those days. Trouble was, fear and adrenaline also burned him out, hence so many off days where he floated through news conferences, pretending to jot things down, covering for the fact that he wasn't all there.

That roller coaster of naturally occurring chemicals led to the drinking, first alone just to come down, sleep, then in the bars where he would increasingly meet sources. Once he realized he could get drunk cops with agendas talking about inside minutia, off the record anyway, and buying him beer, he was drinking just to do the job, picking receipts off the floor and claiming them as expenses, at least until the first DWI. After that, Gordon wasn't supposed to be drinking at all, so he couldn't exactly expense, you know, drinks.

Off in his own little world of blissful regret, the sound of Gordon's work phone going off again put a start into him. He looked at it and didn't recognize the number right away. Given the time, 11:41, he figured, yeah, it was most probably Helen Tyndall. He'd checked her out and she was for real, representing Para-Dice Riders, getting their charges dropped, so of course he answered. "Hello."

"Gordon? Is this Gordon?"

"Yes, Helen?"

"Correct. Um, we do need to talk, as it turns out. Gordon, I'm concerned about our arrangement. I'm not sure it's going to work out after all."

"Our arrangement? I thought Jean-Max arranged everything, payment."

"That's the thing, Gordon. As Jean-Max's attorney, I am extremely limited in what I can say to you."

"About what?"

"Again, I fear that would be beyond the limits of what I can say directly. Just tell me. You're a crime reporter, right?"

"Yes." Gordon put his free hand on the seat next to him, leaning forward. "Like we talked about last week, for *Eye*."

"Well, are you on your way to headquarters for that noon press conference?"

"No, I was just telling my editor I'm skipping it because I have an appointment. And my appointment is I'm sitting in a café awaiting your call so I can give you my undivided attention, respect. Why? What's the presser have to do with it, you and I?"

"It will answer questions you might have of me that I shouldn't be answering, as I am Jean-Max's personal attorney. Merely addressing the subject with you could present a perceived or actual conflict of interest, so just let me say this. Jump in a cab, go to the presser, and I think any questions you might have of me—keeping in mind that I'm Jean-Max's attorney—will be answered there for you."

"You're also supposed to be my attorney."

"Can you pay my retainer? I mean, it's okay if you can't. I can refer you to an excellent public defender."

"Jean-Max is supposed to pay."

"And that's why I'm telling you, attend the press conference. Listen to what the police have to say and you will understand me better. Now, can you pay?"

Helen waited a few seconds for Gordon to answer. When he didn't, she repeated that she would refer Gordon to a public defender, that she would have the public defender call Gordon at this number, bye. He told her, wait, please Helen, please. But she was already gone, leaving Gordon alone in his sea of newspapers.

He reached into his pack for the new burner Jean-Max had couriered over, looking at it. Like the first, Jean-Max had said to only use it in matters of urgency, and well, whatever was going on with this Helen flake, Gordon considered his lack of legal representation a pretty fucking urgent matter, so he punched in the digits to Jean-Max's latest burner, hearing it ring on the other end before someone answered, hello. Right away, Gordon knew it wasn't Jean-Max. First of all, it was not Jean-Max's voice. Second, the person did not say bonjour, and Jean-Max said he would always answer with a bonjour, that he was a Quebecer.

Rather than confirming what he already knew, close enough anyway, Gordon turned the phone off, gathering his pack and heading outside where, as per Jean-Max's instructions, he broke the phone in half with his hands as he walked to Spadina. There, he dropped the top half in one garbage bin, bottom in another, before flagging a Co-op cab and telling the driver to take him to police headquarters, College and Bay. As they turned right, heading east, Gordon thought about how the slow death of real information wasn't exactly a new thing. It was just more apparent now that he was in total crisis.

TWENTY-FOUR

Art and Gervais were laughing at Cecil not knowing MacGyver was a TV character when Alex bent to pick up a Chrysler hood ornament, a chrome-on-black star. Looking at it, tossing it into mounds of screws, plugs, handles, and mirrors, he watched Cecil follow its path, distracted again, always distracted by something. This time, it was an old-style metal tub.

"Wind him up and watch him go," Alex said. "Junior got a bead on something."

"Hey," Gervais said. "I've been wanting to ask. What's with your guy's suit?"

Alex said it was the new casual Tuesdays, first one, but advised Gervais not to go there. Cecil was uptight about the subject. So, if it came up, the suit was not pink, but salmon.

Cecil shouted he could hear everything and to shut the fuck up.

"He ever find anything?" Gervais tapped out a cigarette, opening his Chevy Zippo with a swish, turning the metal wheel, scratching the flint, and lighting up. "I mean, worthwhile."

"Not too, too often, but he is responsible for that big E bust at the raves, so I just let him go off into the poison ivy sometimes." Alex let out a laugh. "Seasoning."

Cecil shouted that he was right here. And poison ivy, huh? Alex was about to pucker up, kiss Cecil's ass. Reaching into the metal tub, he dipped a finger, bringing it to his face.

"Don't eat it." Alex looked at Art. "Watch this. He's gonna taste it, whatever you got in that tub. He's gonna lick it. Watch."

"It's just smelling, is what I'm doing." Cecil didn't look back, staying focused, sniffing, wiping it on his salmon suit as fast as he could, turning, drawing his Glock, and putting it on Art Harwood. "Sick bastard's got a tub here filled with gas."

"Junior." Alex raised his Glock to the sky with his right, put an open left next to it. "Stop. I done told you it's gas on account of it's a service garage for automobiles. Nastiness everywhere,

217

compounds, wash your hands when you leave."

"Yeah." Cecil took his left hand off the gun, pointing over his shoulder. "Well, it's a Michelin soaking in this particular tub, in gasoline. These are for sure the guys doing the Haitian bowties or whatever you call it proper, the necklacings."

Alex opened and closed his mouth like a fish, putting his Glock on Art then Gervais, firmly but politely directing them to the ground, facedown please.

"Must've been something Reggie was working on." Art dropped to his knees slowly. "I don't know anything about that tub or what's in it. Look how I'm dressed. I am the businessman here, doing sales, taxes, payroll. Reggie handles that, the shop."

"What's he trying to do?" Cecil said. "Find a leak?"

"He's working on something." Art was lying on the ground, head sideways away from Cecil. "Reggie's always working on all kinds of things back here, inventions. I don't keep tabs on every job he's doing. I just do my job, let him do his."

"And I got a pretty good idea who the tire job's for," Cecil said. "Pam Jenkins, last of the green hornets. You sickies were going to burn her, too, mock her."

Alex said, "Cecil, you know we're not supposed to name names."

"They already know. Can't keep witnesses safe. Serpico's told 'em already. That's why they're conspiring to make it the necklacing like Doyle and Doris and Venus. Tire in the gas is for Pam Jenkins. Might as well have her damn name on it."

Sideways on the ground, also looking away, Gervais tossed his cigarette and said he didn't know anything about gas, or even this Doyle and Doris. Who was the last colonizer? Planet Venus? Gervais didn't know her, either. And necklacing? Wot dat? What did the Haitians have to do with it anyway? Point was, Gervais didn't do violent deeds. It wasn't in his nature, violence.

"That's what I thought all this time," Alex said. "Just a little gentlemanly fraud. But you know how it looks, everyone here matching the descriptions. You, a gentleman of size, wearing that

Dick Gregory shirt. And in Cecil's defense, who soaks a tire in gas?"

Gervais thought about what they were wearing that night. "Lots of colonizers walking around in suits, coveralls, T-shirts. It's just the wrong place at the wrong time, circumstantial."

At that, Cecil jammed his Glock into the crack of Gervais' buttocks, saying, "Wot dat?" When Gervais didn't respond verbally, Cecil said, "That's more law talk than Reggie talked for a guy had nothing to do with it. But you are going to confess one thing or I'll cure your invisible illness right here, right now. What were Doyle Allenby's last words?"

Gervais said don't ask him. He didn't know. Cecil increased the pressure, grinding the Glock, reminding Gervais his insides were protected only by denim and whatever he was wearing for metrosexual unders, assuming he wasn't going alfresco.

"Goddamn, Gervais," Alex said. "Cecil's got a gun in your butt. Gonna shoot you there."

"Kill you about a week after the fact, proper medical attention, and I will ensure the ambulance gets you to the hospital on time." Cecil was still pushing on his piece, increasing pressure. "I'd answer, I was you. Doyle's last words, what were they?"

Gervais drew in his head like a turtle, his body pulling into the fetal position, reading the T-shirt he was wearing upside down and saying, "Write in Dick Gregory for president." Feeling Cecil's Glock ease up. "Look, it was Renaldo. He made us do this. He was going to kill us if we said no, Jean-Max. He told us to mock them, to sing ironic songs about fire, made requests. This time, we were supposed to sing 'We Didn't Start the Fire' by Billy Joel."

Something gave in all four, a twinge of relief. Nothing else under the hot sun could be as bad as what was now out in the open. Alex told Cecil to kindly remove his Glock from Gervais' cavity. Cecil complied, standing, kicking Gervais in the ribs—*oof, oof, oof*—knocking Gervais' glasses off, then there was only the murmur of traffic from the expressway.

"Cuff 'em," Alex said. "Together on account of I left mine in the car."

"Yeah, well that's where I left mine, under the seat." Cecil trained his gun alternately on the two men. Treading right to Art, then left to Gervais, back to Art and so on. "Damn things were digging into my side, too. Probably because I don't eat right, you know?"

"Okay," Alex said, moving to the door. "Mine are in there for the same reason, give you that. Just keep your piece on 'em while I go to the car." He shook his head looking back at the two men on the ground. "And only shoot 'em if you have to."

Cecil said shut up and get the cuffs. Alex said sure thing, junior, flinching when he opened the back door, setting off the alarm, three dogs barking. When the sounds stopped several seconds after entry, Alex crossed the shop floor thinking this would be his last chance to tinkle for a while, so he hit the can, unzipping, letting go, ahh. Hearing the Supremes—"Where Did Our Love Go"—he sang along softly, wondering what passed for jazz these days. Anything the Supremes did was better than good, their poetry leaving him with imagery of Svetlana, the way he found her on his vacation to get over ex-wife number one at that historic bistro in Vienna, Café Sperl, a dirty refugee girl running away from the war. For a moment, Alex thought maybe they should've stayed where they found each other, as if that was possible. Still, even if the music was giving Alex the warm fuzzies about Svetlana after all she'd done, what Alex was hearing wasn't jazz. It was Motown, he decided, a sound of its own.

Shaking out the last drop, rezipping, he looked at the handle. He didn't want to touch it, other people's miasmas, so he brought up one of his Pumas and flushed with his foot. There.

Through the door, back into the shop, he passed the blue plastic chairs on his way to the front and walked out to the Cougar to find Cecil's cuffs where he said, under the driver's seat. Looking for his own, he opened the glove box, scrounging between cushions, visors, when he remembered, yes, stepping out to retrieve them from the trunk. He thought about calling for back up. But

Cecil really was showing signs of becoming an effective detective on account of they actually solved not just three of murders—Doyle, Doris, and Venus—but some of these auto frauds to boot. What with the tire in the gas, they'd caught the original suspects red-handed, pretty much, or would that expensive white-girl lawyer argue it was, like Gervais said, all circumstantial? Either way, this would get all the suspects off the street, once someone caught up to Reggie, so it didn't really matter for the moment. Only thing that did was that Theodore would be delighted, mostly, and Alex would be back in the fold. Cecil, too. Alex was going to give him another big assist on this one, maybe even put in a kind sidebar with Theodore. And why should Alex and Cecil share credit for the collar when they could march these heathens into headquarters themselves? Shit, Alex was on the way out anyway, so why shouldn't he get his fifteen minutes, too?

Back inside the garage, passing the blue chairs, Alex noticed that the wall clock read minutes past noon. On the radio, Ryan Flanaghan was at police headquarters saying Sheff Dubois was about to read from a prepared statement. After a little rattling near the mics, paper, Sheff said, "The body discovered yesterday on Lake Ontario has been identified as that of multiple-fraud suspect Jean-Max Renaldo." Alex stopped beneath Gervais' T-Bird, listening carefully, processing the information. "Ballistic tests show Renaldo was shot four times with a Firestar M45, common on the street, after being stuffed inside of a very large metal cooler and hogtied."

By the time Sheff was saying it was believed that Renaldo was killed by someone who knew him, someone with knowledge and access, then dumped off his own boat, the *Dine A Shore*, late last week, Alex couldn't help but think how Cecil mentioned that the body had been in the lake but for a few days or so while jousting with Theodore this morning. How did Cecil know? Was he really becoming an effective detective? Or was it just another coinkidink? Probably a little of both, Alex decided. Whatever, Cecil had been alone with Gervais and Art long enough, so Alex made for the door to the back. Reaching for the knob, he knew the sound of three dogs barking was coming, flinching anyway as the recorded dogs erupted again. Then, sweet Jehovah, he jump-stepped through the doorway at what he saw.

Gervais and Art were handcuffed together, one arm each looped through the tire. Flailing one free arm each like a full-grown two-headed monster that couldn't agree on direction, both mouths screamed terrible screams from within their moving flames. Goddammit, Cecil had lit them up with a two-for-one necklacing, or something like that, and he was mocking them as soon as the recorded dogs stopped barking.

"Smells like chicken." Cecil sniffed once, twice. "Rubber chicken."

Pointing at Gervais and Harwood burning up, Alex didn't know where to start. "I thought you forgot your handcuffs, Cecil." Holding two sets up with a thumb, chains dangling. "And you did. We both did, left them in the car, that is."

Cecil opened his suit jacket, showing Alex the secret pockets. "Freida sewed them special for my non-conforming police essentials. The fuck do you think of my pink detective suit now?" Smiling, Cecil turned to Gervais and Art, asking if they had any last requests. They were rolling on their sides, Gervais whimpering it burns, Art coming out for Jesus.

"How about some Evian water?" Cecil said, shaking his Glock at them. "Would you like that, colonizer?" Flicking the Chevy Zippo with his left hand, the metal wheel scratching the flint, shutting it with a swishy click, repeating the drill. "Always wanted one of these."

Alex deposited both sets of cuffs in his back pocket as he walked up saying, "This is some deeply pagan shit to be doing. What am I supposed to do?" Pushing Cecil. "What am I supposed to say?"

Turning to Alex, Cecil said, "I'm putting in my report that we came through the door and found 'em this way, pan-seared, same time as when Reggie was pulling out in the Nomad. That's why

I took the potshots, a clear murder situation, hit the Nomad. So that covers me off for discharging my weapon. Then I'll tell 'em it should all be on tape." Pointing his gun everywhere. "Cameras."

"Only it won't be on tape." Alex chin-nodded about. "They're all decoy cameras."

"So I only thought it was recorded." Cecil took a bow. "See, why would I lie if I thought it was recorded? Speaks to my cred. Whole time, I thought we were being taped, was conscious of my actions. If I think everything's recorded, no way am I going to light these cocksuckers up like a Christmas tree at Mel Lastman Square then lie about it."

Alex considered Cecil's story, processing it until he thought he found a hole. "Okay, only how did Reggie get police cuffs and put 'em on Art and Gervais before we arrived on the scene? How you going to explain that away?"

"You're in shock. You don't understand." Cecil chin-pointed at the bodies moving slowly on the ground, the screams inaudible now. "Those cuffs on Art and Gervais are extras, five bucks at the dollar store. My police cuffs really were in the car. You brought 'em. So, just to be crystal, those ones they're wearing are non-conforming. No way of tracing them."

Alex was trying to say something but couldn't get a handle on his thoughts.

"Just remember what Teddy said." Cecil tucked his gun under his arm long enough to tap a cigarette out of his pack, lighting it with the Zippo, pointing the small flame at the big ones twitching in front of them. "You want to be responsible for this?" Giving Alex a few seconds. "Didn't think so, and that's why you're going to say it must've been Reggie did it, all of it."

Gervais and Art stopped moving, nerves malfunctioning as they whimpered.

"You know what this means?" Alex said.

"Yeah." Cecil pocketed the Zippo, dragging on his cigarette, the nicotine hit releasing dopamine, pleasure. "Means we just solved like six murders. Means we prevented a seventh, Pam Jenkins."

"Excuse me." Alex held his gun out, wait. "We solved how many?"

"Six." Cecil held up a finger each time he added to the checklist until he ran out of free fingers on his left. "Doyle, Doris, Venus, Art, Gervais, Jean-Max—six."

Alex brought both hands behind his back, hiding the gun, looking at Cecil. "And how is it you know Jean-Max is dead? It was just on the radio inside, Sheff Dubois live at headquarters, making the announcement, commenting for the first time."

Cecil paused to suck on his cigarette, more dopamine. "Without the dogs, I can hear the radio from here."

Alex brought a finger to his lips, shush, listening, straining. After a few seconds, he said, "Then how come I can't hear it?"

Cecil brought his gun to his chin, scratching it. Looking at the back door, so far away, then Alex. Looking at him until something made sense. "What took you so long in there? Did you have to pee?"

When Alex admitted he had, Cecil said maybe it was time to invest in some Depends.

"Meaning what?"

"Meaning maybe your hearing is going, too," Cecil said. "What it means is, when you get old, you get cold. Lose your functions, your faculties, your senses. You forget things." Holding out his open left hand. "Like telling Hermosa to check who's paying Doyle's expensive white-girl lawyer." Taking the cigarette out of his mouth. "Shit like that."

"Shit like that?" Alex pointed at the back door. "I was just telling you Hermosa's not talking to me so I can't tell him, empathizing with you that he's difficult to work with."

"Yeah, well maybe if you remembered during the first twenty-four hours, crucial, we wouldn't be here." Cecil fanned his gun over Art and Gervais. "I didn't want to be the one to tell you, but I can't wish it away anymore. You're losing it, pards. This is cognitive shit." Putting the cigarette back in his mouth, snapping his fingers. "Let me ask, you don't use an aluminum frying pan, do you?"

Alex thought on it, said yeah.

"Well there you go." Cecil hit his cigarette, blowing smoke as he spoke. "That's what's causing it. Eating food cooked in aluminum pans causes the Alzheimer's, studies say."

"Alzheimer's now?" Alex pointed west, headquarters. "Well, I was just thinking, remembering actually, how back at the shop, you told Teddy that hogtied floater was dead for but a few days or so. Yes, it's all coming back. How did you know that?"

Cecil shrugged. "It was on the radio this morning."

"No, on the radio this morning they didn't say it was but a few days or so. They just said they found a bloated body. You couldn't have known, even approximately, how many days."

"Yeah, well, maybe you listen to the wrong station," Cecil said. "Maybe I made a lucky guess. Besides, you said yourself when I talked your way out of that stolen car beef, you owe me. That's on top of you're cheating on your mileage. Also, wait until Teddy finds out you've been holding out, gatekeeping not just me, but Hermosa as well. No wonder he's so uppity." Looking at Alex, focusing on his right eye. "And, if you screw me around, I'm telling Teddy you're still calling Angelique Royale the two-hundred-pound rockabilly girl, post-amnesty. Fuck me, I'll tell her myself. Put you in the sensitivity training less than a year before retirement. You want to go out that way, unmanned?"

Alex closed his eyes, Cecil piling it on and calling his chip in over that misunderstanding with Svetlana. And like it would matter that Alex was still calling Angelique the two-hundred-pound rockabilly girl if Theodore even thought Cecil lit these assholes up. Plus, with the paperwork and questions, there was no way Alex was going to get the car back tonight, meaning he'd miss church again, and how was he supposed to talk with Sondra about their relationship without thinking of Cecil? Goddammit, Alex had just told Sondra he had to get away from Cecil and his misdoings, and now look.

"Don't worry." Cecil squinted into the sun. "Everything's going to be fine."

"Yeah." Alex watched Cecil reach into his pocket for Gervais' Zippo, opening it, turning the metal wheel, scratching the flint. "This is going to be okay."

"I'm telling you, by the time this is said and done, we're going to get medals, a command performance. Believe me, Teddy's not going to say anything."

"Cecil, just give me that—Teddy's not going to say anything, right." Alex snatched the Zippo away, untucking his T-shirt to wipe the lighter down, opening it with a swish, and throwing it in the flames. "Theodore's already on about the colonel's talking watches, not a single nerve left. You call him Teddy when you say Reggie must've done it, see what he says."

Cecil took one last hit on his butt and flicked it into the fire. "Teddy already thought maybe Gervais was involved in the neck-lacings, a suspect, so his demise here won't be a stretch." Looking at Alex. "So what are you saying, Teddy's going to know we're lying?"

"Oh, Teddy's gonna know we're lying about something, and that you've been freelancing. Man's been around since long before the best part of you dribbled down the crack of your mama's butt in the tomato field. He just won't be able to prove anything."

"See?"

"See nothing," Alex said. "What I see is spending the rest of my career chasing able-bodied people using wheelchair plates to park in handicap spaces. That's what I see."

Cecil said he wanted his steward present if Alex was going to continue talking so negative and make this official, expose Alex as Serpico. When Alex noted that they were union brothers, Cecil said, so we're brothers now? Not that kind, Alex explained. He was just saying that the union didn't get involved in disputes between members when Cecil remembered something. Reaching into another secret pocket, he withdrew a black phone and tossed it underhand into the fire. Instinctively, Gervais caught it, or at least it seemed that way. Maybe the phone just stuck to his hand

and melted, but it looked like Gervais was holding it, perfect.

"What the fuck, Cecil?" Alex said. "What in the actual fuck?"

"I'm saying that's *his* burner phone." Cecil pointed his gun at what was left of Gervais. "Get it? *His* burner."

Alex moaned as he looked into the clear blue sky, promising Jehovah he wouldn't celebrate Christmas, no matter what Sondra said. In fact, Alex promised to both break up with Sondra, likely a pagan herself, and stop banging bitches entirely if Jehovah would just see him through one last rough patch. No more worshipping false idols ever again, honest. Even Alex's safari sheets, consider them gone. And that was it for the lattes, no more caffeine.

Cecil, he was mildly amused, chuckling until something else caught his attention. Out on the avenue, he heard a car gaining on the address, its stereo growing louder with a two-year-old song by a closeted Puerto Rican homosexual that was still unfairly leaving hetero women all over the world stuck to their seats, Cecil's wife included. And as the car passed out front, Ricky singing about this crazy chick slipping him a roofie, Cecil wasn't sure what kind of guilt he'd been feeling all this time, true or false. Not that it mattered. From here on, he knew he wasn't going to feel either ever again. It wasn't that he thought he should be spared on some vague moral high ground. Just that he was already like Alex and the rest of the vets at the annual retreat, desensitized, and there wasn't anything Angelique Royale could do about it. Yeah, Cecil thought, he was going to run this town one day.

ABOUT THE AUTHOR

Vern Smith is the editor of *Jacked*, a new crime fiction anthology. He is author of the novels *Under the Table* and *The Green Ghetto*. His novelette, *The Gimmick*—a finalist for Canada's highest crime-writing honor, the Arthur Ellis Award—is the title track to his second collection of fiction. A Windsor, Ontario native and longtime resident of downtown Toronto, he now lives on the outskirts of Chicago.

MORE FROM VERN SMITH

"Witty and socially conscious, it's a
needed update for a genre that long ago
rode off into a dire sunset."
—Nick Pearce, **BROKEN PENCIL**

MORE FROM VERN SMITH

"Vern Smith's THE GIMMICK is about a
hard-nosed cop, a bombshell in a belly
shirt, and a bank machine card scam. It's
a complex and intense story, and who can
resist the brilliant opening?"
—Philip Alexander, **FRONT & CENTRE**

"...a high-voltage satire of life behind the scenes of Toronto's 'Hollywood North' in the last days of the analog era. It is, in short, a blast!"
—Steve Venright, **THE LEAST YOU CAN DO IS BE MAGNIFICENT**

"**JACKED** is chock full of white-knuckle stories to propel the reader along at a breakneck pace. Don't sleep on this anthology. It's well worth the price of admission."
—Eli Cranor, author of **DON'T KNOW TOUGH**

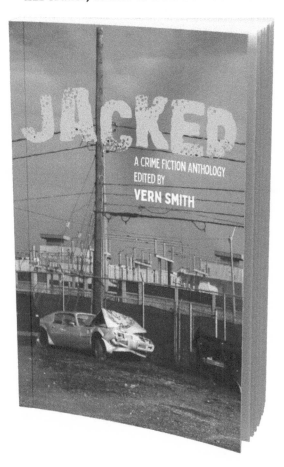

Ingram Content Group UK Ltd.
Milton Keynes UK
UKHW010733070623
423023UK00004B/251

9 798986 993010